A Body in the Auto Body Shop . . .

She clambered over the windowsill and jumped a foot to the concrete floor. She called out again. No answer. Her eyes adjusted to the dim light filtering through the high dusty windows. She could just see her way across the garage without tripping on any of the hoses lying about on the floor. The large empty space was completely still. She moved toward the front of the shop and pushed open the door of the office where Harry worked. A terrible odor assailed her nostrils. Her foot touched something soft. She looked down and gasped. Harry lay on his side, his eyes staring sightlessly at the legs of a chair. Part of his skull was caved in and a pool of now-congealed blood surrounded his head.

Lucky covered her mouth, trying not to scream, but a low gurgle came from her throat. Jack was right. Harry was gone . . .

Berkley Prime Crime titles by Connie Archer

A SPOONFUL OF MURDER
A BROTH OF BETRAYAL

A Broth of Betrayal

Connie Archer

BERKLEY PRIME CRIME, NEW YORK

THE BERKLEY PUBLISHING GROUP
Published by the Penguin Group
Penguin Group (USA) Inc.
375 Hudson Street, New York, New York 10014, USA

USA / Canada / UK / Ireland / Australia / New Zealand / India / South Africa / China

Penguin Books Ltd., Registered Offices: 80 Strand, London WC2R 0RL, England
For more information about the Penguin Group, visit penguin.com

A BROTH OF BETRAYAL

A Berkley Prime Crime Book / published by arrangement with the author

Berkley Prime Crime Books are published by The Berkley Publishing Group.
BERKLEY® PRIME CRIME and the PRIME CRIME logo are trademarks of
Penguin Group (USA) Inc.

For information, address: The Berkley Publishing Group,
a division of Penguin Group (USA) Inc.,
375 Hudson Street, New York, New York 10014.

ISBN: 978-0-425-25208-6

PUBLISHING HISTORY
Berkley Prime Crime mass-market edition / April 2013

PRINTED IN THE UNITED STATES OF AMERICA

10 9 8 7 6 5 4 3 2 1

Cover illustration by Cathy Gendron.
Cover design by Diana Kolsky.
Interior design by Kristin del Rosario.

This is a work of fiction. Names, characters, places, and incidents either are the product
of the author's imagination or are used fictitiously, and any resemblance to actual persons,
living or dead, business establishments, events, or locales is entirely coincidental.
The publisher does not have any control over and does not assume any responsibility for
author or third-party websites or their content.

PUBLISHER'S NOTE: The recipes contained in this book are to be followed exactly
as written. The publisher is not responsible for your specific health or allergy needs that
may require medical supervision. The publisher is not responsible for any adverse reactions
to the recipes contained in this book.

ALWAYS LEARNING · PEARSON

In loving memory of Gale Hyatt.
You will live in our hearts always.

Acknowledgments

With thanks and appreciation to Paige Wheeler of Folio Literary Management for her hard work, good advice and expertise and to Emily Beth Rapoport, Faith Black, and Kayleigh Clark of Berkley Prime Crime for their enthusiasm and support for the Soup Lover's Mysteries. Thank you to Marianne Grace for her copyediting skill in making this book the best it could be; and to everyone at Berkley Prime Crime who had a hand in bringing this series to life.

Many thanks as well to the writers' group—Cheryl Brughelli, Don Fedosiuk, Paula Freedman, R. B. Lodge, and Marguerite Summers—for their criticism and encouragement, and last, but certainly not least, special thanks to my family and my wonderful husband for their tolerance in living with a woman who is always thinking about ways to kill people.

CONNIE ARCHER
WWW.CONNIEARCHERMYSTERIES.COM
WWW.FACEBOOK.COM/CONNIEARCHERMYSTERIES
TWITTER: @SNOWFLAKEVT

Chapter 1

Neigeville 1777

NATHANAEL COOPER CREPT slowly, staying as close as possible to the trunks of the larger trees. He moved silently, fearful of giving his presence away. His heart beat so heavily he thought his chest would burst. Fragrant pine needles and dead leaves, dry and crumbled from the summer heat, carpeted the forest floor. A small twig crackled beneath his feet. He uttered a curse under his breath and froze. There were watchers now—watchers everywhere—on both sides. The town of Neigeville had formed a committee of volunteers to monitor the roads and report all movement, particularly British, immediately. At the slightest alarm, the church bells would be rung to wake the countryside.

He had lain awake that night until he was certain everyone in the house was asleep—his mother, father and sisters. He hoped they'd sleep deeply and not wake to find him gone. He did not want to explain to anyone what he was about. Once certain it was safe, he crept softly down the stairs and out into the fragrant, humid night. No one must know. He would never be forgiven. He would be killed, no doubt about that, and most likely his entire family as well. At the very least, their home and all their goods would be confiscated by the militia.

His feet were encased in gray homespun socks and soft leather boots that made little noise, but even so, a chorus of cricket song quieted at each step he took. A small animal scurried away through the underbrush. It was the dark of the moon, just a day or two to the new moon. Hard to see anything at all, much less among the trees. He edged closer to the clearing where only thin saplings would offer him protection, careful not to step out of the shelter of the dark. A single lantern burned in the window of the tavern below where the British officer had approached him that very afternoon. Somehow the man knew about his brother, knew that Jonathan was missing. Nathanael had last seen his brother driving away in the family's horse-drawn cart to deliver ale to a neighboring town. The family had asked everyone in town if they had seen Jonathan or heard any news of him. They had searched for him but had learned nothing. His mother was consumed with worry, sure her missing son had been shot by the British. At best, Nathanael's brother had been taken prisoner. At the very worst, he was dead.

His family was terrified by the events unfolding around them, as were many others. Angry at the arrogance of the British regulars, the townspeople wanted to drive them out. Yet many believed that as British citizens they still owed allegiance to the King. Feelings had reached a boiling point and now there was no more time to debate. Everyone must choose a side. Nathanael's father was eager to fight, held in check only by his mother's fears. It was his father's hesitation that had caused the town to turn a suspicious eye in their direction. Against his mother's wishes Nathanael himself had joined the militia, more in an effort to protect his family than for any other reason. He had no desire to fight, to kill other men, even if they were British. Like his brother, he had little interest in politics and wished only to live the quiet life of a farmer. He hoped he'd never be forced to kill anyone, British or Yankee.

The strange man with information about Jonathan had worn the clothing of a local, short trousers and a coat of homespun cloth, in shades of brown, but there was no mistaking him for a colonial. His manner was high-handed and arrogant, used to giving orders. He hadn't fooled anyone in the tavern, not even the young boy who swept the floor. Another man followed in his footsteps and took orders from him—a servant. Only a British officer would keep a servant. Perhaps the pastor was correct—if the town did not take up arms, if the rebellion were quashed, they'd be slaves to the crown forever. Nathanael was torn—stay loyal to the King and hope for peace, or join the rebels in their hatred of the King's authority? An iron fist was closing over all their land. The loyalists were called traitors and the rebels were at risk of their lives. To be hesitant to take a side might mean death at the hands of a neighbor.

The man had accosted him that afternoon outside the tavern. He had news. His brother Jonathan had been taken prisoner on the road to Bournmouth, his cart, ale and horses confiscated. The officer swore to Nathanael that Jonathan was still alive and promised to reveal where his brother was being held. In exchange, he wanted information. Young as he was, Nathanael was no fool. He knew there'd be a price to pay, but gasped when he learned what the man wanted. He demanded to know where in the town the gunpowder and arms were hidden. Even more, he wanted details about the stores at Bennington, and how many rebels would march to defend the armory.

The Committee of Safety formed in Neigeville was certain the British, approaching from the north, planned to confiscate all the guns and ammunition that had been so carefully stockpiled, and ultimately gain control of the

armory at Bennington. At meetings, townspeople had
learned that the ranks of Burgoyne, the hated British general, were swelled with Hessians, loyalist Canadians, Indians and French. They knew their horses and cattle would
be taken to feed the soldiers on their march. A fierce battle
was coming, if not here in Neigeville, then closer to
Bennington.

Nathanael knew that, with the blessing of their minister,
guns and powder were hidden under the pulpit of the
white-steepled church on the Village Green, but he was not
privy to any information about the armory at Bennington.
Nathanael would happily give the lobsterback all the
details he wanted, if only he could free his brother and
bring him home. But did he know enough?

He shivered in spite of the warm night. *Where was the
man?* He was terrified of the officer, but far more terrified
of discovery by his fellow townsmen. He hated to think
what would happen to him if it were known he had pro-
vided information to the enemy. A branch crackled and
Nathanael jumped in terror. The man had come through
the woods behind him and now had stepped out into the
clearing. Nathanael watched and waited. His heart finally
slowed its rhythm. He took a deep breath and moved out
of the shadow of the trees. He recognized the linen shirt and
brown vest, the wide-brimmed hat, but when the figure
turned toward him, his blood ran cold. This was a different
man, shorter and stockier, not the officer he had promised
to meet. The man raised his gun. A shot rang out. Nathanael
reeled back, falling against a tree. More surprised than in
pain, he looked down at his chest to see his life's blood flow-
ing from a wound. The last word he heard was *"Traitor."*

Chapter 2

"HOW DID YOU ever manage it?"

Lucky stopped in her tracks, almost losing control of the dolly loaded with bottled and canned drinks. "Manage what?"

Sophie smiled. "Getting Pastor Wilson to host the demonstration. Unbelievable."

"Well, I don't know about hosting, but he's volunteered the meeting hall."

Sophie shook her head. "Amazing. I mean, he's so stuck in another century, and you've virtually talked him into rabble-rousing."

Lucky smiled. "He's not a bad sort at all. I really like him."

Sophie wrinkled her nose. "He smells of mothballs."

Lucky laughed. "Maybe that's why I like him. I love the smell of mothballs."

"Nobody loves that smell. You must be kidding."

"I do. Really. Always makes me think of summertime . . .

you know, when everyone puts away their wool clothes and stuffs mothballs into drawers and closets."

Sophie guffawed. "Maybe you do. I sure never did. Just the same, you charmed him."

Lucky smiled, shrugged her shoulders and grasped the handle of the dolly more firmly. She was thrilled that her friendship with Sophie Colgan had been renewed. Several years before when she had left their small Vermont hometown to attend college, Sophie had taken it very badly, reacting with coldness and cutting remarks. A serious rift had formed between them. Now, all that was past and Lucky couldn't have been happier. Months before, Sage DuBois, the chef at Lucky's restaurant, and the love of Sophie's life, had been arrested for the murder of a winter tourist. Lucky had uncovered the real murderer and Sage was freed. She and Sophie had mended their fences and Lucky could count her a close friend once again.

"Pastor Wilson's just providing a space at the church for the demonstrators to take breaks. We'll bring over half sandwiches tomorrow and part of the profits will go to the church. But that's not why he agreed. He believes in the demonstration—no one wants to see a car wash built in the middle of town."

Sophie shook her head. "I'd like to see all those town council people recalled. How they ever . . . *why* they ever voted for that disgusting thing, I'll never understand. It'd make much more sense to build it up at the Resort."

In winter months Sophie was a top ski instructor at the Snowflake Resort perched halfway up the mountain from the town. During the summer, her schedule was much lighter—giving occasional swimming lessons to summer tourists. That left plenty of time for Sophie to visit the Spoonful, help Sage with his chores and spend more time with Lucky. Right now she was wheeling a dolly of her own, identical to Lucky's, loaded with drinks for the start of the demonstration the next day.

"I really appreciate your help with this." Lucky paused to wipe her brow with the back of her hand. Temperatures had soared on the first day of August and the heat had shown no signs of abating. The morning had the stillness that comes when summer heat is at its peak, no crickets, no birds, the heat rising off the asphalt in waves. "Can you believe this weather? And it's still early in the day too." She checked her bare arms quickly. She'd have to remember her sunblock when she was out running errands.

They had managed to maneuver their carts to the edge of the Village Green and now, single file, navigated the path to the Congregational Church, a white-steepled building erected in 1749 that sat at the head of the Green. Lucky took a deep breath, relishing the smell of freshly mown grass. "That's my other favorite summer smell."

"What's that?" Sophie didn't look up. She was focused on making sure none of her crates slid to the ground.

"Grass—the way it smells when it's just been cut."

"Hmmm. Okay. I'll buy that. I like that smell. So . . . cut grass and mothballs . . . anything else remind you of summer?"

"Remember that white cream we used to put all over us when we were kids whenever we got sunburned?"

Sophie laughed. "Oh, I remember. We'd always peel after we had worked so hard to get a tan. Don't tell me you *liked* the way that stuff smelled? It stunk. We used it 'cause it was all we could find in our parents' medicine cabinets." Sophie stopped and looked toward the other end of the path. "And speaking of stinky . . ."

Lucky spotted a woman with bright strawberry blonde hair leaving the church. Rowena Nash—her hair was unmistakable.

"What's she doing here?" Sophie whispered. "I can't stand her."

"Shush . . . she'll hear you." Rowena looked in their

direction and waved energetically. Changing course, she walked straight toward them. "We're about to find out."

Lucky and Sophie had both attended school with Rowena, who now worked for the *Snowflake Gazette*. Rowena's zeal in chasing down a story made it clear her sights were set far beyond the *Gazette*.

"Hey, Lucky. Hi, Sophie. You setting up for tomorrow?" Rowena bestowed a large smile on Lucky while her gaze slid over Sophie.

"What are *you* doing here?" Sophie asked.

"Oh, I just came over to talk to Pastor Wilson but he's busy right now. I saw Harry Hodges go into his office. I was thinking of writing something about the demonstration and hopefully getting an interview with Richard Rowland too—you know, the developer of the car wash—kind of airing both sides of the dispute."

"That sounds interesting," Lucky offered, sure that no one in town had one ounce of interest in hearing Richard Rowland's point of view.

"Since you're here, Rowena, you want to give us a hand with this stuff?" Sophie smiled sweetly.

"Oh, sorry. Love to. But I can't right now. I have a meeting with my editor. I'll catch you later." Rowena flounced off with a last beaming smile and continued across the Village Green.

Lucky turned to Sophie. "You're incorrigible, you know that, don't you?"

Sophie smiled impishly. "I thought the prospect of actual work might send her scurrying." Sophie shook her head. "She hasn't changed a bit since we were in school. She was a self-important little snob then and she's worse now."

"Come on. Let's move this stuff inside. I have to get back to the Spoonful before the lunch crowd hits." They reached the church and navigated the pathway to the side door that led to the meeting hall. Lucky pushed open the heavy wooden door and held it while Sophie bumped her dolly over the threshold. The smell of polished floors and chalk-covered erasers hovered in the air. Sophie held the door for Lucky in turn. They wheeled their carts through the meeting hall and into the large kitchen.

"Where should we put this stuff?"

"Hang on. There are some long tables in the storage room we can set up." With Sophie's help, she hauled out two long folding tables. Sophie lifted one end and together they pulled the retractable legs open, setting both tables up by the entry to the kitchen. Lucky searched the kitchen drawers and found long paper tablecloths in plastic wrappers. Ripping them open, she shook out the paper cloths and spread them over the long tables, placing stacks of napkins at each end. She opened the refrigerator. "Let's cram as many drinks as we can in here, and I'll bring a couple of big plastic bins tomorrow for the ice. Can you dig out the coffee urn?"

"Sure. I'll find it," Sophie replied, opening and closing cupboard doors in her search.

Lucky unloaded canned and bottled drinks from the carts until the refrigerator would hold no more. "That should do it for now. I should let Pastor Wilson know the drinks are here and the ice will be delivered early tomorrow."

"I'll rummage around and see what other supplies are on hand."

"Be right back." Lucky pushed through the door leading to the main part of the church. She followed the corridor to the end hoping to find the Pastor in his office. As she approached the door, she halted. She heard voices. Pastor Wilson wasn't alone. She listened, certain she had heard the unmistakable sound of sobbing. Then silence. Someone was having a very emotional conversation with the Pastor. She tiptoed back a few steps, but before she could retreat from the corridor, the office door opened. It was Harry

Hodges, the town's auto mechanic and one of the major forces behind the demonstration. Harry's voice carried clearly through the partially open door. "I had to talk to someone."

The Pastor's voice was closer now. "You did the right thing. Be calm. We can talk again . . . whenever you're ready."

It was too late to retreat. Harry stepped into the corridor. He started visibly when he saw her standing nearby. His face darkened. Pastor Wilson peeked around the doorjamb. "Lucky! Hello. I didn't know you were here."

"I didn't mean to interrupt. We just came over to unload drinks. I wanted to alert you that an ice delivery would be coming tomorrow."

"Oh, good, good. That's wonderful. Harry and I . . . well, we were just discussing the plans . . ." Lucky suspected the Pastor was making an effort to cover for Harry, who seemed embarrassed she might have overheard his conversation.

Harry glanced at the Pastor. "I'll call you very soon." Without a backward glance, he turned away and left by the door leading into the church.

Pastor Wilson cleared his throat and opened the office door wider. "I can't thank you enough. This is truly wonderful what the Spoonful is doing. It'll really help keep everyone's spirits up tomorrow."

"I am sorry if I interrupted anything."

"That's quite all right. Harry and I were just finishing our little chat. Anything I can do for you?"

"No, thank you. I have a helper today. But you might want to lock that side door now that the drinks are there."

"Good idea. I'll just get my keys." Lucky stood in the doorway and watched the Pastor as he scanned his desk, littered with papers, books, a Bible and remnants of a piece of toast. Pastor Wilson was tall and thin with a prominent Adam's apple. His face was pale, his hair a shade between sand and gray. His movements were disjointed, as though confused by the objects around him—as if the furniture of his life belonged to someone else. She detected a faint whiff of naphthalene. She smiled to herself. Sophie was right about the mothballs.

"Now what did I do with those keys?" Pastor Wilson brushed a few wisps of hair from his forehead and replastered them over a bald spot on the top of his head.

Realizing this search could take quite a while, Lucky said, "I'll be on my way then."

"Oh yes, yes, my dear . . . you go on. I'll find them eventually."

Lucky headed back down the corridor to the meeting hall and pushed through the swinging doors. Sophie was leaning against one of the dollies, waiting for her. "Ready?" Lucky nodded, grabbed her dolly and followed Sophie out the door. She was silent as they headed across the Village Green to Broadway.

"Something wrong?" Sophie watched her critically.

"Oh, no. Nothing." Sophie waited, aware that something was on her friend's mind.

"Well, actually, I think I overheard something I wasn't supposed to hear." Lucky repeated the exchange between Harry Hodges and the Pastor as they walked.

Sophie shrugged. "Probably nothing at all. Maybe Harry wanted to confess he had dipped into the collection box."

Lucky didn't respond to Sophie's gibe. "It was more than that. There seemed to be a . . ." She hesitated. ". . . an emotional charge to the words, I guess. I could have sworn Harry was crying. More than that—Harry almost jumped out of his skin when he saw me standing in the corridor."

"Hard to imagine him being emotional. The most excited I've ever seen him was when he was staring under the hood of my car."

Lucky chewed her lip. Sophie was right, of course. Harry definitely took more interest in the workings of internal combustion engines than in people. She pictured his shocked look when he saw her in the corridor—as if afraid she might have overheard something. Harry was a man of few words, not rude but taciturn, definitely not forthcoming. All the same, Harry's tone hinted at a very painful subject—something deeply buried.

Chapter 3

"CAN YOU TELL Sage I'll see him later? I've got to get up the hill. I have two classes and a private this afternoon and I'm running late."

"I will. Thanks again." Lucky waved as Sophie hopped in her car and pulled out of the small parking lot behind the restaurant. She dragged both dollies up to the door and over the threshold, wheeling them into the storage closet. Then she headed down the hall, grabbed a fresh apron from the closet and slipped it over her head. Her mother had designed the Spoonful's aprons—yellow, like the checked café curtains at the front windows, with an outline in dark blue of a steaming bowl of soup. They echoed the neon sign at the front window that her Dad had designed. It hardly seemed possible that only eight months had passed since her parents had died on an icy road and she had inherited their business. Last winter, when the Spoonful was on the verge of bankruptcy, seemed a universe away, yet her parents' deaths were still fresh in her heart.

She peeked into the kitchen. Sage was at the stove, stirring a simmering pot of one of his daily specials.

"Sophie had to run. She'll call you later."

"Okay." Sage didn't turn his head, but held up a wooden spoon to acknowledge the news. He was sprinkling flecks of fresh thyme into the broth.

Lucky pushed through the swinging door into the main room of the restaurant, cooler here, thanks to ceiling fans and air-conditioning. Soft piano music filled the space. Once her grandfather Jack had gotten used to the CD player, he went out of his way to buy more music. Jack's taste ran to forties' sounds, which Lucky had come to love as much as Jack did. He could name all the top hits and musicians of the day. A tinkling piano solo was just the thing. R&B and rock were great for the winter when people needed to move just to keep warm, but not on a steamy August day like today.

Her grandfather, Jack Jamieson, and three of the Spoonful's regulars, Hank Northcross, Barry Sanders and Horace Winthorpe, had taken over one of the corner tables. Normally, Hank and Barry would have been engrossed in a game of Connect Four or chess, but now their attention was focused on the demonstration against the car wash planned for the following day.

In summer months, the By the Spoonful Soup Shop usually enjoyed a lull when winter visitors to the ski slopes abandoned the town. Lucky had been toying with the idea of taking a few days off to go camping and swimming, but was finally forced to postpone her plans. Over the last month, the Spoonful had become a meeting place for angry discussions about the proposed construction—no longer proposed, but actually commencing—on the other side of the Village Green, just a block or two from the Spoonful itself.

Snowflake, Vermont, prided itself on preserving its heritage. The town was united in its disapproval of the car wash. Even though most of the town's tourist business came from the ski resort, many people arrived in August to celebrate the Reenactment of the Battle of Bennington, a battle crucial in the ultimate defeat of British forces in the Revolutionary War. No one wanted an ugly industrial edifice that would mar the quaint charm of their town.

"Something has to be done to stop this. We can't have a *car wash* in the center of town. It's downright blasphemous. What barbarian would even think of erecting such an eyesore here?" Barry fumed.

"You know, he's originally from Snowflake," Hank volunteered, looking over his pince-nez glasses at his friend.

"Who? That Philistine? What's his name again?"

"Rowland, Richard Rowland," Jack volunteered. "And yes, Hank's right. He's a Snowflake boy. Born and raised here. Well, I should say, originally from here. His family moved away when he was a young kid."

"Hmph." Barry snorted. "So wouldn't you think he'd have a bit more taste, now that's he's such a big-shot developer? But no, he plans to inflict a disgusting, noisy car wash on us. Why not stick it up at the Resort in one of their huge parking lots?"

"It's the Resort that's been pushing the town council to put it down here. They're afraid it might ruin the ambience of their buildings," Hank said.

"Oh my," Barry replied sarcastically. "We wouldn't want that. Heaven forbid it wouldn't look like an overgrown collection of Swiss chalets! It's a much better idea to put an ugly, square, hissing, concrete-block monstrosity right in the center of our little town." Barry's plaid cotton shirt threatened to burst. One very strained buttonhole was keeping it together. "We wouldn't want to ruin the *ambience* of the Resort, now, would we?" Barry slammed his coffee cup down on the table, causing some of the liquid to splash over the edge of his cup.

Horace Winthorpe sat quietly, offering no comment. He

took off his glasses and wiped them carefully with a tissue. A retired professor now living in Snowflake, and renting Lucky's parents' home, Horace had become one of the Spoonful's regulars. Lucky and Jack had welcomed him to town and had grown very fond of him. When Lucky took over the restaurant, she was struggling with grief. She couldn't bring herself to live in her childhood home, nor was she able to afford to do so with the restaurant doing poorly. When their local Realtor found Horace, Lucky was delighted and relieved he wanted to rent the house on a long-term basis. Horace had taught history all his life and was now working on a book about his particular field of interest—the Revolutionary War years in New England. He, like many others before him, had fallen in love with Snowflake and had settled happily into Lucky's family home to enjoy his retirement and begin work on his long-desired project.

"Horace, you haven't said very much all morning," Hank said.

Horace slipped on his wire rim glasses. The sun streaming in through the gingham curtains lit up his mane of white hair. He was a big man, slightly portly, who had been enjoying most of his meals at the Spoonful and had put on several pounds since living in Snowflake. "I, like you, am terribly saddened to see this happening. I haven't said very much—after all, I don't have a long history here—but I so appreciate this town and the efforts everyone has made to keep the old buildings and restore so many of them."

"Are you willing to join us, then?" Barry asked.

"Well, yes, if you'll have me. I would be honored." He smiled sweetly. "Nothing like a good demonstration to remind ourselves we were all rebels once. Besides, the Reenactment of the Battle is only a few days away and I for one would prefer to have something more dignified than a car wash as a backdrop for our town celebration. After all, I've been asked to play a Hessian and I'd much rather like to do so without bulldozers growling in the background—really interferes with the willing suspension of disbelief."

"Well, that's it then," Barry said. "We're starting tomorrow at nine o'clock. I'll give your name to Harry Hodges to add to the list."

"Harry from the Auto Shop?" Horace asked. "I know him. He put in a new alternator for me a few months ago."

"Good then. We're agreed. The plan is to do whatever we can to halt or delay construction. Demonstrating with signs and all that is fine, but it's gonna take more than that. If our own town council can be swayed into voting for this, the hell with 'em."

Hank grimaced. "Swayed! That's a nice way to put it. Bought off, more likely. Every single one of them, except Edward Embry, the only honorable man on the council in my opinion. Maybe we should be working on a recall vote of the rest of those corrupt twits."

"I agree. But first we have to do whatever it takes to stop this project. Even if it means we block the big equipment from getting in or out with our cars, or we lie down in the dirt. They won't be able to carry us all away. And there isn't enough room in the two cells at the police station to hold all of us anyway." Barry's face had grown flushed and angry.

"Jack. You with us?" Hank turned to Jack.

"You bet I am."

Lucky glanced at her grandfather and exchanged a look with Sage through the kitchen hatch. Jack's health had steadily improved over the last few months, but she wanted to keep a close eye on him. When she had first returned to Snowflake, her grandfather was suffering from a constellation of health problems—heart palpitations, fatigue, memory lapses and actual episodes of dementia. It was Dr. Elias Scott at the Snowflake Medical Clinic who had diagnosed Jack's problems as a severe vitamin B deficiency. Now, after six months of treatment, Jack was strong and healthy. He occasionally suffered from his wartime memories, but even these seemed to be lessened with his medical treatments. He was getting older, there was no denying that, and Lucky worried about him. Jack was the only family she had now, and at his age, she was thankful he wanted to run the Spoonful with her. She didn't like the thought that he could be involved in physical confrontations at the demonstration. She had seen Richard Rowland, the developer, around town and took an instant dislike to him. He was a man as nasty and sleek as a shark, determined to push his agenda through.

Sage shrugged his shoulders in response to Lucky's quick look, as if to say, *What can you do? He's a grown man.* Lucky accepted the truth of it. Most of Jack's life had been spent in the Navy. He had always been tough and fearless. She had to bite her tongue. Getting old was tough enough. The last thing she wanted to do was cause him to feel less than powerful now that he was aging.

Chapter 4

HARRY HODGES HIT the control button for the garage bay door. He took two steps back and watched as it rumbled shut. Other than a stack of paperwork on his desk, he was done for the day. His assistant mechanic, Guy Bessette, stood at the utility sink scrubbing his hands, anxious to be on his way.

"Harry . . ." Guy approached, wiping his hands on a paper towel. "You sure you don't mind if I take a few days off? I'm playing a militiaman in the Reenactment and it's just . . . well, the rehearsals are in the afternoon, and the Reenactment is at midday. If you need me . . . I can come in earlier and come back to the shop when rehearsals are over."

"Nah, that's fine, Guy. You go ahead. Have some fun. I can manage on my own, and all the big jobs are done now anyway."

"I finished Mr. Rank's car."

"Good. I told him it'd be done. He might stop by tonight

to pick it up. I'm gonna stay late and try to clear up some of that paperwork. Piles up so fast."

"Thanks, Harry. I really appreciate it." Guy smiled and pushed a stray lock of hair off his forehead. His front teeth were crooked and he was self-conscious about smiling widely—at least when he was in unfamiliar company. In front of his boss, though, it didn't matter. His boss liked him, and as long as he worked hard, Harry didn't care anything about how his teeth looked. Guy hesitated. He couldn't help but notice his employer was distracted. Maybe asking for a whole week off was too much. "You sure you don't mind, Harry?"

"No, Guy. For the last time. Be on your way and don't worry about it. I'll call you if I need you."

"Okay then." Guy tossed the paper towel into the round metal trash bin and grabbed his backpack. "I'll see you next week." Guy left by the small side door and made sure the lock clicked behind him. Once on the sidewalk, he hesitated. Something wasn't right. He could feel it, but he couldn't imagine what it was. Harry said he was okay with his taking a few days off, but something was definitely troubling him. Guy just hoped it had nothing to do with him or his work.

Harry heard the lock click on the door as Guy stepped out to the sidewalk. He walked into his small office and sat heavily in the chair behind the desk. It creaked loudly as he leaned back. *Soon it will all be over,* he thought. He heaved a sigh and reached for the nearest stack of paperwork. After an hour, he had managed to clear most of it away. He set the unpaid invoices to the side in a neat pile, placing a heavy wrench on top to keep the papers secure. It had been a very long day. He was hungry, but every time he thought of eating, his stomach cramped and the hunger was forgotten. He'd feel better when it was over. Just one more thing to take care of before he broke his silence.

A sharp rap at the door caused him to jump. He rose from his chair slowly and approached the door. There was no turning back now. He took a deep breath to steel himself and turned the lock. A solitary streetlight cast a jaundiced glow over the visitor standing on the sidewalk. His face was in darkness but that didn't matter. Harry would have known him anywhere. Leopards didn't change their spots, and the years hadn't changed this man one bit.

"What did you want to talk to me about?"

"Come into the office and grab a seat," Harry answered.

"I don't have time for this. Get to the point," the man spat.

Harry turned away without responding and walked back into the office. A heavy oak desk and two large filing cabinets dominated the small space. A metal gooseneck lamp shone a harsh light over the stacks of paper and order forms. The smell of motor oil hung heavy in the room. Harry took a deep breath. Now that he had made his decision, he felt years younger. An enormous weight had lifted from his shoulders. He turned to his guest. "I'm not keeping it any longer."

"What the hell does that mean?" The man had followed him into the small room.

"You heard me. I can't carry it anymore. It's ruined my life. It's gonna hurt a lot of people, you most of all, but I don't care."

His visitor stood silently, a slow rage building inside him. A vein in his forehead throbbed. "What are you thinking?" He hissed. "Don't you know what they'll do to you?"

"I don't care anymore. I told you—I made my decision. I just wanted to give you fair warning." Harry sighed and turned away. There was nothing more he could say. He'd done his best. He was tired, so tired, but relieved he had come to this point. He reached across the desk to grab his keys. The blow came so quickly, he barely felt it. He was dead before he hit the floor.

ARNIE HICKS GRABBED on to the lamppost to steady the street. It moved like an undulating river of concrete. He wasn't sure where he was exactly—somewhere near the Village Green. He knew he had had too much to drink, but he didn't care. Today was his birthday—August 9— and he deserved to celebrate. He didn't want to think how many years had passed since he was born, but he was still above ground—which was more than a lot of his cronies could say. He giggled at the thought of his dead friends talking. *"Arnie,"* they'd say, *"can't believe you're still kickin' around. Thought for sure you'd be the first to go."*

Arnie launched himself away from the lamppost and stumbled across Broadway. He tripped over the curb and fell facedown on grass of the Village Green. Lifting himself on one elbow, he rolled over and took another swig from his bottle of whiskey. Some of the liquid dribbled down his shirt. He coughed and sat up and began to sing off-key at the top of his lungs. *"She wheeled her wheelbarrow . . . through streets broad and narrow . . ."* He stopped. Couldn't remember the rest of the words. Oh yes, it was coming back to him now. He took another swig, the last one. He squinted at the bottle. Empty. He flung it at the statue of the Revolutionary War soldier, hitting the pedestal. The bottle shattered loudly in the quiet night. *". . . crying cockles and mussels aliiive alive-o-o-o."*

A car turned the corner on the far side of the Green. The police cruiser. Arnie knew it well. They were looking for him. Couldn't let him have a little fun, not even on this one night, could they? But this year was going to be different, he promised himself. They weren't gonna catch him and lock him up where he'd wake with a colossal hangover in a jail cell, lying on a hard wooden bench. Oh no, not this year. This year was special—it was the big seven-oh. He was determined to outwit Nate Edgerton, Snowflake's Chief of Police, and have a little fun.

He crawled on all fours, giggling and hiccupping, and ducked behind the statue. Nate was peering out the window of the cruiser trying to spot him. Arnie slowly dragged himself to a kneeling position and peeked out from behind the granite pedestal. Nate's cruiser continued on. Once Arnie was sure it was gone, he took up his song again, stumbling to the other side of the Green.

"Alive alive-o-o, alive aliiive-o-o, crying cockles and mussels . . ." He wobbled across Water Street and reached the construction site. They were building something here, but he couldn't remember right now what it was. Something the town was up in arms about. He crashed into the chain-link fence and, kneeling down, crawled through an opening where the fence had torn away from its post. He stumbled across the dirt lot, doing his best to stay upright, but the world was spinning around him. Heavy earthmoving equipment loomed in the night like prehistoric beasts waiting to maul unsuspecting humans. His feet were mired in soft dirt. Losing his balance, he fell back into an earthen depression. He struggled to sit up, but he was so tired and the dirt so soft, he might just as well lie down and have a little rest.

Chapter 5

NATE EDGERTON, SNOWFLAKE'S Chief of Police, turned on his siren as he pulled up to the curb—an action he generally had no need for, but now the crowd had grown and several people were shouting at one another from opposite sides of the fence. One man was beating on a drum while the rest of the protesters were chanting, "*Car Wash—Hog Wash*," over and over. Many of them carried large placards that read, "*Go away—wash your car another day*." A few people had crawled through the torn chain-link fence and were attempting to block some of the workers with their signs. Jack Jamieson and Barry Sanders had managed to crawl through the fence before one of the workmen manned the opening. The worker stood, a large hammer in hand, discouraging anyone else from slipping through.

Richard Rowland slammed shut the door of the construction trailer and picked his way across the muddy site. He wore an expensively tailored suit and highly polished shoes. Reaching a bulldozer that had come to a stop, he shouted at the driver, ordering him to resume earth removal. The worker shook his head, crossed his arms and ignored Rowland's orders, unwilling to rev up his equipment with civilians on-site.

A woman in the crowd screamed at the developer, "Get out of town or you'll regret it! You'll be sorry you ever came to Snowflake!"

Rowland turned to stare at her, then awkwardly slogged his way through mud and dirt toward the fence. He grasped the links of the fence with both hands and shouted, his voice rising in pitch, "Is that a threat? Are you threatening me?" Spittle ran down his chin.

The woman jumped away from the fence. "You're a mad dog. You know that?" she declared contemptuously. A few of the protestors overheard the exchange and picked up the phrase, chanting, "*Mad Dog . . . Mad Dog*," while others moved closer to the fence, barking and howling at Rowland.

Nate Edgerton climbed out of his cruiser and approached the group by the fence. "All right everyone," he shouted. "Just back off. You have a right to demonstrate. You do not have the right to trespass or create obstructions." The crowd booed him.

Edward Embry, the lone councilman who had voted against the construction proposal, called out, "Nate, whose side are you on?"

"I'm on the side of law and order, Ed. This vote's gone through and there's nothing I can do about it. But I am gonna make sure nobody gets hurt."

"We're not leaving, Nate. We'll be here every day," Rod Thibeault hollered, glaring at the developer. Rod was a young lawyer from Lincoln Falls, frustrated that his attempted injunction to halt the construction had failed.

The drums and chanting ceased. The crowd had hushed to listen to the exchange between Embry and Nate. In that moment of relative quiet, a shout rang out from the construction site. The urgency in the worker's voice grabbed the crowd's attention. The workman stood next to the bulldozer pointing at something a few yards away, an alarmed look on his face. The demonstrators drew closer to the fence. A pile of old clothing lay in the dirt. As they watched, the clothing moved and morphed into human form. Arnie Hicks sat up and struggled to his feet.

Nate made a disgusted sound. "Arnie. What the hell . . . I looked for you last night. You woke up half the town."

Arnie, now on his feet, wobbling but upright, smiled at Nate and the demonstrators.

"You get out of there, Arnie. You coulda been hurt." Nate looked around for a way through the chain-link fence.

"I'm comin' out, Nate. No need to get testy. I fooled ya last night, didn't I?" Arnie laughed and raised his hand. He clutched something long and dark.

Nate narrowed his eyes. "What have you got there?"

Confused, Arnie looked at the object in his hand.

Nate's face blanched. "Damn it, Arnie. That's a bone!"

Somewhere in the crowd a woman cried out, "Is it human?"

THE BELL OVER the door rang and Meg rushed into the Spoonful. "Hi, Lucky. I'm late. Sorry. My Mom is picketing and I wanted to watch for a bit."

"How's it going up there?"

"Getting really noisy. Everyone's angry, but not as angry as that creepy developer guy."

Janie, taking an order from a table of lunchtime customers, looked up and raised her hand in greeting. Meg stuck her purse under the counter and tied an apron on. She slipped her glasses into a pocket and stood on tiptoe to peer through the hatch into the kitchen. "Hi, Sage." She smiled hopefully. Meg had nursed a crush on Sage for several months to no avail. Besides the fact that Meg was ten years too young for Sage, Sage was committed to his relationship with Sophie.

Lucky smiled, thinking about her schoolgirl crush on Dr. Elias Scott. She had never dared hope he would take an interest in her, but amazingly, now that she was several years out of college, and the difference in their ages wasn't such an overwhelming gap, they were actually dating. After several months, they were considered a couple by the town, and Lucky, as private as she was, could finally admit that, yes, they "liked" each other. Her schoolgirl fantasies had grown into a real relationship. All the same, her knees still became weak when Elias walked into a room. She was the last person on earth to judge Meg.

"Hi, Meg," Sage called in return. Meg waited for more of a response and when it wasn't forthcoming, heaved a sigh, put her glasses back on and started to arrange napkins and silverware behind the counter.

Janie stuck her order slip at the kitchen hatch and Sage grabbed it immediately. She turned to Lucky. "We're not exactly slow, but nowhere near what you'd expect this time of day."

"I think everyone's busy picketing at the construction site."

"After lunchtime, when it slows down, why don't I check with Sophie at the church and see if she needs help?"

"Oh, would you? That would be great. I'll pop over later to give you a break." Sophie's help had been invaluable this summer. Lucky had offered to pay her, explaining it wouldn't be a large sum, although she certainly deserved it. Sophie refused, adamant that she couldn't accept money. She had part-time work in the summer season and, in any event, couldn't commit to being an employee. She'd help out wherever she could, particularly where Sage was concerned, but mostly she was enjoying her time at the Spoonful and was happy to be hanging out with everyone.

The bell rang again and Lucky looked up. Marjorie and Cecily, the two sisters who ran the Off Broadway ladies' clothing store, came through the door. Cecily waved and headed for her regular stool at the counter. "My, it's quiet in here today." Cecily was outgoing and ebullient, her dark hair chopped in a pixie cut. Her sister, Marjorie, her polar opposite, was reserved and cool, her blonde hair always perfectly in place. She followed gracefully in Cecily's wake.

"Where is everyone?" she asked. "Are they all up at the demonstration?"

"Yes," Lucky replied. "Jack's up there with Hank and Barry and Horace. They expect this to go on most of the day."

"Wouldn't it be wonderful if they have some success in shutting it down? Although I don't hold out much hope," Marjorie replied.

Cecily pursed her lips and shook her head. "Try to be positive, dear. Just once."

"Why, what do you mean? I'm always positive."

Cecily shot a meaningful look at Lucky and remained silent.

"The usual?" Lucky asked. The sisters nodded in assent. Lucky quickly prepared two plates with croissants and jam, the sisters' favorite, and two cups of herbal tea. As she placed the dishes in front of them, she heard the phone ringing in the office.

"I'll be right back," she called to Janie and hurried down the corridor. She grabbed the phone on the third ring.

"Is Jack with you now?" It was Elizabeth Dove, her parents' oldest and dearest friend.

"No. He's at the demonstration."

"Oh." Lucky knew that Elizabeth loved her and worried about her. She was truly a surrogate mother since the death of Lucky's own mother, but it was strange to think Elizabeth included Jack on her worry list, especially now that she had been elected Mayor of Snowflake, with all the duties that office entailed.

"Why? What's going on?"

"I just got a call. A couple of fights have broken out and Nate's threatening arrests. *And* a skeleton's been discovered. How's that for news?"

"Did you say a *skeleton*?" Lucky cried. "I better take a walk up there and make sure Jack's not in trouble."

"I'm on my way too. I'll see you there." Elizabeth hung up without further ado.

Lucky pulled off her apron and placed it on a hook by the door. Sage, Janie and Meg would be fine on their own for a while. Now that Meg was on duty, Janie could man the cash register and Meg could handle the few customers. If Lucky had to take a break, there couldn't be a better time. She brushed off her skirt, returned to the front of the restaurant and pulled Janie aside. "Can you handle things for a bit? I'm going up to the Green to make sure Jack's okay."

"Sure, no worries. We can manage." Janie looked concerned. "Has something happened up there?"

Lucky leaned closer to her and whispered, not wanting the few nearby customers to hear. "Elizabeth just called. They've discovered a skeleton."

"Whaaat?" Janie inhaled deeply.

"Shhhh." Lucky glanced around to make certain no one in the restaurant had heard. Whatever had happened, everyone would know about it soon enough. "I'll be back as soon as I can."

She rushed out the front door and hurried to the corner of Main and across the Village Green to the construction site. She pushed through the crowd as far as she could go and stood on her toes, straining to locate Jack in the crowd. Several people called out to her but she didn't bother to respond. She pushed farther in until she reached the chain-link fence. Her grandfather was inside the site with Barry

Sanders, talking to Nate. She breathed a sigh of relief that Jack wasn't hurt or under arrest. Hank Northcross and a few other men were nearby. They were staring down at a shallow hole in the dirt. A young man and woman standing next to her peered through the fence. They looked like college students and were definitely summer tourists.

The woman said, "Wow. This *is* exciting."

The young man replied, "And you thought you'd be bored. See? Told you it'd be interesting." He chuckled.

Lucky felt a tap on her shoulder and turned to see Horace. "Horace, what's all the excitement?"

"Apparently Arnie Hicks spent the night right there. As your grandfather would say, he was three sheets to the wind, and probably still is." He pointed to the earthen depression that Nate and the other men were studying. "When he woke up, he was holding what looked like a femur in his hand."

Lucky's eyes widened. "A *human* femur?"

Horace nodded. "I doubt they know for sure yet, but it shocked everyone, I can tell you. I'm going to try to get a closer look." He moved away and maneuvered carefully through the crush of people to reach the spot where the fence was loose. He carefully bent down and struggled to get through the opening. Lucky watched him as he approached the group inside the site.

She heard a woman's raised voice. It was Elizabeth, standing at the edge of the crowd. Lucky turned and spotted her silvery white bob. "Everyone, please. Move away from the fence and let the police do their job."

Several people called out. "What's going on? What did they find?"

Elizabeth answered, "We're not exactly sure just yet. But as soon as we find out, you'll know too. Now, I suggest that under the circumstances, everyone should go home. This will have to be investigated. I've asked Nate to shut down construction for the time being until this is sorted out."

"Too bad you didn't shut the site down permanently," one angry man yelled out. The crowd had lost interest in the discovery and was straggling in Elizabeth's direction, surrounding her.

A woman hollered, "You should have done something about this!"

"This was not within my power. You all know that. It was voted on by the town council. I didn't approve of it, but it wasn't my decision to make. You'll have to take it up with them."

"We have. They won't listen to us," the same woman called out.

"Then I'm sorry. There's nothing I can do. But I can tell you the work on this site will stop for the time being until we look into this." Elizabeth's words didn't seem to calm the demonstrators. In fact, they were getting angrier. Lucky could tell from Elizabeth's expression she was becoming worried by the energy of the crowd. Lucky had clung to the chain-link fence to keep her balance in the jostling mass of people, but now she moved away from the fence and pushed through the mob to stand next to Elizabeth.

She shouted, "Back off everyone. She's already told you there's nothing she can do. Go home." Lucky blocked several people from coming closer to Elizabeth and put a protective arm around the older woman's shoulders. A few people glared at her, but they backed away.

"Thanks, Lucky," Elizabeth whispered, breathing a sigh of relief. "I know everyone's very upset about this. I am too. I wish this were being built somewhere else, but my hands are tied."

A tall, slender man with silver hair slipped through the crowd and joined them. He had a distinguished air in spite of the fact that he wore sandals and Bermuda shorts in deference to the heat. He held tightly to a leash attached to the collar of a black and tan dog with a white patch of fur over one eye. He turned to the demonstrators. "Please don't blame the Mayor. She's absolutely right. You all know I'm the one man who refused to vote for this disgusting project, but I was outnumbered. You know that."

"We know, Ed," a burly man called out. "And we know where the rest of the people on the council live, too. Maybe we oughta pay 'em all a visit. Believe me, none of 'em will have our vote at the next election." A few voices called out their agreement.

Lucky realized the tall man had to be Edward Embry, now a local hero for attempting to stop the car wash project. He turned back to Lucky and Elizabeth with a mischievous smile on his face. "What do you say we climb through the fence and see what's going on? At least we won't be pushed around in there."

"Good idea. I am curious," Elizabeth responded. "Oh, please excuse my manners. Lucky, this is Edward Embry, who's on our town council. Ed, Lucky Jamieson owns the By the Spoonful Soup Shop."

Lucky extended her hand. "Very nice to meet you."

"And you too." He shook the proffered hand. "And this is Cicero. He seems to like you."

Lucky reached down to pat Cicero's head. The dog's tail wagged furiously. "That's an unusual name." Lucky smiled up at Edward while Cicero planted a wet kiss on her hand.

"He talks a lot. I thought the name was appropriate." Edward's face had a rather careworn expression, but Lucky noted the sparkle in his eyes when he looked at Elizabeth.

Nate's deputy, Bradley Moffitt, now guarded the opening in the fence. He pulled the fence back for the Mayor and the town councilman. Bradley was proud of his law enforcement credentials and could be insufferably pompous at times. Lucky was afraid he'd try to bar her, but he said nothing as she followed Elizabeth onto the site.

Lucky heard her name called and turned around. Rowena Nash stood at the opening, waving to her, obviously wanting to be admitted to the site. Lucky sighed.

Rowena had the knack of always turning up when she was least wanted. Smiling provocatively at Bradley, Rowena put her hand on his arm, obviously pleading with him to let her through. Bradley pulled himself up to his full height of five feet seven inches in an attempt to look authoritative. Lucky watched the exchange. Bradley didn't stand a chance. Rowena smiled wider, and with a last caress to Bradley's arm, scrambled through the opening. Bradley gallantly held back the fence for her. Rowena was breathless as she caught up with them.

"Okay if I tag along?"

Elizabeth turned around. "Rowena, you shouldn't be here."

"But I want to write this up for the *Gazette*. This is news!"

"That might not be such a good idea. Can you wait a bit until we have more information?"

"We can't just ignore this. It's intriguing. I promise to just stick to the facts if you promise to share what you figure out. Deal?" Rowena smiled ingratiatingly.

Lucky could see the shifting emotions on Elizabeth's face. Rowena was beside herself at the prospect of actually having a novel story to cover, but Elizabeth was unwilling to totally trust Rowena's word.

Elizabeth shrugged. "All right. As long as Nate doesn't kick you out. Just remember, it's an investigation. I want your solemn promise you won't submit anything until Nate or I give it an okay."

"I promise." Rowena nodded seriously.

"All right then. Follow us. Let's see if we can find out what's happening."

Rowena dutifully followed Elizabeth, Edward Embry and Lucky to the group standing over the depression.

Nate was kneeling on the ground, gently moving clumps of dirt away with his hands. "Somebody have a clean brush?" he asked without looking up. One of the workers hurried away and returned a few moments later, brush in hand. Nate grabbed it, gently sweeping off another layer of dirt. He uttered an oath and stood up. The shape was unmistakable. An eye socket displaying a long tendril of tree root peered blindly from the earth. Nate had uncovered a skull.

Chapter 6

"ELIZABETH." NATE NODDED to the Mayor. "We're gonna need some help. I'm not sure what we have here. Judging by the color of the bone, I suspect this must be very old." Nate noticed Rowena and frowned. He looked as though he intended to order her from the site.

Elizabeth caught Nate's expression. "I gave Rowena permission. She's promised not to submit anything until you or I approve it."

Nate shrugged his shoulders. "Good enough." He took off his cap and scratched his head. "I'm waiting for Elias. He should be here any minute."

A door slammed in the distance and Richard Rowland, his expensive shoes now covered with lumps of mud, stormed out of the construction trailer and charged toward Nate. "I want that damn thing out of here." He attempted to take an authoritative pose, but his highly polished shoe stuck in the mud. He tripped and stumbled, quickly righting himself.

"Calm down, Mr. Rowland," Nate responded. "It will be. Just as soon as we have it looked at."

"That's not good enough," he hissed. "I have workers here. I'm on a tight schedule and I have to complete this on time. I need to know when I can start work again. And you!" He pointed at Edward Embry, who had remained silent until now. "What do you think you're doing on my site?"

Edward's expression was grim. "You know damn well why I'm here. I'm going to make sure we see the last of you in this town."

"Are you threatening me?" Rowland stuck his chin out, his voice rising in pitch.

"Take that any way you want," Edward replied calmly. Something in his tone caused Rowland to take a step back.

Horace cleared his throat and addressed the developer. "Sir, I don't think you understand. This is something the coroner will have to examine, and if this is very old, the anthropologists will also have to have a look. Perhaps this site is an old burial ground. If these bones turn out to be Native American remains, that's a whole different kettle of fish. They're protected by the Native American Graves Protection and Repatriation Act. And, at the very least, someone will certainly need to contact the Vermont Division for Historic Preservation."

Rowland ignored Horace. "You!" He pointed in Nate's direction. "I asked you a question!"

Nate took a deep breath, struggling to remain patient. He turned and shot Rowland a withering look. "Your schedule is not my concern. My concern is dealing with these human remains, so I suggest you go right back to your trailer and I'll let you know when you can resume work. Is that clear enough?"

"Like hell it is. I own this parcel and what I say goes. I want that thing out of here and I intend to continue this project."

Nate's eyes narrowed. Rowland was treading on dangerous ground. "Mr. Rowland—understand this—it is against state law to disturb burial sites of any kind. It doesn't matter if it's privately held land. Until we investigate further, you can consider your project shut down."

"You can't do that!"

"I just did, Mr. Rowland."

"You'll hear from my lawyers."

"You do that. You give them a call. I'm sure they'll tell you the very same thing." Nate, seemingly unperturbed by Rowland's outburst, turned back to the bones in the earth.

Rowena had foolishly positioned herself in front of Rowland before he could move away. "Excuse me. I wonder if you could give me a few minutes for an interview for the *Gazette*. At your convenience, of course." She smiled broadly, completely ignoring the heated altercation that had just taken place between the two men.

Rowland stared at her for a long minute and then, without a word, turned on his heel and strode back to his construction trailer, his dignity compromised once again by the mud.

Horace spotted Elias coming through the fence and waved to him. "Over here, Elias." Carrying a heavy black bag, Elias hurried over to join their small group. Dr. Elias Scott was not only the head of the Snowflake Clinic but the county coroner.

"I got here as soon as I could, Nate. Full house this morning." He passed Lucky, and reached out to squeeze her hand quickly. She smiled in return. Then he bent down next to the partially uncovered skull and whistled softly. A tiny flake of black material started to lift in the breeze. Elias grabbed a pair of tweezers from his bag and pushed it back into its original position. No one spoke. Elias continued to stare at the remains and said nothing.

Finally, Nate broke the silence. "What do you think, Elias? How long has this been in the ground?"

Elias stood and brushed off his clothes. "This is extremely old, Nate. Look at the pitting and discoloration of the bone tissue. The surface is heavily flaked and abraded. I'm sure the mandible has separated from the skull. All the material has rotted away of course, although there could be tiny fragments underneath."

"Any guess as to whether this skeleton is Native American?"

"You'd need to take cranial metrics to determine that. I don't want to jump the gun, but judging by the shape of the skull and eye sockets, I'd say offhand this skeleton is Caucasoid."

"Can you tell how long it's been here?"

Elias turned and smiled. "Oh, my guess is a very, very long time. There's mineralization on that bone, and you'll find more tree roots as you dig down. There's no way of telling if there's a complete skeleton there. Obviously the site's been disturbed already. Maybe there'll be a lot of difficulty if the bones have bonded with the soil. That can be like extracting them from concrete. Animals could have carried off some of the bones too. You'll need to notify the University. This is something the forensic anthropologists should look at." Elias replaced the tweezers in a side pocket of his bag. "Don't think I can be of much use here, but I'll be at the Clinic if anyone needs me."

Lucky hated to admit it, but she felt a thrill every time Elias was near. Had she fallen in love? Probably, she thought, head over heels. She only hoped it was returned as deeply. She walked with him back to the opening in the fence. "You think this might have been an old burial ground?"

He shook his head. "I really don't know. That's for the anthropologists to decide, but my guess is no. I don't see any remnant of a casket. If he was shrouded, that material would have completely rotted away. If he was a victim of war he might have been buried in a hurry. I'll be curious to hear what the experts have to say."

He touched her arm lightly and a thrill ran through her. "I'll give you a call tonight." He turned and crossed Water Street, heading across the Village Green to return to the Clinic. Lucky watched him until he reached Broadway then she returned to the group at the gravesite.

Horace was elated at the discovery. "I knew it. I just knew it. I know some people at Bennington. I can make some calls. I'm sure they'll get here as soon as they can."

"You're just the man," Nate replied. "Now, it's getting on in the day. We'll have to erect a small tent over this," he said, indicating the pile of bones. "I doubt it'll be raining tonight, but I don't want anyone poking around."

"Perhaps we can form a little team. Myself. Jack?" Horace looked questioningly at Jack.

Jack nodded his agreement. "Hank and Barry will donate some time, I'm sure."

"We can split it up into four-hour increments. We should camp out here and make sure no one disturbs anything," Horace responded.

"Good. My deputy can do a shift too. You men work it out with him."

Lucky said, "I'll send one of the girls over with a basket of sandwiches and drinks. Jack, can you help me with that?" Her grandfather had always insisted she call him by his name. He cringed at the thought of any title he thought was for old men. He wasn't ever going to be old and insisted he always be called "Jack."

"Sure will, my girl. Right now, it's just about five bells."

Barry smiled. "What he said . . ."

"He means it's two thirty." As a young girl Lucky had learned to tell time Navy style, thanks to Jack. It was

second nature to her now, especially when she was talking
to her grandfather.

Jack ignored Barry's comment. "Barry, why don't you
take the first watch while Horace calls the University, and
I'll be back with some food and a couple of folding chairs."
Barry nodded in agreement and plopped down awkwardly
on a small piece of discarded plywood.

Nate said, "I'll send Bradley to the station and have
him bring back something we can use as a kind of a tent.
Or maybe the workmen have some tarps. We'll figure
it out."

Most of the crowd had dissipated by the time everyone
climbed back through the fence and reached the sidewalk
on Water Street. Lucky realized that Edward Embry had
slipped away after his confrontation with the developer.
Bradley had already left for the police station, and Lucky
and Elizabeth were the last ones to leave the site, other than
Barry, who sat cross-legged at attention.

Jack was waiting for them on the sidewalk. He nodded
to Elizabeth and then turned to Lucky. "I'll head back to
the Spoonful and get some sandwiches ready."

"I'll catch up in a minute, Jack. Sage and the girls are
there. I'm sure they're fine, but they'll wonder what happened to us."

Jack hurried away while Lucky strolled slowly across
the Village Green with Elizabeth. Since Elizabeth Dove
had been elected Mayor, her schedule was tight. Lucky
didn't often have a chance for an impromptu chat with her.
She had always felt close to the older woman, as though
she were an aunt, but now, with her mother gone, the connection with Elizabeth had grown deeper. Elizabeth had
never married or had children of her own. She thought of
Lucky as the daughter she never had, especially now that
Lucky's parents were gone.

"I'll never be able to figure that out." Elizabeth smiled.

"What's that?" Lucky asked.

"Telling time by the bells."

"Oh—it's very simple really. You see, the day is divided into six sections and each section into eight time frames . . ."

"Enough!" Elizabeth covered her ears. "I'll never get it. Save your breath." She burst out laughing.

"Just don't try to tell Jack the time using any other method." Lucky linked her arm through Elizabeth's as they walked. "Edward Embry seems like a very nice man." She watched Elizabeth to gauge her reaction. "I think he's a little sweet on you."

Elizabeth shook her head. "Once, perhaps."

"Once?" Lucky felt as if she had trod on a private area. "I'm sorry. I didn't mean to pry."

Elizabeth smiled. "That's quite all right." She glanced at Lucky's concerned expression. "Really, it's all right. You weren't prying. Besides, it's no secret. A long time ago . . ." Elizabeth trailed off. She was silent for a few moments. "A long time ago . . . oh," Elizabeth laughed. "More than twenty years ago now, that might have been possible, but it just didn't work out. Edward has had a very sad life. He lost a child years ago, and his wife shortly after. It didn't work out for the two of us, but we're on good terms. He devotes all his time now to town business."

Lucky glanced back at the group still inside the chain-link fence. Barry and two of Rowland's workers were erecting a rather efficient tent out of boards and plastic sheeting. A movement next to the fence caught her eye. She stopped to get a better look.

Elizabeth turned as well. "What is it?"

"I . . . somebody there, on the other side of the fence. Not where the men are standing. See?" Lucky indicated a huddled figure, wrapped in a loose coat, at the far end of the site.

"Oh . . . how strange." Elizabeth followed Lucky's gaze. "That's Maggie. Maggie Harkins. I didn't think she ever came into town anymore. That poor soul. How strange it is . . . to see them all here again after so many years . . ."

"I've never seen her. Who is she?"

"She's a dreadful creature who should be put away." Lucky jumped involuntarily at the harsh voice. Cordelia Rank blocked their path. Cordelia was dressed in a spotless white skirt and a linen navy jacket. Her two-toned shoes and purse coordinated perfectly with her outfit.

"Now, Cordelia. Try to have some compassion, for heaven's sake," Elizabeth replied.

"Compassion?" Cordelia's voice had risen. "If this town had compassion, she'd be locked up and cared for. That would be the humane thing to do—not allowing her to wander the roads and the town at all hours doing who knows what. Why, she's not fit to take care of herself. Look at the way she's dressed."

"Please keep your voice down. I wouldn't want her to hear you."

"Someone has to take charge of her. She's obviously dotty."

"On what grounds would you suggest we do that? She may not meet your strict standards, but she bothers no one. She has her own home and income. Frankly, Cordelia, it really is none of your business if Maggie Harkins chooses to wander the town looking disheveled."

"People like that"—Cordelia's lip curled—"make our town look bad. As you must know, my ancestor was a Vermont militiaman and this is a very important celebration for me and my sisters. I have several guests from the Daughters of the American Revolution arriving for our Reenactment of the Battle and it simply creates the wrong impression."

"I realize that, Cordelia, and I'm sorry Maggie doesn't meet with your approval, but whether the DAR approves of her or not, she is a resident of Snowflake and has committed no crime. She needs to be left in peace."

Cordelia glared at Elizabeth, while Elizabeth maintained a calm and reasonable composure, letting her words sink in. Cordelia's cheeks were flushed, and she was obviously chagrined that Elizabeth had bucked her. She turned on a pristine heel and headed toward the white-steepled church at the end of the Green.

"Whew," Elizabeth said when Cordelia was a good fifty feet away. "That woman." She shook her head.

"What was all that about the Daughters of the American Revolution?"

Elizabeth groaned. "Cordelia Cooper Rank is a DAR and she never ever lets anyone forget it. Her husband, Norman, is from a very old, wealthy family. Although why all that is so important, I have no idea. Half the people in this town can point to ancestors that go back just as far. So what? What's important is how you behave in the twenty-first century, if you ask me. And that woman needs to learn some manners."

"Well, I certainly know her husband. He's our landlord at the Spoonful. All the same, I don't know how you do it." Lucky marveled. "How you handle the politics, the budget, the town council, the voters and the personalities. I stand in awe."

"Not at all. I've just lived a long time and I can smell the lawn fertilizer a mile away. And now that I'm an old lady . . ."

"You're hardly old."

"I'll be sixty in a couple of years and I've earned the right to say what I please and talk like a longshoreman. Maybe I should learn some good old Navy cuss words from Jack, even if I can't tell time to suit him."

Lucky laughed. "Why don't you take a break? Come on back with me. We have a fabulous celery and green onion soup that Sage serves cold. Just the thing for a hot day."

"All right, I will. Thanks, Lucky. But after that, I'll have to get back to the office. I just know that Cordelia Cooper Rank, DAR extraordinaire, will have left several messages to torture me further."

Chapter 7

THE SPOONFUL WAS noisy and packed with customers by the time Lucky and Elizabeth arrived. The room was bright with afternoon sunshine, but the ceiling fans kept the cool air circulating. The aroma of soups and breads filled the room, and Jack's favorite CD with a clarinet solo played in the background, softening the clatter of dishes and trays. A large group of demonstrators had descended on the Spoonful. They were elated that the discovery of a body had put an end, however temporary, to construction. Judging by some of the conversations Lucky overheard, the group was planning its next onslaught against Richard Rowland's construction project.

She glanced around the restaurant searching for a quiet table for Elizabeth. Elizabeth touched her arm. "I'll just grab a stool at the counter. I can't stay very long anyway. You'll be busy with this crowd. We can catch up later."

Lucky hurried down the corridor and pulled an apron

from the shelf. She slipped behind the counter to relieve Meg. Janie and Meg were both just out of high school. Janie was tall and thin with an electric energy. She moved quickly, whisking away dishes, resetting the tables and taking orders. Meg's movements were slower and calmer, yet she almost never made a mistake.

The day's specials were cream of asparagus soup and a celery and green onion soup served chilled. Sage had agreed that adding salads for the summer was a good idea, so in addition to sandwiches, the Spoonful was offering a walnut apple salad with crumbled bleu cheese, a roasted vegetable salad with a peanut dressing and a thinly sliced beef salad with vinaigrette dressing. Elizabeth ordered the chilled celery and green onion soup with a serving of crispy flatbread baked with feta cheese. As soon as she finished her lunch, Elizabeth blew a kiss in Lucky's direction and headed for her office. The next two hours flew by, and once the rush was over, Lucky poured a glass of iced tea and joined the men at their table.

"I thought he was with us," Barry grumbled. He had tucked his napkin in under his chin, and now pulled it off and dabbed at his mouth. The buttons on his plaid shirt were still holding firm.

Hank looked across the table, peering over his glasses. "He is with us. He's in complete agreement. Why would you think otherwise?"

"Because he didn't even show up today." Barry shook his head. "Harry's the one who organized everyone and he couldn't find a few minutes to turn up on the first day? And at the last meeting, he seemed kind of . . . I don't know . . . held back, like maybe he was having second thoughts."

"Hmm." Hank rubbed his chin. "He was quiet. But I know he agrees with us. Maybe he got stuck at the shop— maybe somebody needed a tow."

Barry grumbled. "I can't put my finger on it, but it seems like more than that."

Jack spoke up. "Don't worry about Harry. He'll turn up next time. And speaking of Harry, I've gotta pick up my car. I put it in the shop for an oil change but I need to get over to Lincoln Falls tomorrow to get supplies."

The bell over the door rang as Rod Thibeault stepped inside. Lucky had noticed him speaking with Nate's deputy, Bradley, at the construction site after the demonstration broke up, but hadn't seen him since. He smiled in their direction and headed for the large table to join them. Rod's hair was carrot red and his face was sprinkled with freckles. Lucky had a hard time believing he was old enough to have graduated law school and been in practice for several years. He wiped his brow. "Nice and cool in here. Mind if I join you?"

"Not at all, Rod. Have a seat." Barry slid his chair closer to Lucky to make room for the attorney. "Thanks for coming out with us today."

Rod grabbed a chair from another table and slid it over. "Quite a surprise." He laughed. "Of all the things that could have happened today." He shook his head.

"The good news is it threw a monkey wrench into Rowland's plans."

Rod nodded. "And no doubt will crank up his lawyer's fees. Couldn't wish it on a better fellow."

"Yeah, well, the law didn't do much for us, did it?" Hank remarked.

Rod's face fell but Hank immediately rushed to apologize. "Not your fault, Rod. You did a good job. That guy just had the damn town council on his side."

"And maybe the judge too, for all I know," Rod said. "Except for Edward Embry—more power to him."

Lucky rose and started to gather up some of the dishes. "Would you like something cold, Rod? An iced tea?"

"That sounds great. Thanks, Lucky."

Lucky returned to the counter and slid the dishes and glassware into a plastic bin. The front door opened and she looked up to see Elias. He smiled and headed for the counter.

"You must be starving. You didn't get any lunch, did you?"

"You got that right. What a day!" Elias sighed, collapsing on a stool at the counter.

"What would you like?"

"Some time with you." He smiled.

Lucky blushed. "Shhh, big ears are in the room." She couldn't help but grin from ear to ear.

"I'll behave myself. I promise. Anything is fine."

"Hang on for a sec." She filled two tall glasses with ice and poured the iced tea, adding a lemon wedge. One she passed to Elias and the other she carried to Rod at the table. She headed for the kitchen where Sage was chopping vegetables.

"Hey, Lucky, need anything?"

"I'll take care of it." She enjoyed the fact that Sage now always called her by her name. When she had first come home from Madison and taken over the restaurant he'd consistently kept his distance, calling her "boss." Whether that was because he worried she wouldn't keep him on, or perhaps due to resentment at taking orders from someone slightly younger, she never knew. But since her efforts last winter resulted in his release from jail, their relationship was on solid footing. Now he always called her by her name.

She brought Elias a large bowl of the chilled celery and green onion soup and a cream cheese, red onion and watercress sandwich on dark rye. His schedule had been far too busy and pressured. Even with an assistant, a nurse, a records clerk and two receptionists at the Clinic, he was still the only doctor in town and had to travel to Lincoln Falls when his patients were admitted to the hospital. The schedule was taking its toll on him. They managed to get together at least twice a week and saw each other, if not every day, close to it, but she knew he was overworked and needed a vacation.

"Let's have dinner this week. I've promised myself a night off. No trudging over to the hospital, no reading, nothing. And I'll cook."

"Sounds lovely. Any luck finding a new doctor?" She felt a twinge of guilt, or perhaps responsibility. Because of her, Elias had lost his partner at the Clinic. When it came to light that his partner's wife was guilty of murder, the man was compelled to leave town. Lucky still had nightmares about the events of the previous winter.

Elias looked up at her. "Don't go there. I know you're feeling responsible, but it's not your fault."

"I know that," she replied. "If only . . ."

"If only, what? It had to happen the way it happened. The truth had to come out. What would you rather? That Sage go to jail for the rest of his life?"

Lucky glanced through the hatch at Sage, busy at work in the kitchen. "Of course not," she said vehemently.

Elias reached across the counter and squeezed her hand. "There's nothing nice about emotions that would drive a normally decent person to murder. But you did nothing wrong, just remember that."

Lucky looked into Elias's eyes and her heart melted. She finally smiled.

"That's better," he said. Lucky reached out and touched the dimple on his chin.

"I hate to interrupt you two lovebirds," Barry announced, heading for the counter and grabbing the stool next to Elias. Lucky blushed furiously and pulled her hand away. "Tell me something, Elias. How could those bones still be preserved if they're so old?"

Elias wiped his chin and turned to face Barry. "It has a lot to do with the pH of the soil. Generally speaking, soil with neutral acidity, or even alkalinity, will preserve bone. With the right pH balance, bones can last for hundreds of years—even longer. On the other side of the argument, there are scientists who don't agree that soil conditions have that much to do with preservation. You've heard of bog bodies, of course?"

"Oh yes. Pretty amazing."

"Those bodies were buried in acidic sphagnum bogs, mostly in northern Europe. The skin is severely tanned, but it's preserved. Even facial features are obvious. That happens because of the high acidity, low temperature and lack of oxygen. However, the bones in that type of soil aren't preserved very well at all because the acid in the peat dissolves the calcium phosphate in the bone tissue, while the skin and internal organs remain intact. I'm sure the anthropologists will want to take measurements of the pH of that soil. As I said, some experts claim pH is irrelevant, while others swear by it."

"To think some poor soul was lying under the ground near the Village Green all these years. I can't wait to hear what the University people have to say."

"Hopefully, most of the skeleton can be retrieved. They should be able to figure out if this individual was male or female and its age at the time of death fairly quickly. Any other tests will take a little longer."

Lucky cleared the dishes away as Barry returned to his chair at the big table. Elias looked up and squeezed her hand. "Sorry. I have to rush off."

Lucky nodded, disappointed he was leaving, but at least they had made a plan to have dinner together this week.

Chapter 8

ELIZABETH RINSED OFF her breakfast dishes and placed them in the strainer. Cordelia Rank's remarks still haunted her. She had taken offense at Cordelia's snobbery, but all the same, perhaps the woman had a point—not that Maggie should be locked away, but that she might very well need help. Had anyone checked on her lately? Perhaps Cordelia was right and Maggie wasn't able to take very good care of herself. Before yesterday, when was the last time Maggie had been seen in town? And when was the last time she had received a visit from a neighbor?

Elizabeth, in her former life, had taught elementary school and remembered Maggie as she had once been—a young mother with a little boy—her son Danny. Elizabeth knew Maggie Harkins's history and was well aware of the forces that had shaped her life. There no longer was a reason for Elizabeth to stay in touch, but what kind of a Mayor was she if she didn't worry about the least protected of her citizens? What kind of a woman was she not to take an

interest, and at least make sure that Maggie had food in her
house and heat in the winter? Her conscience had bothered
her no end since she had seen Maggie skulking around the
Village Green.

She took a last sip of coffee and rinsed her cup in the
sink, placing it neatly in the dish strainer. Charlie, her cat,
brushed up against her legs in the knowledge that Elizabeth was getting ready to leave. She reached down and
scratched his head. He purred in response. She checked
that Charlie had enough food and water to last the day, and
shut the kitty door to keep him safely in the house and out
of the summer heat.

"I'm sorry, Charlie. It's too hot today. You can go out
this evening." Charlie was older now and didn't need to be
constantly roaming. Besides, he had a big two-story house
to roam in while she was at work. Taking her purse and car
keys, she locked the front door and climbed into her car. It
wouldn't hurt to check on Maggie. It was just a few miles
in the other direction. Then she could head to her office.
Won't take any time at all, she thought.

PASTOR EARL WILSON stood close to the head of the
earthen depression, a prayer book in hand, and surveyed
the group. Horace Winthorpe had made all the arrange-
ments and now, Professor Daniel Arnold, the head of the
Archaeology Department at the University, had arrived
early in the morning following the discovery of the
remains. With him were three graduate students in work
clothes, armed with shovels, trowels and brushes. They had
quickly dismantled the temporary shelter of boards and
plastic and now, eager to begin their work, stared in fascination at the remains still lodged in the earth.

Pastor Wilson had insisted that no soul should be buried
or dug up without prayers for the afterlife, and since this

soul more than likely hadn't been properly buried to begin with, he certainly needed some good words to speed him on his way. He had made a point of calling some of his steadfast parishioners as well as the Spoonful's regulars to request attendance at his service. Lucky agreed to come in Jack's place, since he had errands to run. Sophie, curious about the discovery, decided to tag along.

Lucky and Sophie, along with Hank, Barry and Horace waited for the ceremony to begin. The Professor and his three charges, and Nate Edgerton and others of the Pastor's flock stood close by the grave. In addition, a small, curious crowd had gathered outside the fence along Water Street to watch the proceedings. Everyone waited in respectful silence.

Pastor Wilson stood, his hands clasped in front of him, and spoke. "In the presence of death, we must continue to sing the song of life. We must be able to accept death and go from its presence better able to bear our burdens and to lighten the load of others." When he had finished, a hush fell over the small group. In all likelihood, one of their own was being exhumed. Everyone watched while the graduate students began their work, gently brushing dirt away, slowly creating pedestals of earth around each fragment—a long, slow, laborious process.

Nate Edgerton viewed the scene for several minutes and then signaled to Bradley, who waited outside the fence. Together they cut and pulled back the chain-link fence to allow easy removal of the remains later in the day. Nate returned to the sidewalk, while Bradley stood guard at the opening to keep the curious at a distance.

Horace, watching the proceedings carefully, moved closer. Something had caught his eye. "What is that?" He pointed to a dark curved shape lying slightly deeper in the earth. One student, her hair pulled back in a bun under a baseball cap, looked up.

"Not sure." She brushed away the dirt carefully, better exposing the shape of the object. She turned back to Horace. "Looks like it might be a . . . maybe a powder horn?"

"It might have some carvings—perhaps even a name. If it does . . . and I'm assuming this person is a 'he' . . . we might actually be able to find out who this fellow was," Professor Arnold offered, grinning broadly at Horace.

"You're right." Horace nodded. "It was common for people to carve their names, sometimes even drawings of their homes, on powder horns—if that's what it is—like scrimshaw. It's not likely, but perhaps we might find a weapon nearby. This is terribly exciting!" Horace turned to Lucky and Sophie. "You see, not everyone could afford a rifle or other type of gun. During the Revolutionary War, small towns kept a common stock that the men, and even women, would use in case of an attack, but most men did carry their own powder horns."

Professor Arnold spoke. "Let's not get ahead of ourselves. This body could be much older—pre–Revolutionary War, or even much younger. Eventually we'll be able to date the bones."

As the work progressed and no further finds seemed likely, people drifted away, back to their jobs and homes. There wasn't much to interest the onlookers in the slow, tedious work taking place. Nate released Bradley from guard duty, sending him back to the station. Nate said good-bye and drove away in his cruiser. Hank and Barry lingered by the fence until the crowd had completely dispersed.

Barry turned and scanned the spectators drifting away. "I didn't see Harry. Did you?"

Hank shook his head. "No."

"I'm telling you, it's strange the way he's been acting."

Hank replied, "Harry's right where he should be. At his shop. Working."

"Speaking of who wasn't here today, I'm sure glad that Rowland character didn't show up," Barry said.

"Why should he? He doesn't care about this town. If he did, he wouldn't be building this concrete blight in the middle of it."

Lucky checked her watch. It was time to get to the restaurant. She turned to leave and a movement across the street caught her eye. Her grandfather Jack was on the Green, stumbling toward them. His face was pale and he was in obvious distress. Before Lucky could react, Jack's knees buckled and he collapsed on the grass.

Chapter 9

LUCKY RUSHED THROUGH the fence and raced across the street to reach Jack. Her heart was in her throat. Was he ill or having a flashback to his days in the war? Sophie ran to catch up with her. When they reached Jack, Lucky grasped his arm gently and helped him to his feet.

"Are you hurt?" she asked. Jack shook his head. He opened his mouth to speak, but couldn't seem to form any words. He looked helplessly at Lucky.

She took his hands in hers. "Take a deep breath. Tell me what happened." Together, Lucky and Sophie led him slowly to a nearby bench. Sophie sat next to Jack holding his hand, and Lucky knelt on the grass to get a better look at his face. He swallowed with difficulty and raised his arm, pointing toward Spruce Street.

Sophie looked questioningly at Lucky. In answer to her silent question, Lucky said, "He was heading for Harry's Auto Shop to pick up his car." She turned to Jack. "Did something happen there?"

Jack covered his face with his hands, leaving a smear of blood on his cheek. "Harry's gone."

Hank and Barry, also realizing that something was terribly wrong, had rushed across the street. "Jack, what's happened?" Hank asked, placing a hand on Jack's shoulder.

Lucky looked up at them and said softly, "He said, 'Harry's gone.' Can you find Nate and ask him to get to Harry's right away?"

Hank and Barry looked up and down the street, half hoping that Nate would magically appear. Hank patted his pockets. "I don't have my phone with me."

Barry pulled his cell out of his pocket. "I do. I'll call the station. Bradley can reach Nate quicker than we can."

Jack's breathing was starting to return to normal. Lucky watched him carefully. "Do you want to go to the Clinic?"

"No," Jack grumbled. "I'm fine now. Almost. Just the shock . . . the blood. I just want to go back to the Spoonful." Lucky knew that certain things set off Jack's reaction, particularly the sight of blood. It carried with it nightmares of his time in the Pacific attempting to rescue men at sea attacked by sharks. Even though his flashbacks had decreased in their occurrence and severity now that his health had improved, she knew it could still be very difficult for him to hold on to reality and not let the past flood his mind.

Lucky caught Sophie's eye. "Sophie's going that way. She'll walk back with you." Sophie nodded affirmatively.

Jack squeezed her hand. He seemed a bit more in control. "I don't want to be any trouble."

"It's no trouble, Jack," Sophie offered. "I have to go that way anyway. My car's there."

Jack looked at Lucky. "I'm sorry. I'm a useless old man."

"Oh, Jack." Lucky reached up to give him a hug. "Don't say that. It's not true. There's nothing to be sorry about."

Jack stood and took a deep breath. He started to walk

slowly across the Green. Lucky edged closer to Sophie and whispered, "It could be Harry's had an accident. If you walk back to the Spoonful with Jack, I'll go check." If Harry were hurt and unable to reach help, she didn't want to wait until a message reached Nate. Who knew how long it would take for Nate to get there? Jack might just have overreacted at the sight of blood. Harry might need an ambulance, in which case she could call Elias at the Clinic and he could arrange one.

Sophie hurried to catch up with Jack. Lucky watched them until they crossed the street and turned the corner on Broadway. She left Hank and Barry, still waiting to speak to Nate, by the park bench and hurried across the Green, turning down Spruce Street. She ran the three blocks to the end and came to a quick halt on the sidewalk in front of the Auto Shop. The bay doors were closed. They were never closed except on Sundays. When Harry was there, they were always open. She tried the side door. Locked. Could Harry be inside? Unconscious? She banged on the door. Perhaps if he were hurt, he could call out. She waited a moment, her ear pressed against the wooden door, but heard nothing. In frustration, she ran down the alleyway at the side of the old brick building, which had once housed a bakery. At the rear, a window at street level was wide open. She peered into the interior, but the brightness of the sun and the dimness inside made it impossible to see anything. Had Jack climbed through this window with the same thought?

She clambered over the windowsill and jumped a foot to the concrete floor. She called out again. No answer. Her eyes adjusted to the dim light filtering through the high, dusty windows. She could just see her way across the garage without tripping on any of the hoses lying about on the floor. The large, empty space was completely still. She moved toward the front of the shop and pushed open the door of the office where Harry worked. A terrible odor assailed her nostrils. Her foot touched something soft. She looked down and gasped. Harry lay on his side, his eyes staring sightlessly at the legs of a chair. Part of his skull was caved in and a pool of now-congealed blood surrounded his head.

Lucky covered her mouth, trying not to scream, but a low gurgle came from her throat. Jack was right. Harry was gone. She felt blood rushing through her ears. The room was spinning around. She heard a shout. It was Nate. She backed out of the office leaving the door ajar and managed to call to him.

"In here, Nate. I climbed through the window."

She heard Nate mutter as he scrambled over the windowsill, his heavy shoes hitting the concrete floor. "In the office." Her voice trembled.

Nate moved past her and gently pushed the door of the office open. He stared for a long moment at the body of Harry Hodges. He backed across the threshold and gave her a studied look. "Jack just found him?"

Lucky nodded her head, not trusting herself to speak. "He came over to pick up his car. He couldn't talk at first. He said Harry was gone. I ran over in case he was just hurt and needed help."

"You should have called me first."

"I would have but I didn't have my phone. Barry promised to find you."

"Well, that's it, then. Just what Snowflake didn't need—another murder."

"Can you be sure? Could he have been hurt under the lift?"

"He could have, but I doubt he could have walked into the office with that head wound. I'm no expert, but I really don't think so. Looks like somebody bashed his head in right here. But you listen to me, young lady. I don't want you involved—not like before. I want you as far away from this as possible. You hear me?"

Lucky gulped. "Fine with me. You're in charge."

"Glad you agree," Nate replied sarcastically. "Now, can I take you home or back to the restaurant? There's nothing we can do for Harry now."

"No. I'll be okay. I just want to get to the Spoonful to see how Jack's doing. Sophie walked back with him. I only meant to go to Pastor Wilson's ceremony and then get to work."

Nate pulled his cell phone out. "I'll start with a call to Elias and go from there. You sure you're all right?"

Lucky nodded. Nate led her to the door that gave access to the street. He pulled a white handkerchief from his pocket and carefully turned the lock, holding the door open for her. She stumbled out into the hot summer morning, blinded at first by the bright sunlight. Soon everyone would know about Harry—another murder in their midst.

Chapter 10

ELIZABETH CLIMBED THE steps of Maggie's house carefully, fearful that the damaged wood might give way beneath her feet. She held tightly to the shaky railing. One or two boards had nearly rotted away leaving only a jagged edge still nailed to its support. The house was in terrible repair. So much paint had peeled from the clapboards that layers of brown and gray were exposed. This wasn't the cheerful cottage Elizabeth remembered from years ago. No one had cared for or maintained this place for a long time.

When Elizabeth was still teaching, and both she and Maggie were young women, the house had been yellow, with white shutters. Now several of those shutters had fallen away. The window boxes were still in place, but the white paint had worn off, eroded by harsh weather. Any semblance of plant life had long since disappeared. She hated to think it, but Cordelia might be correct. Maggie really shouldn't be on her own.

She reached the front door and took a deep breath. Fearful of what she might find inside, she knocked. The door swung slowly open. It was unlatched. Elizabeth stood quietly, looking into the entry hall of the cottage. She called Maggie's name, hesitant to enter without permission. There was no response.

She called again. "Maggie? Are you here?" She stepped across the threshold. The door listed slightly, as though not hung properly on its frame. She wondered if it shut tight during the long winters. Then she wondered if Maggie had any source of heat. She looked through an archway into the small parlor. The floor was bare. A couch was pushed against the wall, several springs sticking up from one of the cushions. There was no other furniture in the room— no bookcases or small end tables. Surprisingly, there was no dust. Every surface appeared clean. A stairway to the right led to a second story where Elizabeth knew there were three small bedrooms. Many of the rungs in the banister were missing. Had Maggie been burning interior wood to keep warm in winter? The thought horrified her. She needed to make sure someone was delivering oil for the furnace. Elizabeth walked slowly into the living room and called out again.

"Maggie? It's Elizabeth. I was just driving past and thought I'd stop in." She waited. There was a stillness in the air, but the house didn't feel empty. It felt as if someone were watching and waiting, holding their breath. "Maggie, are you here?" Finally, Elizabeth heard a quavering voice. It came from the entry hall.

Elizabeth returned to the hallway and approached the cellar door tucked under the stairway. She pulled the door open. Was Maggie down there? She heard rustling sounds at the bottom of the stairs. A breeze of damp and moldy air arose. "Maggie, are you down in the cellar? Where are you?"

"Help." The voice was weak.

Elizabeth shuddered. The poor woman must have fallen

down the stairs. "I'm coming," she answered. Elizabeth grasped a splintered wooden railing and descended the narrow stairs carefully. A spiderweb brushed her cheek. The stairwell was dark but a tiny amount of light filtered through an opening high in the wall of the cellar. "Maggie, where are you? I can't see a thing. Is there a light switch?"

She heard no further sound. Elizabeth descended the rest of the way very slowly, still clinging to the railing. There had to be a light source down here. She felt along the wall and reached up to see if a hanging string might turn on a light. She stopped and stood still for a moment, her eyes slowly adjusting to the dark. A thin sliver of daylight was visible at the other end of the cellar. It was the opening of a hatch to the backyard. Next to that she could make out the shape of a rough workbench.

"Maggie. Please. Where are you?" She took the last step and reached the bottom. The air moved near her cheek. Instinctively she knew someone was close by. Elizabeth turned her head. A cloth was pressed forcefully against her face. She struggled to breathe. Terrified, her heart racing, she lashed out to free herself from the firm hands gripping her. She was falling. Her brain was going numb. She felt her body weaken and collapse as she finally lost consciousness.

THE NEWS OF Harry's death had spread like wildfire throughout Snowflake. It seemed appropriate that everyone, not just those involved with Harry and the demonstration, but all the restaurant's regulars and concerned citizens, should gather at the Spoonful throughout the day. Unlike the anger and excitement of the demonstration, this was a quiet group, shocked and numb, confused that anyone could have wanted to hurt Harry Hodges.

Barry and Hank, both very upset, had held court all day, as townspeople stopped by, stayed for a time then quietly left. Jack joined them occasionally, while Lucky, Janie and Meg handled customers. As far as Lucky could tell, the summer visitors appeared oblivious to what had happened in their midst. From experience, she knew this wouldn't last long.

Finally she decided to close the Spoonful an hour earlier than usual and sent Janie and Meg home. Hank and Barry remained at their table. Jack seemed to be stronger now, but she thought that giving him an excuse to go home early and get some rest after his shock was the best thing to do. She had riffled through a stack of CDs and found a harp instrumental. She plugged it in hoping it might soothe their spirits.

A loud knock came at the front door and everyone turned. Nate Edgerton stood outside on the threshold. Lucky walked over and unlocked the door for him. Nate entered without a word and sat at the table with the men. Without asking, Lucky poured an iced tea with a slice of lemon and brought it over to Nate.

He looked up. "You read my mind. Thanks."

Everyone at the table looked expectantly at Nate as if he could explain Harry's death to them. Nate shook his head. "There's not much I can tell any of you. In fact, I'm here to ask a few questions myself."

"Now, Jack." Nate pulled a small notebook out of his pocket. "I'm sorry to put you through this." Nate was being very gentle with Jack. He had always looked up to the older man. "I'm just hoping there might be some little detail that would help me out."

"Not much to tell." Jack shrugged. "I went over to see if my car was ready—that was right around one bell."

Nate paused with his pen over the notebook and looked at Lucky.

"He means eight thirty," Lucky offered.

"The place was locked up, which was strange, 'cause Harry starts his day early. I banged on the door, thinking he might be in the office, but nobody came. So then I went down the alley. I figured I'd take my car and leave Harry a note. Maybe he had just stepped out for a minute. I knew he wouldn't mind if I paid him later."

"Was that back window unlocked?"

"Closed, but not locked. I wouldn't have gone in like that, through the window, but I needed my car to drive over to Lincoln Falls. Had to get some supplies for the Spoonful." Jack rubbed his forehead and took a shaky breath. "Harry had told me the car would be ready. I thought I could just grab my keys and catch up with him later to pay him."

"When did you talk to him?"

"Oh, let's see . . . musta been the day before the demonstration."

"What time was that?"

"Right about four bells."

Nate sighed and looked across the table at Lucky.

"Two o'clock," she answered.

"Did you notice anything else? Anything strange or out of place?"

Jack shook his head slowly. "If I did, I'd never remember. It was seeing all that blood. I started to . . . you know . . . it always brings back things." Nate nodded sympathetically. "I could feel one of my spells coming on, but I knew I had to . . . I think I knew it was too late, but I wasn't thinking clearly. I . . . that's when I got the blood on me." Jack closed his eyes. "It was real bad."

Lucky interjected, "Nate, any idea when this might have happened?"

Nate shook his head. "Not sure. Elias thinks he might have been dead more than a day. It's hard to say. The weather's been hot, but the interior of that shop stays pretty cool. The techs from Lincoln Falls are working there now. They'll go over everything and then arrange an autopsy. We'll know more then."

"I feel just awful." Barry spoke. "I've been criticizing Harry for not showing up, accusing him of flaking out on the demonstration. And all the time . . ." Barry trailed off, unable to complete his thought.

Hank reached over and patted Barry on the shoulder. "How could you have ever known? You couldn't." Hank looked at Nate. "I don't understand why someone didn't find him right away. Where was Guy Bessette? Didn't he show up for work this morning?"

"I've already talked to Guy. They had just finished a couple of big jobs and Harry said he'd be fine on his own for the rest of the week. Guy wanted a few days off for the rehearsals and the Reenactment. He's pretty broken up right now. If you have a chance to talk to him, make sure he knows it wasn't his fault. Right now, he's thinking that if he hadn't taken time off, Harry might still be alive."

"What do you think, Nate?" Hank asked.

Nate was silent for a moment, staring off into space. "I doubt it. The place was locked up. The lamp on Harry's desk was still on. Looks to me, at least on the surface, like whatever happened, happened at night, well after Guy would have quit work for the day. But, Guy was probably the last one to see Harry alive . . . that we know of. And that was the night before last. There were a few messages on the answering machine from yesterday. I think if Harry were still alive then he would have hit the button and listened to 'em, even if he didn't return the calls right away."

"You think someone came to the shop at night then? Maybe somebody Harry knew?" Jack asked.

"Looks that way."

"Any money missing? Was it a robbery, you think?" Barry said.

"Nope. Plenty of cash on hand." Nate shrugged. "But I gotta ask you. Can you tell me when *you* last saw Harry?"

Barry rubbed his chin thoughtfully. "I guess it had to be the day before the demonstration. I mean, I didn't see him. I talked to him on the phone and gave him the names of a few more people who had promised to show up. He seemed fine."

"Anybody know of anything going on in his life that might have brought this about?"

Jack heaved a sigh. "Harry . . . well, you know how Harry was. If you didn't know him, you'd call him cranky. He wasn't a man who talked about himself or his feelings. Pretty much a loner. But I can't imagine anybody who would have wanted to hurt him."

"Taciturn might be a better way to describe Harry," Hank volunteered. "He was a good man, real straight arrow, hardworking, but Jack's right. Harry never talked about himself at all."

"I told him my car was no hurry. It wasn't till I needed to pick up some supplies that I went over there to get it." Jack shuddered. "Were there any other cars there being worked on?"

"Just yours and Norman Rank's fancy car. Both ready to go. That's why Guy says Harry didn't object to his taking some days off. It was a slow time."

Lucky pulled her chair closer to the table. "I saw Harry the day before the demonstration. He was talking to Pastor Wilson at the church. Sophie and I had gone over there to set up for the next day."

"Pastor Wilson, you say?"

Lucky nodded. She didn't want to repeat the conversation she had overheard in front of the whole table. She could tell Nate her impressions later, but she was sure he'd find out from the Pastor what Harry had said in more detail.

Nate took a last swallow of his iced tea. "I'll stop by and have a word with the Pastor before I head home. I'll see you folks later. If you think of anything I should know, you know where to find me."

"We will, Nate," Jack said.

Nate shoved his chair back and stood. "Thanks for the iced tea." Lucky followed him to the door and locked it behind him.

Everyone fell silent. Hank finally pushed his chair away from the table. "I'll be on my way, Jack. I guess there's not much we can do about any of this. It's a terrible shock. Nothing like this has ever happened in Snowflake. Not that I can remember. I mean there was that winter tourist, but this is different. Harry was a local."

"It's gonna hit everybody real hard," Jack replied.

Once the men were gone, Lucky moved around the room, turning off all but one of the lamps, and returned to the table to sit with Jack. "We should call it a night."

Jack peered out the window at the darkening street. "Not so fast. We've got an important customer on his way."

Lucky craned her neck to see. She smiled when she saw Elias approaching. She hopped up to open the door for him. Elias kissed her quickly on the cheek as he entered and headed for the table to join Jack. Lucky went into the kitchen and quickly fixed a sandwich for him. She was sure he had spent a good part of the day and evening dealing with Harry's death, on top of his patients at the Clinic. She made a large wrap of tomatoes, sprouts and avocado with cubes of chicken and chopped walnuts and brought it to the table with a small serving of Sage's potato salad with asparagus.

Elias looked drained, dark circles under his eyes. "Thank you," he said, squeezing her hand. "How are you feeling, Jack?" Elias looked at him carefully.

"I'm fine. Well, better really. Just tough—finding Harry like that."

Elias nodded in sympathy. "You knew him a long time?"

"I guess you could say that. Ever since he's been in business for . . . what? Maybe almost twenty-five years now."

"How old was he?" Lucky asked.

"Don't really know exactly. He was real young when he first opened his shop. So maybe he's about forty-six, forty-seven . . . was . . ." Jack trailed off.

"Really? He seemed so much older."

"Harry was always a real serious man, but something like this . . . it makes you realize maybe we didn't know him all that well after all. He wasn't close to anyone that I know of. Never got married or had kids. Come to think of it, maybe he was lonely, but it never seemed that way. Always seemed more like he didn't want any company."

Elias nodded sympathetically and took a large bite out of the wrap. A piece of tomato fell onto the tablecloth. "Sorry. I'm eating like I haven't seen food in a day or so. Come to think of it, maybe I haven't."

"We're all out of sorts," Jack replied. "Now that Elias is here, I'm gonna head home. It's just gone three bells."

"Would you like a ride?"

"Nah." He shook his head. "It's a beautiful night. I feel like walking."

Lucky reached over and grasped his hand. "Are you sure you're all right?"

"I'll be fine. You two stay. Enjoy the evening. I'll swab the deck in the morning." He leaned over and kissed the top of her head. "See you tomorrow."

"'Night, Jack." Lucky's eyes followed him as he left by the front door, pulling it shut behind him.

Elias had wolfed down the rest of his food. "Let me help you close up."

"Not much to do. We closed officially a while ago," she said, clearing off the table. "People kept stopping in. Everyone's in shock. It was pretty sad." She carried the tray of dishes to the counter. "All I have to do now is take out the trash. I'll run the dishwasher in the morning."

Elias waited while Lucky turned off the last lamp and the blue and yellow neon sign in the window. He lifted two trash bags while Lucky grabbed her purse in the office and followed him down the corridor. She locked the door behind them and lifted the lid of the Dumpster while Elias threw the trash bags in. She took his arm as they headed down the short alleyway to Broadway. In the shadows, he pulled her close and kissed her tenderly. She felt the heat of his body through the thin cloth of her summer dress.

"Can you come home with me tonight?"

She reluctantly pulled herself away and took a deep breath. "I'd love to, believe me, but I'm so exhausted for some reason. And so are you. I can see it in your eyes."

"I am, you're right. But I'm walking you home. Until we know what really happened to Harry, I don't want to let you out of my sight."

Chapter 11

THE FIRST SENSATION that came to Elizabeth was the smell of damp and musty earth. Her head throbbed. Her mouth was dry. Her neck was so stiff she could barely turn her head. She knew her eyes were wide open but still there wasn't any light. It must be evening. Her wrists were bound behind the chair on which she was seated. She barely had feeling in her arms. The binding was thin and smooth, like electrical wire or telephone cord. When she shifted her weight on the wooden chair, it creaked and wriggled, as if about to collapse. Her ankles were tied together with cord just as tight. She was in the cellar—Maggie's cellar. A wave of panic swelled in her chest. What had happened to her? She had been on her way to the office and instead had driven to Maggie's farmhouse. She remembered walking slowly down the wooden stairs. Strong hands had held a pungent cloth to her face. She struggled as long as she could but finally her limbs would not obey. That was her last memory. How long had she been unconscious? It was morning when she had arrived. Had she lost a few hours or a day? Panic rose again.

She had called out to Maggie. A quavering voice had responded. Had it really been Maggie who answered? She had been frightened that Maggie might have been hurt, might have fallen down the cellar stairs and been unable to get up. She cast her mind back. At that moment, she had been sure it was Maggie's voice calling. But perhaps it wasn't. She hadn't actually spoken to Maggie in many years. Had someone else been here, pretending to be Maggie? Had someone hurt the woman? She hated to think how isolated the farmhouse was. If Maggie had been in trouble, no one would have known. No one would have checked on her. Maggie would never have done this. She could think of no earthly reason why Maggie would wish to hurt her.

The throbbing behind her eyes was terrible. She made a conscious effort to sharpen her senses. She took a deep breath. The chair squeaked loudly. She prayed it wouldn't collapse and send her sprawling to the floor with the dirt and the spiders. The joists of the house creaked slightly as someone walked above her. Footsteps! She tried to call out, but managed only a croaking sound. She licked her lips and tried again. "Maggie . . ." she cried. Her voice was weak. Even if Maggie were above her, she'd never be able to hear this pathetic sound. Elizabeth stifled a sob. She had been so foolish to come here alone. Worse yet, she hadn't let anyone know her plan. Surely if she didn't turn up at the office, someone would worry—her secretary or Lucky, someone would sound the alarm. Her car was parked in front of Maggie's house, but the house was well off the road up a lengthy dirt drive. How long would it take anyone to realize she was gone? She breathed deeply to quell the rising anxiety and called out again, stronger this time.

"Maggie!" She waited. The footsteps stopped, but no one answered.

Elizabeth forced herself to take deep breaths. She knew it was the only way to control her fear. It was imperative she maintain her sensibilities. She would need all her wits to comprehend what was happening and to escape. Her clothes, so fresh the morning she had left for work, were grimy and wrinkled. If only she hadn't decided to take a detour. What had possessed her to check on Maggie after all these years? Cordelia! It was Cordelia Rank who had ignited the worry that led her here to this lonely house.

It must be possible to try to reason with Maggie. If she could only understand the woman's motives, then perhaps she could talk to her, convince Maggie to let her go free. What possible delusion had caused Maggie to attack her and keep her locked in the cellar? Or was it really Maggie who had pressed that cloth against her face? If so, her slight frame gave no hint of such strength. The hands that had grasped her head and held a cloth to her face were large and strong. And there was something else. A whiff of . . . aftershave? Someone other than Maggie had waited for her to descend the cellar stairs. Had something happened to the woman? Had someone hurt her? Or did Maggie harbor anger toward her from the past? Anger perhaps that Elizabeth hadn't stayed in touch all these years or made sure she was doing well? Had Maggie dropped out of society so far that she had lost normal human connections? Was she insane?

Elizabeth gritted her teeth to keep from screaming in frustration. She knew where she was, but she didn't know who was keeping her prisoner, or why. She cast her mind back as far as she could remember. Years before, Elizabeth had spent many days and hours with Maggie when Maggie had lost her son. It was true that as time goes by, people fall away, lose connections, but Elizabeth had done more to stay close to Maggie than anyone else in town. She couldn't imagine why Maggie would bear her any animosity. Her behavior made no sense.

The door at the top of the stairs creaked loudly. Then footsteps, cautious ones as though of someone afraid to trip and fall. Elizabeth listened carefully and finally the door to the small room swung open. Maggie stood in the doorway holding a wooden tray. A light shone behind her. She placed the tray carefully on the dusty floor just inside the door. The aroma of warm vegetables filled the room. Elizabeth's stomach rumbled loudly. When had she last eaten? She was ravenously hungry. Maggie moved closer to the chair where Elizabeth was bound. She reached up and pulled a string that hung from the ceiling. A weak overhead light flickered on. Hardly enough to dispel the gloom. Maggie turned back without looking at her and started to close the door. Elizabeth wriggled her wrists and pulled against the cord in an attempt to free her hands. Surely Maggie wouldn't place tempting food so close and yet leave her like this, bound to a chair?

"Maggie. Please. Let me go," Elizabeth croaked. Her throat was so dry.

Maggie halted, but said nothing. She shut the door behind her and Elizabeth heard her footsteps as she climbed the stairs. Elizabeth felt a sob rise in her throat. She fought against the tears that threatened. She was helpless, bound and terrified. She pulled at the cord that cut painfully into her skin. Perhaps if she kept working at it, it might give and she could at least free her hands. She gritted her teeth against the pain.

The footsteps were returning. The door swung open. Maggie held a jug of water in one hand and a large bundle under her arm. A sleeping bag. She placed the water jug on the floor, then spread the sleeping bag near the wall. She reached into a pocket of her faded sundress and extracted a sharp kitchen knife. She approached Elizabeth slowly, knife in hand. Elizabeth stopped breathing. Maggie wouldn't stab her, would she? But then why was she keeping her here in the first place? And if she intended to kill her, why had she brought food and water and a sleeping bag?

Elizabeth could barely form the words. "Maggie. Talk to me, please. Why are you doing this?"

Maggie cocked her head to the side and stared into Elizabeth's eyes. Elizabeth remembered those striking blue eyes. The tears she had shed when she learned her son Danny had died in a car wreck. As she stared into Maggie's eyes, something changed. A dullness came over them. Whatever spark had been there was gone now. Maggie shuffled behind her and stood at the back of the chair. Elizabeth held her breath, waiting, terrified that Maggie might plunge the knife into her. She felt the cold blade against her wrist. With one quick slash, Maggie sliced through the cord binding Elizabeth's wrists.

Elizabeth let her breath escape. She tried to turn her head to look at Maggie. "Are you letting me go?" she asked hopefully.

Maggie stared back at her wordlessly. Did she still have the power of speech? Had she not spoken to another soul all these years? Elizabeth recalled seeing Maggie at the construction site. At a distance, she seemed to be muttering to herself. Perhaps that was it—her ability to speak normally had atrophied.

Maggie shuffled to the door and turned back. She looked like a frightened animal. "You have to stay. He won't hurt me then." She mumbled quickly.

Elizabeth stared, unable to speak at first. Finally, she managed to croak, "Who? Who'll hurt you?"

The door closed. Elizabeth heard the boards creak once again as Maggie climbed the cellar stairs.

"Maggie!" she called desperately. The door slammed at the top of the stairs. Elizabeth's head dropped to her chest as she sobbed quietly.

Chapter 12

LUCKY DIALED ELIZABETH'S number for the second time that morning. She knew the number by heart and her fingers quickly hit the buttons. She had left one message already and still Elizabeth hadn't returned her call. Maybe she had gone to her office earlier than usual? She'd try the office number later in the day. Right now, she just wanted to hear Elizabeth's voice. Like everyone else in town, she couldn't seem to think about anything except the discovery of Harry's body the day before. She was anxious to hear Elizabeth's thoughts and was more than surprised that Elizabeth hadn't called her already. She waited impatiently while the phone rang four times. Finally, the answering machine clicked on and the outgoing message played. Lucky left another quick message, promising to try to reach Elizabeth at her office later in the day.

The Spoonful was crowded with people grabbing a bite before the dress rehearsal of the Reenactment. Hank, Barry and Horace were at one table, dressed for their roles, as were many other men and women. Hank wore garments of linen in varying shades of brown with a vest the color of butternut squash and a large floppy hat. Barry was decked out as an Indian, with, fortunately, a long tunic over his protruding belly. War paint was streaked on his face, and his outfit was topped with a braided wig, bandanna and feather. Jack was assisting with props in the Reenactment, but not playing a role, and Horace looked quite impressive as a Hessian in white breeches, a long blue coat with gold buttons and a small hat with a brass insignia.

"Horace, your outfit is striking. But I thought Hessians wore those funny tall conical hats?"

"Oh, some did. But most Hessians wore tricorn hats or a small cap like this. The tall, pointy caps were developed so they could throw their grenades and sling their muskets without knocking off a floppy hat. The conical hats also had the added benefit of terrifying the enemy, and since most battles were fought close-up with bayonets, you might frighten a rebel soldier into running away before you even engaged him. The battle would be quickly won."

"Ah, ha. Well, you look terrific, and thankfully not terrifying," she said as she headed back to the counter. Horace bowed and smiled shyly.

Barry took a last bite of his cream cheese and red onion sandwich on dark rye. "I guess we'll just have to keep our spirits up today and do our best. I'm certainly not in a festive mood."

"I'm with you." Hank sighed. "There's nothing we can do for poor Harry now."

The bell over the door rang and Hank raised his hand to catch Rod Thibeault's eye. The young lawyer waved in return and joined the motley crew. "Great outfits, guys."

"You're not gonna take part, Rod?"

"Can't." He shook his head. "Got too many cases to handle right now, and I have to get back to Lincoln Falls.

I've got court appearances all week. Wish I could stay and watch the dress rehearsal though."

"Well, come on over on the sixteenth—that's the big day. You don't want to miss that."

"I'll definitely try. I drove over to Snowflake 'cause Nate wanted to ask me some questions about . . . you know." The men nodded sadly in response.

Meg approached their table to take Rod's order. He smiled up at her. "I'll have a roasted vegetable salad with the vinaigrette dressing." Meg scribbled his order and returned to the hatch where she placed her slip.

Marjorie and Cecily bustled in and surveyed the crowd. All the counter seats were taken. Cecily waved to the men at the table and pushed her more reserved sister in their direction.

"My, look at all of you. I can't wait to see the real show," Cecily gushed.

Horace stood and offered his chair to Cecily. He reached across to another table and pulled up a chair for Marjorie.

"Thank you, Horace," Marjorie replied. "You're a real gentleman, even if you are a Hessian."

Horace smiled. "On your way to the shop?"

"Yes. We just stopped in for our tea and croissants. We've been very busy this summer. Seems like we have more tourists here every year." She leaned closer to the group. "Any news about Harry?"

Barry shook his head. "No. We saw Nate yesterday. Stopped in here to ask us all when we had last seen him."

"It's just terrible," Cecily said, shaking her napkin onto her lap. "I don't even know what to say. It had to be a robbery. So many strangers in town."

"Nate doesn't think so. Said there was plenty of cash left untouched."

"Really?" Marjorie's eyebrows shot up. "Then it must

have been personal, although I can't imagine why. Everyone got along fine with Harry. Now that he's gone, what are we going to do? Will his business be sold?"

"I doubt anyone knows." Barry took a sip of his coffee. "Harry didn't have anybody. We all liked him just fine, but if you asked me who his closest friend was, I couldn't tell you."

"I didn't really know him at all. We just connected over the demonstration and the lawsuit," Rod offered. "I'm sure there must have been someone in town he was close to. After all, he lived here his whole life." He looked around the table. Everyone stared blankly at Rod, realizing the import of his words.

"That's just awful," Marjorie said. "I never really thought much about it, about Harry's personal life, I mean. If he spent his whole life in Snowflake and was never really close to anyone, I find that very hard to believe. But you men would probably know him better than I."

Meg arrived with Rod's order and buttered croissants with jelly and a pot of tea for the sisters.

Barry checked his watch. "Sorry to cut this short, but we should go. It's time." The men rose from the table. If they had been real soldiers preparing for battle, their expressions couldn't have been more serious.

Jack called to Lucky at the counter. "We'll be back later, my girl—around six bells for sure."

Lucky waved to him. Jack would return at three o'clock. "See you then." The bell rang as the door slammed shut behind the men. Lucky left the counter and moved to the big glass window to watch their progress as they headed toward the Village Green. Several summer tourists stopped to point and stare at the men in their costumes. An older couple asked the three of them to pose for a picture. Hank and Barry struck a pose on either side of Horace while Jack moved out of the frame. Lucky smiled. She had always enjoyed the Reenactment. Not only was it fun for everyone in town, but it attracted tourists and lots of business. She had been looking up Broadway toward the Village Green and hadn't seen Elias approach from the direction of the Clinic. She turned when she heard the bell over the door jingle.

"Hey, Lucky." He stood close to her at the window. "What's so interesting?"

She laughed. "Just watching Hank, Barry and Horace ham it up for the tourists. They really look great."

Elias followed her back to the counter and grabbed a recently vacated stool. "I've promised myself a whole hour for lunch today. What do you say I grab a bite and we walk over to watch the rehearsal?"

"Love to. I can take a break in a little while. What would you like to eat?"

"Hmmm. Let me try the cream of asparagus soup and the mushroom feta wrap with an iced tea."

"Coming right up." Lucky placed the order slip on the hatch and Sage grabbed it quickly. She was thankful for one thing—she no longer blushed horribly when Elias was around, or when asked about their relationship. Well, not all the time. She had always been attracted to him, even when she was very young. But now, it was hard to hide the powerful effect he had on her.

The lunch rush finally died down, and just in time. Lucky slipped into the corridor and hung her apron on a hook inside the closet door. She pulled the elastic out of her hair and brushed it quickly, adding a little touch of lipstick. Always a tomboy, she had had to learn things that came easily to most young women—like using lipstick and a little eye shadow or blush occasionally. She had never had an interest in fashion or makeup, but it seemed that everyone in her life—Elizabeth, Sophie, even Jack—urged her to be a little more aware of her appearance. When she returned to the restaurant, Elias had settled his bill. Only a few customers remained. She leaned over the cash register and told Janie she'd be back in an hour and headed up Broadway with Elias.

The Village Green was a shifting tableau of controlled chaos. Not everyone was in costume as yet, but volunteers had been sorted into groups—the men playing British soldiers, Hessians, loyalist colonials and Indians were on one side. The townspeople playing militiamen were on the other. Cordelia Rank, using her bullhorn, shouted instructions about movement and blocking to the players who would move onto the Green. She reminded them of the signal for the militiamen to attack the incoming column of troops.

Vermont's battles were not as well-known as the celebrations in Concord and Lexington on Patriots' Day in Massachusetts, but true Vermonters never forgot the part their ancestors had played in the birth of America. Even though the actual battle occurred a few miles from Bennington in what was then and is now New York State, it was still an event in which Vermonters took great pride.

Lucky stood on tiptoe and spotted Hank and Barry. Barry stood among the Indians and Hank at the other end of the Green with the group that would play militiamen. She couldn't see her grandfather in the crush of people. Many of the actors milled around in a confused fashion, ignoring Cordelia's bellowed instructions. Women would also take part, most of them pretending to reload prop rifles and pass ammunition. No one would carry a weapon with a live round, not even blanks, for safety's sake, but a volunteer with sound equipment would provide the effects of gunfire. Another volunteer would operate a smoke machine.

Lucky spotted the top of Sophie's head, as she pushed through the crowd to join them. "Hey, Lucky. Hi, Elias."

"Sophie—good to see you. Are you off for the summer?" Elias asked.

"Part-time. I'm teaching swimming classes up at the Resort, but it's not a heavy schedule at all. I'm enjoying some free time." She turned to watch the rehearsal. "I feel sorry for those guys having to wear heavy outfits on such a hot day." She nodded in the direction of the local actors.

"Lucky!" Lucky heard her name shouted and saw Rowena's strawberry blonde head bobbing through the crowd.

"I think you're being paged," Sophie muttered under her breath. "She must know what a pain she is."

Lucky was sympathetic to Sophie's feelings but hoped her animosity didn't create a scene. Sophie came from a large family—too poor to afford stylish clothing and other accessories that teenagers felt so important. Rowena in her school days had been the leader of a tight clique that looked down their collective noses at those less fortunate. Lucky always stood up for Sophie at school, but Sophie had borne the brunt of that disdain. As Rowena drew near, Sophie indicated an invisible watch on her wrist. "Well, nice seeing you. My! Look at the time." Sophie ducked through the crowd just as Rowena reached Lucky and Elias.

"Oh, Lucky, I'm so glad I ran into you." Rowena's face was blotchy. She was on the verge of tears.

"What's wrong?"

"That developer guy, Rowland. I just saw him go into his trailer on the site, so I thought, hey, maybe I could talk to him. He completely ignored me the other day. So I climbed through the hole in the fence hoping he'd talk to me then and there. He agreed to give me an interview. I explained how the editor wanted to lay the article out. You know, run some old town pictures with the article—kind of a 'local boy makes good' theme. After all, Richard Rowland has been so successful, he could probably buy this whole town. But when I told him that, he just clammed right up. He couldn't get me out of there fast enough—as soon as I mentioned the pictures. He was downright nasty and then he told one of the workmen to throw me out!" Rowena stifled a sob. "Can you imagine? I don't know what

I'm gonna do now. I had my heart set on that article. There's not much I can say about the skeleton they discovered—not yet anyway, and Nate won't let me write anything about Harry."

"I'm sorry, Rowena. Maybe something better will come up."

Lucky spotted Guy Bessette as he peered over the heads of the milling crowd. He pushed his way through several people to join them. Lucky wasn't surprised. Guy could usually be found somewhere in the vicinity of Rowena, hoping she would notice him. He was dressed in rough homespun pants and coat with a large floppy hat.

"Hi, Rowena." Rowena glanced haughtily at him without acknowledging his greeting. Guy's fascination with Rowena was painfully obvious. Rowena, on her part, was either oblivious or disinterested. Guy's face fell and Lucky felt terribly embarrassed for him.

"Guy, we're so sorry about Harry. Are you all right?"

"I'm okay. Thanks, Lucky. I just don't know what I'm gonna do now. I feel pretty bad. Harry was always good to me, he taught me everything I know about cars. It's really the only job I've ever had."

Lucky nodded sympathetically. Rowena rolled her eyes and looked annoyed that she had been interrupted. She turned back to Lucky. "I still have all those old photos of the town and the school. Maybe I could write something about town architecture."

Elias nodded in the direction of the construction site. "Let's just hope that little pile of architecture across the street doesn't get built at all."

"I agree." Rowena's face was flushed. "I'm definitely going to join the next demonstration. Here I was trying to be nice to the guy and he throws me out! What a jerk," she fumed. "I'll see you later, Lucky. Elias." She ducked back into the crowd. Guy bobbed and weaved a few times and finally followed in Rowena's wake.

"I'm always amazed when all this comes together. You have to hand it to Cordelia, she really gets everyone mobilized," Lucky observed.

Elias put his arm around her shoulder. Lucky resisted the urge to kiss him. Not in front of the entire town. She was far too shy for that. "Cordelia lives for this stuff. It's a good thing we have a famous battle to celebrate, otherwise she'd have to reorganize the DC branch of the DAR and tell the Secretary of the Navy how to run his department more efficiently."

Lucky heard her name called again. Edward Embry emerged from a cluster of onlookers. Cicero, on his leash, sat dutifully next to Edward, wagging his tail hopefully. "Lucky! How nice to see you. This is surely a lot more fun than the day of the demonstration."

"Hello." Lucky smiled in return. "Edward, do you know Elias . . ."

Edward laughed. "I sure do. Everyone does. How are you, Elias? You manage to get a little time off from the Clinic?"

"Barely. I'm taking a little time, in spite of my patient load."

"You're not volunteering to dress up for the Reenactment?" Lucky asked Edward.

"No. Please. I love this stuff, but I'm too old to go rolling around on the grass, pretending I've just been shot. I only popped over to watch and maybe catch Elizabeth here. Have you seen her around?"

"No. And I've been keeping an eye out for her too."

"I didn't see her in the office earlier. Must have just missed her." Edward reached down to pat Cicero's head. Once again, Lucky thought she detected Edward's affection for and interest in Elizabeth. "Well, nice seeing you both, but I've got to get back. I have a pile of complaint letters to read this afternoon."

"About the car wash?"

"Mostly. And perhaps a few others—we'll see. Should make for a pleasant afternoon," he replied ruefully. "If you see Elizabeth, tell her I was looking for her," he said as he moved away through the crowd, Cicero following dutifully.

Lucky had been more or less scanning the crowd herself since they had arrived, also hoping to spot Elizabeth. She felt a flutter of anxiety. Elias glanced at her.

"What's wrong?"

She smiled up at him quickly. "Nothing."

"It must be something." He grasped her shoulders and turned her toward him. "Out with it."

"I've been trying to reach Elizabeth. She hasn't called me back and I'm sure she must have heard about Harry by now." She smiled apologetically. "And I guess I've been hoping I might spot her here."

"This time of day, she's probably at her office. Have you tried there?"

To her relief, Elias didn't minimize her anxiety. "It was too early when I called before. But you're right. I'm being silly. It's just . . ."

Elias waited patiently for her to continue.

"I've just had this nervous feeling since yesterday. Can't put my finger on it. I know it's silly . . ." Lucky stopped in midsentence.

"It's not silly. Cut yourself some slack. You're probably suffering from a little PTSD yourself. Keep that in mind." Lucky stiffened at the allusion to her parents' death only months earlier. Elias felt the change immediately.

"I'm sorry. I didn't mean to . . ."

"No, you're right." Lucky closed her eyes and took a deep breath. "You're right. I think I've been handling everything just fine, but maybe I haven't. Maybe I've just shoved all that fear inside. I'm feeling almost phobic . . . that people can just disappear from your life."

"Quite a common reaction after the shock you've had."

"It was months ago."

"Doesn't matter. It takes a long time. It happens to a lot of people by the way, so don't beat yourself up. I didn't mean to imply that you weren't handling your feelings well. I think you are . . . admirably so. But dealing with the sudden death of the people you were closest to in the world . . ." Elias trailed off. "It's got to be dreadful."

"Everyone keeps telling me it gets easier," she replied uncertainly.

"It will." He pulled her closer. "But now—with what happened to Harry . . . no one in town is feeling safe."

Chapter 13

ELIZABETH MASSAGED HER wrists, grateful that Maggie had cut her loose from the chair. Red welts were still visible where the cord had chafed. At least now she could stretch her arms. Her shoulders were cramped with strain and fear. She took a deep breath and rubbed the back of her neck hoping to relieve her headache.

It had taken what seemed an eternity the night before to undo the thin cord around her ankles. The nerves in her fingers still tingled. When she had tried to stand and reach the tray of food, her right leg had buckled beneath her. She had fallen to the floor but managed to push herself up. When she had finally reached the food, she sat, leaning against the wall, and lifted the tray onto her lap.

Maggie had fed her a generous serving of vegetables— sweet potato, chard and turnip. She must grow her own food in the summer. Maggie's behavior was so outside the norm, the thought had occurred to her the food might be poisoned. Elizabeth had carefully scooped a small piece

of sweet potato and tasted it. It was warm and delicious.
There had been no choice but to eat the food and hope
for the best. It was the only way she could regain her
strength.

She looked around the room in which she was a prisoner. A stained and filthy remnant of carpeting covered the
concrete floor. The walls had been finished with a sort of
wallboard that had long ago been painted green. Ripped
and molding rock-and-roll posters were pinned to the
walls. Some of the names Elizabeth recognized—groups
that were well-known more than twenty years ago. Had
this been a room Danny used in his teen years? It was
devoid of furniture. Other than the chair she sat on, the
sleeping bag that Maggie had left behind and the stained
carpeting covering the floor, the room was empty. A narrow window near the ceiling allowed a small amount of
dusty light to filter into the room. Boards had been nailed
over the window on the exterior of the house, but a space
of a few inches showed a gap. Elizabeth was sure it was
morning. If only she could reach that window, she might
find a way to escape.

She breathed deeply to stanch the fear that was just
under the surface. What had she done to deserve this treatment? She, a middle-aged woman, a retired teacher, she
had always led such a careful life. Things like this simply
didn't happen to people like her. She had never been reckless . . . about anything. Yet here she was, the Mayor of
Snowflake, locked in a cellar like an unwanted animal. She
thought of Charlie, all alone with no food. What if his
water ran out? Who would take care of him? Who would
miss her? Surely, Lucky would notice she was gone, and
Jack, and her nearest neighbors. The people at the town
office, her assistant Jessie, and Edward. They would realize
something had happened to her. People would look for her,
but how would they know where to look? She had told no
one where she was headed. *So foolish*, she thought. *So*

foolish. Elizabeth stifled another sob. No one would ever focus on Maggie Harkins's house.

Even more perplexing, she couldn't imagine what Maggie meant when she said, "He won't hurt me then." Who was she referring to? Was someone coercing her or was she delusional? There was no logical reason Maggie should want to keep her prisoner. She had always been kind to her and her son Danny when he was in her classes years ago. Danny was a difficult kid for a woman to raise alone. He had often been the instigator of trouble at school but Elizabeth had never reported him. She had always been convinced that whatever commotion Danny stirred up, he had a good heart. He was mischievous, but never mean.

She wondered if Maggie would bring more food today. Perhaps if Maggie opened the door she could overpower her and force her way out. She hated to think about hurting another human being, but if Maggie brought food she might leave a real fork that could be used as a weapon. How quickly we descend to the lowest level of human survival, she thought—struggling to keep body and soul together and fighting to be free.

Chapter 14

LUCKY REPLACED THE receiver and looked up. Jack was standing in the doorway of the office.

"What's up?" he asked.

"I just tried Elizabeth's number again. I called her office today and no one answered, and there's still no answer at her house."

"Maybe she's out for the evening. Even old people sometimes have a life, you know."

Lucky did her best to smile in spite of her anxiety. "I haven't seen her since the day of the demonstration—and that was two days ago. I'm sure she's heard about Harry but I can't understand why she hasn't called us."

"You need some cheering up. Can I treat you to an ice cream down the street?"

"Only if you buy me two scoops." As far back as she could remember, it was her grandfather who would take the time to treat her to ice cream. Her parents were always busy with the restaurant. A vivid memory flashed before her eyes—her child's hand grasped by a huge rough paw, and the cold sweetness of two scoops of chocolate ice cream. "I'll just turn off the lights."

Lucky followed the corridor to the front room and turned off the lamps one by one. She approached the window to turn off the last lamp. A peripheral movement caught her eye—a shadowy figure across the street. She moved closer to the window and, shading her eyes, peered out. "Jack?"

"Right here." Jack had followed her to the front room.

"Come over here," she whispered. Jack moved toward the window and stood next to her in the dimly lit room. "Look across the street. Someone is skulking around and going through garbage cans. It's the woman I saw at the construction site the other day. Who is she?"

Jack turned off the last lamp and stared across at the opposite sidewalk. "I see her now. That's Maggie Harkins."

"Oh, that's right. Elizabeth mentioned her name the other day too. Does she not have any money or enough to eat?"

"It's not that. She's got her house and her husband's pension and all. I don't think it has anything to do with money."

"Is she mentally disturbed?" Lucky continued to gaze as the disheveled woman investigated the next garbage can and tucked a rolled-up newspaper under her arm. Her lips were moving as though she carried on a dialogue with herself.

"In a way, maybe. She was a widow for years and then she lost her only child—a boy—oh, maybe, let's see, twenty-five years ago, I guess. Really pushed her over the edge. Sad . . . don't think she ever got over it."

"You think she needs help?"

"I doubt she'd take it. The thing is . . ." Jack continued to stare at the figure in the shadows. "She usually doesn't come into town, not that I can recall. Always thought maybe a neighbor did errands for her. You say you saw her at the construction site?" He turned to Lucky with a puzzled frown.

"She wasn't part of the demonstration, but she was sort of hanging around by the chain-link fence afterward. Elizabeth knew who she was."

"Elizabeth knew her and her son years back. Danny was one of her pupils when she was still teaching." Jack heaved a sigh. "Very sad. So lonely, that poor woman."

Lucky flicked off the blue and yellow neon sign in the front window. "It's a beautiful night. Let's go for a walk and get that ice cream."

"Two scoops, as promised." Jack locked the front door behind them and Lucky slipped her arm through his as they headed down Broadway. Outside the air was moist and fragrant. Moths fluttered in the halos of light around the streetlamps. Lucky stole a glance over her shoulder as the figure in the shadows melted away.

Chapter 15

TUCKING HER SKIRT between her knees, Lucky knelt on the grass and pulled a gardening trowel from her basket. It was early morning yet but the day promised to be another scorcher. The morning had that stillness that comes when the air doesn't move and even the birds are silent. Lucky breathed in the aroma of cut grass. The clumps of dirt in her hands felt warm and fragrant.

Using the sharp edge of her tool, she carved a neat trench at the base of the gravestone, pulling up clods of grass and shaking off the loose dirt. When she was satisfied with the space she had created, she added rich potting soil and carefully slipped the containers of bright purple phlox out of their small plastic pots, padding them into the soft earth. It was late in the season to plant these, but they were hardy perennials and should last through the fall. With luck, they'd return in profusion in the spring. She patted the earth gently around the blossoms and moistened the flower bed generously with a watering can. Satisfied with her efforts, she wiped perspiration from her forehead and washed her gardening tools off at a nearby spigot, dumping the grassy clods into a green container. She stripped off her gloves and tucked them into the basket with her trowel.

She stood up and admired her handiwork. The sun had moved and now shone directly on her parents' gravesite. She walked a few feet to the shade of a nearby maple tree and sat on the ground, leaning against the rough trunk. The air dripped with humidity and a distant rumbling heralded a possible thunderstorm. If only. A rainstorm would bring cool air. She closed her eyes for a moment, mentally picturing her mother and father. She whispered a silent prayer for them as she always did every time she came here, and often at night in her room. They were beyond harm now, but she prayed for them and for Jack.

Lucky made it a point to stop at the cemetery once a week. She held one-sided conversations with both her parents, keeping them up to date about her life, about Jack and the Spoonful, and the deepening relationship with Elias. She looked forward to these visits, as she thought of them. She imagined her parents in her mind's eye and the responses they would have made to her mental chatter. It was good to get away from the bustle of the restaurant, to be able to sit and think quietly. Her parents weren't here, of that she was sure. But she could still talk to them and pretend they were able to listen. Perhaps the ancients were right to place coins on the closed eyes of the dead. Coins that would pay the ferryman for the journey across the river. Were the dead on the other side of an unseen river, always there, always waiting, just invisible to those on earth? Wherever the spirits of the departed were, Lucky had never believed they could be found at a gravesite, but she wanted to do her best to remember her parents, to make sure their resting place was well tended and cared for. For herself, she would choose cremation and have her ashes scattered at the top of the mountain in the cleansing cold of winter.

A tingling at the base of her neck alerted her. She was sure she was being watched. Instantly she was on guard. She slowly turned her head and scanned the area. No one. Was she imagining things? Was someone hiding behind a headstone or bush watching her? She stood, her reverie broken. Scanning the cemetery, she watched and waited. A movement several yards away caught her eye. Who else would be in the cemetery so early in the morning? Not even the caretakers came this early in the day. And why would they be watching her? She held very still and waited. Finally she spotted a figure standing in the shadow of another large tree several yards away. She squinted, adjusting her eyes to the difference between shadow and bright sunlight. The small figure was wrapped in a large coat. Maggie Harkins. The woman she had seen at the demonstration, the woman she had seen last night, investigating garbage cans across the street from the Spoonful. Lucky stepped out of the shadow of the maple tree and started walking toward her. She called out, "Hello."

The figure froze. The woman peered across the distance at Lucky. When Lucky had gone a few yards, the woman scampered away toward the exit to the road. Lucky started to follow, realizing she must have frightened the woman. "Don't run away . . . please. I didn't mean to scare you."

Maggie broke into a wobbling run, and Lucky halted, watching her until she disappeared from sight. *Such a peculiar character,* she thought. *I must have scared her more than she scared me.* Lucky sighed and turned back, heading for the shelter of the tree and her gardening tools. She glanced down at the marble slabs sunk in the grass near the pathway. A name caught her eye. HARKINS. She stopped and stared. The name was carved on two slabs with first names ROBERT and DANIEL. Given their birth and death ages, they were of two different generations. Robert had died at age forty-one. Maggie's husband? Daniel Harkins was twenty when he died. He was the son Maggie Harkins had lost—the son Jack had mentioned.

Elizabeth's words on the Village Green came back to her. She had said of Maggie, *"That poor soul."* Poor soul indeed, a husband gone for many years and then the heartbreak of losing a child who had grown to manhood. Lucky had been stricken by her parents' sudden death, but at least they had lived the greater part of their lives. Maggie Harkins had lost a son who was barely out of his teenage years.

It was Elizabeth who had compassion for Maggie, while everyone else saw only a ragged old lady. Elizabeth. *Why hadn't she returned her calls?* She pushed away the thought that something might be wrong. Anyone could forget to return a phone call. Lucky checked her watch. She had to hurry or she'd be late getting to the Spoonful before opening. She grabbed her basket and started down the road toward town. Maggie Harkins was nowhere in sight.

ELIZABETH LEANED AGAINST the wall and stretched her legs out. Her ankles still chafed a bit, but at least the soreness was gone. There was nothing for her to do all day but think. And think she did, and then think some more. It took all her courage not to break down and cry. Surely Maggie would release her, but what in heaven's name had caused the woman to hold her hostage in the cellar? It made no sense. All Maggie had said was *"He won't hurt me then."* Who was this mysterious "he," or was this "he" a figment of Maggie's imagination? Had she had no social contact all these years? Had the woman lost her mind? Elizabeth cringed when she thought how she had scoffed at Cordelia Rank, but obviously Cordelia had been right. Perhaps Maggie should be institutionalized. She simply couldn't be in her right mind.

The pins and needles had abated once her ankles and

wrists were freed. Feeling had returned to her limbs. She
was able to explore the small room that imprisoned her. A
short door made of sturdy pine boards opened into a washroom the size of a closet. She ducked her head and stepped
into the miniscule bath. The small amount of light from
the dusty cellar window couldn't penetrate into this room.
Elizabeth felt for the top of the toilet tank and lifted it.
Gingerly, she reached inside until her fingers touched
water. The tank was full. That was hopeful. The toilet was
connected to a water supply for the house. The tiny porcelain sink, what she could see of it, was chipped and stained
with rust and hard water spots. The faucets were caked
with deposits and so rusty they looked as if they would
break if too much pressure were applied. She reached for
one and tried to turn it. It wouldn't budge. If only she could
splash cold water on her face. She was sure the temperature
outside was in the high nineties, but the cellar room was
damp and cool. Nonetheless, her skin felt hot and grimy.
She cringed at the thought of cooling her brow with water
from the toilet tank. Who knew when the toilet had last
been cleaned. What she wouldn't give for a shower. What
she wouldn't give to escape from this room. She leaned
into the faucet and struggled to turn it. A slight movement
of the metal indicated it might give. She retrieved a shoe
from the floor next to the sleeping bag—a low-heeled shoe
with a sturdy heel. Using it like a hammer, she banged on
the side of the faucet, willing it to budge. A metallic echo
rang through the room. Touching the wall, she felt exposed
pipes. They ran up through a hole in the ceiling. She beat
the faucet again with the heel of her shoe and finally heard
a screech as the faucet gave way. A trickle of rusty water
ran into the sink and air in the pipes made a moaning
sound. Elizabeth turned the faucet on as far as it would go.
She pushed the pine door open all the way to catch the
small amount of light. She let the water run until she was
able to see that it flowed in a clear stream. After another

minute, when she was sure it was fresh, she splashed cool water on her face.

She caught a partial glimpse of herself in a shard of broken mirror on the wall over the sink. She looked dreadful. Dark circles outlined her eyes, her hair stuck up in clumps. She brushed water over her hair and smoothed it down until it looked almost normal. Maggie had taken her purse and watch. Now she wasn't even able to brush her hair or tell the time. Her clothing was streaked with grime, her white blouse that she had ironed so carefully the morning she left her house was wrinkled and dirty. At least Maggie had fed her more steamed vegetables and yesterday a tomato. The food was plain, but it was fresh and healthy—for all that meant. What difference did it make if the food was wholesome if Maggie had no intention of releasing her? Whatever Maggie's intent, it wasn't to kill her by starvation or dying a slow death of thirst. But why, oh why, had Maggie done this?

Chapter 16

ONCE THE LAST of the midday customers were gone, Lucky wiped off the counter and carried the basin of dishes into the kitchen, loading them into the dishwasher. Sage sat on a stool scribbling in his notebook. Lucky poured a tall glass of iced coffee and joined him at the work table.

He looked up and grinned. "Just working something out. I had an idea for a soup—something I came across a long time ago and I'm just trying to remember what went into it—based on peanut butter."

"Really?" Lucky raised her eyebrows. "Go for it. Anything you want to do is fine with me."

Sage looked across the work table. "You okay?" His face was serious.

"Sure. I'm fine."

"You don't exactly look fine. You look like you haven't slept in a couple of days." Lucky didn't answer. "You're worried about something." It was a statement, not a question.

Lucky nodded. "I've had a couple of bad dreams. Keep waking up and then can't go back to sleep very easily."

"Tell me about the dreams." He clipped his pen to the notebook and gave her his full attention.

"Crazy dreams. I'm in my apartment and someone knocks on the door. I don't know who it is but I have a feeling of dread. Next, a man, I can't see his face, is in my living room and he tells me my mother is waiting for me. 'Why haven't you gone to see her?' he asks me. 'But my mother is dead,' I say, and he says, 'No, she's not, she's right here.' He opens a door in the wall that I never noticed before, that I didn't know was there, and I'm scared but I follow him through the door. My mother is sitting in a chair. But in the dream I know it's not really my mother. She looks exactly like my mother but I don't feel anything and so I know it's not her. I ask him where my father is, and the strange man says, 'He's on his way.' I start screaming, 'That's not my mother' and I wake up." Lucky paused and took a deep breath. "On the one hand I know in the dream that I'm dreaming, but a part of me is afraid that I'm really awake and have forgotten my parents."

"I'm sorry, Lucky. Sorry you're going through this— especially now when your life should be settling down." Sage was a handsome man. His looks had brought him a lot of unwanted attention from people who couldn't see past the façade to realize what a sensitive individual he was, a man who had overcome abuse as a child and false accusations as an adult. His relationship with Sophie, she knew, was a good thing. Sophie could be a bit hard-boiled at times, but she had softened of late and Sage's anxiety and fear of persecution had almost completely disappeared.

"I've been worrying about Elizabeth too. I'm going to try her office again before we get hit with another rush." She slipped away and headed down the corridor, shutting the office door behind her. She dialed the familiar number. Elizabeth's assistant Jessie answered on the first ring.

"Jessie, it's Lucky Jamieson. I was just trying to reach Elizabeth if she has a moment."

"Lucky?" Jessie squeaked. "I'm so glad you called." Jessie's voice had risen in pitch. "She's not here and she didn't come in yesterday or the day before. I don't know where she is."

"What?" Lucky felt a sickening dread in her gut. "You haven't heard from her?"

"No. And it's getting really embarrassing. I've been telling people she's in a meeting, and then today I decided to say she had to go out of town for a day or so. She'd call them as soon as she could. I didn't know what else to do. At first, I thought it was my mistake, you know, that I'd forgotten she had told me something. That maybe she was taking a day off or had to go away. I wracked my brain. Checked her calendar and everything, but I'm not going crazy. I'd remember if she'd told me something like that."

"Jessie, I've been worried about her too. I've called her house twice, no three times yesterday, but she didn't answer. I left messages but she hasn't called me back. And I tried your number too, but no one answered. It's just that I would have expected to hear from her after what happened to Harry."

"It's horrible about Harry. It really scares me. You must have called when I was at lunch. I'm sorry I missed you. I just don't know what I should do." Jessie sounded on the verge of panic.

"Call Nate Edgerton right away. This isn't like Elizabeth at all. Maybe there's been a car accident." Lucky shivered. The vision of her parents dead by the side of an icy road, their car crushed, flashed in front of her eyes. "I'll go over to her house right now. Maybe she's there and hurt and can't get to a phone." Lucky took a deep breath and tried to quiet the panic she was feeling. Elizabeth lived alone.

She was in her late fifties, and very strong and healthy, but all the same, anyone could have an accident. She whipped off her apron and, grabbing her purse, ducked into the kitchen.

Sage looked up. "What's wrong?" Obviously her panic showed on her face.

"It's Elizabeth. Her assistant just told me she hasn't been in the office for a couple of days. I'm going over to her house—I'm worried she might have had an accident and can't get to a phone."

"That doesn't sound good. Want me to come with you? There's nothing on the stove now and Janie and Meg can handle everything."

"Thanks, it's all right. Her house is close and I'll be fine. But can you let Jack know?"

"Will do." Sage followed her to the kitchen door and watched as she hurried down the corridor and out the back exit. "But call us and let us know what you find out," he called after her.

Lucky raised her hand in response and hurried to her car. Elizabeth's house was at the north end of town. She could have walked just as easily, but driving would be quicker. She kicked herself for not checking on Elizabeth yesterday. She should have trusted her instincts to begin with.

A FEW MINUTES later Lucky pulled up in front of the small gingerbread Victorian and turned off the engine. Elizabeth's house was white with black trim and shutters. It had always reminded Lucky of a doll's house. A wide porch ran across the front. The yard, enclosed by a wrought iron fence, bloomed with hydrangeas and pink roses. A climbing vine of wild roses twined around the banisters of the porch and up a column. Lucky pushed the gate open and approached the front door. A swinging bench hung on chains attached to the ceiling of the porch. On the flowered cushions were two magazines and a flyer, too large to fit in the mail slot. She rang the doorbell and heard it echoing inside. The house felt empty. She rang a second time and called Elizabeth's name. No one answered. She knelt and pushed open the brass mail slot. Cool air greeted her. On the floor she could see two envelopes that the mailman had pushed through the slot on his route. If Elizabeth were home, she'd never leave her mail on the floor or on the porch swing.

She scanned the little she could see of the front hall. Everything seemed to be in place. A whiff of something reminiscent of oranges filtered out. It was the fragrant smell of orange oil. Had Elizabeth recently polished her furniture? Mixed with the aroma of oranges was the smell of yeasty dough. Houses have their own unique atmospheres created by their owners—cooking smells, cleaning products, old books, baby powder, dog kibble. Lucky had always thought one could tell a lot about the inhabitants of a house if one simply inhaled. She called once more, although now she was certain the house was empty.

She descended the porch stairs and followed the paving stones to the driveway. Elizabeth's car was gone. In the summer, she always left her car outside on the drive. Wherever she had gone, she had driven. Only in the coldest days of winter would she use her garage. Lucky walked the length of the driveway and peeked in the side window of the garage. Empty. No car.

She heard a small mewing sound from the kitchen door. She walked up the back steps to the kitchen door. It was Charlie. His kitty door was closed. He was locked inside and probably hadn't been fed. How long had it been since anyone had seen Elizabeth? Three days?

"Hang on, Charlie," she whispered at the door. She hurried to the garage and pulled open one of the wooden doors. Even the garage was as neat as a pin. Gardening implements hung in the cabinet and small household tools were displayed above a corner workbench. Lucky opened the cabinet and felt in back on the left side for the house key she knew Elizabeth kept hidden there. She returned to the kitchen door and unlocked it. Charlie rushed at her legs. She dropped her purse and kneeled down to hug the cat. He climbed onto her lap, meowing and purring, thrilled that someone had come home. "Oh, poor Charlie. You poor thing. You must be starving." Elizabeth's cat was a sweet-tempered gray-striped tiger cat with huge paws. Elizabeth babied him to death.

"It's all right now, Charlie," she murmured to the cat as she opened the refrigerator and pulled out a can that was almost full. She scooped a large chunk of wet food into a clean dish. Fortunately, Charlie still had a good-sized bowl of dry food, but Lucky added more pellets just in case and gave him fresh water with an ice cube in it to keep the water cool.

The house had high ceilings and eaves that kept the temperature moderate even on the hottest days, so Charlie hadn't been suffering from the weather. Elizabeth usually kept him inside during the day while she was at the office, and let him come and go at will when she was home. At night, she closed the kitty door to keep Charlie safe from raccoons. Lucky knew Elizabeth worried about him when she was at work. She would never have left Charlie on his own. She would have asked someone—Lucky, a neighbor, someone—to keep an eye on Charlie and feed him.

Charlie hunkered down and made loud slurping sounds in his bowl. Lucky picked her purse up off the floor and dropped it in a kitchen chair. Maybe there was something here that could tell her where Elizabeth had gone. She walked out to the front hall and opened the door. She scooped up the magazines and flyer and the two bills that lay inside on the floor and placed them on the library table in the hallway. She walked through the small parlor and dining room, checked the hall closet and then climbed the stairs to the second story. Elizabeth's house was warm and charming, nothing out of place. No dust had accumulated. The bed was covered with a crocheted spread that Elizabeth had made herself. A sprinkling of gray Charlie hairs at the foot of the bed indicated his favorite place to nap.

Elizabeth used the second bedroom as a combination office and guest room. Everything looked completely normal and undisturbed. The daybed was neat, its cushions perfectly placed. Lucky checked the calendar above the desk. No appointments had been marked for today, yesterday or the day before. The light on the answering machine was blinking. Lucky hit the button and listened to messages from Jessie, sounding more and more worried, her own voice messages and finally one from Marjorie at the Off Broadway ladies' clothing store, reminding Elizabeth that her order had arrived.

Lucky slumped into the desk chair and looked around. Nothing terrible had happened to Elizabeth here. Everything was in order, as if she had just prepared for work, made her bed and washed her breakfast dishes before she left for the office. She had just never arrived.

Where could she be?

Lucky dialed Nate's number at the station. It rang twice before Bradley picked up.

"Snowflake Police. Deputy Moffitt."

"Bradley, it's Lucky Jamieson. I have to speak to Nate right away. It's important."

She heard a slight poof of air through the telephone, as if Bradley considered her call an annoyance.

"It's *very* important."

"Just a minute," he replied in an officious tone. Lucky bit her tongue. One of these days she would march to the police station and personally throttle Bradley. Nate could arrest her but it would be justifiable homicide and she could prove it. She amused herself with the vision of Bradley gasping for air on the floor of the Snowflake Police Station until she heard Nate's voice.

"Chief Edgerton."

Lucky snapped out of her homicidal fantasy. "Nate, it's me. Lucky. I'm at Elizabeth Dove's house. Something's really wrong." Lucky tried to keep the panic out of her voice. Nate never responded well to an excess of emotion.

"Just got a call from Jessie at her office. Did you tell her to call me?"

"Yes. I'm terribly worried."

"Now what makes you think she's missing, and not just out somewhere?"

"I haven't seen her for the last three days. She hasn't been to her office and her assistant has no idea where she is. Her car's gone and she left her cat with no one to feed him."

Nate took a deep breath. "She could have just gone out of town for a day or two."

"Without telling her secretary? Without someone taking care of her cat? That's not like her Nate and you know it. What if she's had an accident on the road?"

Nate was silent a moment, all too aware of what Lucky had gone through with her parents' car crash. His voice was slightly warmer. "Okay. You're right, that doesn't sound like Elizabeth. Tell you what, I'll go over to her office and I'll make inquiries about her car. But I doubt there's been an accident. If there had been, I would have been contacted about any car registered in Snowflake. Do you know the year, make and license plate?"

"Hang on. Her files are right here. I know it's a dark blue Toyota sedan, probably about six years old, I'm guessing." Lucky pulled open the top drawer of the filing cabinet and riffled through the folders. She wasn't sure what Elizabeth's filing system was. "Don't hang up, Nate. Just give me a minute." She rested the phone on the desk and opened the second drawer of the cabinet. She found what she was

looking for. Balancing the file on her lap, she opened it.
Several papers slipped to the floor before she could grab
them. Her hands were shaking slightly as she tried to
quell her growing fear. "Here it is—her plate number is
on her auto policy. It's 501293. Nate, I am really worried
about her."

"I know you are. But there *could* be a logical explanation. In the meantime, I'll call over to the hospital in Lincoln Falls and check out her car license with the police
there. I can send Bradley out to drive around and look for
her car."

"Is there anything else you can do?"

"Lucky . . . look . . . I'm not minimizing this, but I have
a murder investigation going on right now. If you're right
about Elizabeth, that something might have happened to
her, I'll get the State Police on it. Just give me a couple of
hours to try everything else, okay? And try not to panic."

"Okay. Thanks, Nate." Lucky took a deep breath and
replaced the receiver, not feeling the least bit better. She
picked up the papers that had fallen to the floor and
returned them to the folder, setting it neatly in the filing
cabinet. She took a last look around and trudged down-
stairs. She double-checked that the lamp in the front room
was still on its timer, as Elizabeth always left it.

Charlie was now purring and circling her legs. She
picked him up and carried him back to the kitchen. His
bowl was empty. She dished out another smaller bowl of
wet food in case he grew hungry later. Charlie showed no
interest in the additional food but sat next to his dish and
meowed. Lucky knew he expected a treat. Elizabeth
always gave him one after feeding him. She found the bag
of treats in a kitchen drawer and doled out two. Charlie
snapped them up. She turned on the radio that sat on the
kitchen counter and found an easy listening station, setting
the volume low. It might keep Charlie company. She took
a last look around the kitchen. A bowl and a cup, freshly

washed, sat in the dish strainer. If there was a clue here as to where Elizabeth had gone, she hadn't found it.

She leaned down to pat Charlie. "I'll be back tomorrow morning to check on you."

"Elizabeth, where are you?" she whispered softly to herself as she slipped out the door.

Chapter 17

"IS THERE ANYONE she's close to? A relative maybe we could call?" Sophie asked as she reached over to pour another glass of wine. She was seated cross-legged on a large cushion on the floor of Lucky's living room.

"More?" she asked, holding the bottle over Lucky's glass.

Lucky shook her head to indicate no. Sophie ignored her and poured another full glass. "Drink up. There's nothing else you can do right now. You need to relax."

Sophie had knocked on the door of Lucky's apartment unexpectedly a half hour before, a bottle of wine in her hand. She had come, no doubt, because she knew Lucky was worried sick about Elizabeth. She claimed that Sage was busy tonight and she had popped over because she thought a girls' night would be a great idea.

"Relax? How can I relax? It's just too weird, Sophie. People don't just vanish . . . or do they?"

"You've done everything you can. You've notified Nate and now it's in his hands. Look—tomorrow I'll go over to her house with you. We'll search everywhere. I can knock on her neighbors' doors and see if they've seen her or seen *anything*. We'll stay in touch with Nate and find out what he's doing about the situation. Someone must know something. Someone must have seen something."

"Talking to the neighbors is a good idea. Maybe they saw her leave the house. Maybe they noticed if she was with someone. And to answer your earlier question, no. Her family is gone. She has no brothers or sisters. No one. She was closest to my Mom and Dad . . . and me and Jack. That's why I'm sure something's happened to her. She would never have gone away without at the very least letting me or Jack know—not to mention Jessie, her assistant."

"How do you know she left in the morning? She could have gone out at night."

"I don't. I'm just guessing. There was a cup and a bowl in the strainer. Like she might have had breakfast before heading to her office."

"Hate to say this, but it doesn't really prove anything, Lucky. She could just as easily have had a cup of tea and a bowl of soup at night. She could have gone out anytime. When was the last time you actually spoke to her?"

"The day of the demonstration. There was a lot of yelling and carrying on at the construction site and then the bones were discovered. Elizabeth was trying to calm everyone down but they were pressing in on her. They were shouting at her as if she were responsible for how the town council voted."

Lucky glanced around her small living room. Everything she had now she owed to Elizabeth—the apartment she rented in the building that Elizabeth owned, the car Elizabeth had given her. Even most of her furnishings had come from Elizabeth's hand-me-downs.

"What happened then?"

"Edward Embry came over and Elizabeth introduced us. We chatted for a bit and then she and I walked back to the Spoonful. Oh, and we ran into Cordelia Rank, who was going on about the DAR and that's it."

"And you haven't talked to her since?"

"No," Lucky moaned. "Not once. The next day I was pretty busy. I didn't expect to see her. And then Jack discovered Harry in his shop and you know the rest. I thought I'd talk to her after that, even the next day, but I didn't hear from her. I called a few times but just got her machine. I knew she'd be very upset about what happened to Harry. I thought she'd certainly want to talk to Jack or me. It seems that's all anyone wants to talk about anyway . . ." Lucky trailed off. "Well, you know what I'm saying." Lucky took a sip of the unwanted wine. "Sophie, do you think her disappearance could have something to do with Harry's murder?"

"What makes you say that?" Sophie furrowed her brow.

"No reason. It's just too coincidental for my taste. And speaking of Harry, I told Nate about what happened at the church the morning we were there unloading drinks."

"Refresh my memory. What happened at the church?" Sophie looked blank. "Oh, that's right. I remember now. You said you overheard Harry confessing something to Pastor Wilson. You really think that might have had something to do with his murder?"

"It's unusual. Harry never talked to anyone. We've all been sitting around trying to figure out who knew Harry best, and even though everybody knew him, we really didn't know anything about his life. Who his friends were. Who he had a beer with. Nothing. Probably Guy Bessette knew more about Harry than anyone and even he admits he didn't know him very well. He was here, in this town, his whole life, and it's as if he was invisible, living under the radar. He doesn't seem to have had any deep connections with anyone."

"I know you told me what you heard at the church, but tell me again."

"I've done my best to recall." Lucky cast her mind back. "I was standing in the corridor near the door to Pastor Wilson's office. It sounded like someone was sobbing and then I heard Harry say, '*I just had to tell someone.*' Pastor Wilson said, '*You did the right thing. We can talk again . . . whenever you're ready.*'"

"Look, I'm not pooh-poohing your intuition. Couldn't they have been talking about anything? Maybe Harry was concerned about something to do with the demonstration. Maybe you heard something that just sounded like crying."

"I could be wrong, I admit. It's hard to describe the feeling. It was something . . . There was an emotional charge in the air. It was obvious the Pastor was trying to soothe and encourage Harry to come back and talk again. Maybe he hadn't made up his mind. That's what I felt. The Pastor said, '*Whenever you're ready*' as if Harry had to prepare to talk to the Pastor again. It felt like Harry had a secret, something he wanted to get off his chest."

Sophie leaned back against the arm of the chair, staring into her wineglass. "Too bad he didn't get it off his chest sooner. If you're right, I'd be willing to bet it's what got him killed."

Chapter 18

LUCKY LOOKED UP from the counter. Two tall figures were dark shadows against the sunlight. The Spoonful was packed with morning customers and so noisy she hadn't heard the bell over the door jingle. Nate stood with another man in a State Police uniform. A frisson of fear ran up her spine and her throat caught. Had they found Elizabeth? Were they here to deliver bad news? Her hands started to shake. She placed the dishes she was holding on the counter and watched as the men headed in Jack's direction where he sat on his stool behind the cash register. Lucky couldn't hear what they were saying over the din of the restaurant. It was obvious they wanted a quiet place to talk. She signaled to Sage that she was heading for the office and called Meg over to take care of the counter. Jack spoke to Nate and the other man and then pointed in her direction. She stood at the doorway to the corridor, and when they reached her, she led them down the hall to the office. She offered them seats on the other side of the desk. When she closed the door behind her, the room was almost completely quiet.

"Lucky, this is Sergeant Woczinski of the State Police. He's based in Bennington, but he's very familiar with this area and has had a lot of experience in missing person cases."

The man nodded without smiling. "Call me Steve." He was in his midthirties with a ruddy complexion and blond hair cropped so close to his skull, he appeared to be bald at first glance.

Lucky shook the Sergeant's hand and took a seat in the cracked leather chair, her Dad's chair, behind the desk. "No news?"

Nate shook his head. "That's maybe a good thing, Lucky. I wanted the Sergeant to meet you and Jack, and try to gather all the information he can. He's already spoken to Jessie at Elizabeth's office. We're heading back to her office again to try and locate anyone else who's around who might know something we don't already know."

"Sophie's knocking on doors on Elizabeth's street this morning. She promised to ask all the neighbors if anyone had seen Elizabeth, or seen anything unusual."

"Great. We'll talk to her too. And question the neighbors ourselves. You never know what information a few nosy neighbors can give you," the Sergeant agreed. "So, let's start at the beginning. When was the last time you saw Elizabeth Dove?"

"The day of the demonstration. That was . . ." Lucky quickly checked the desk calendar. "August tenth—we walked back to the Spoonful together. She had a quick lunch at the counter and said she was heading back to her office."

"Jessie's confirmed that she returned and worked until five o'clock. Do you know if she had any plans for that evening?" Nate asked.

"Not that she mentioned . . ."

The Sergeant interrupted. "When did you first become alarmed?"

"I was a little surprised I didn't see her the next day. Pastor Wilson held a short service at the construction site before they moved the skeleton."

Sergeant Woczinski raised his eyebrows. Nate caught his look and rushed into the breach. "Quite by accident. We discovered a very old skeleton. It was uncovered during construction of the car wash over on Water Street."

"Okay," the Sergeant replied cautiously.

Lucky continued. "A few people stopped by to attend the Pastor's ceremony. It wasn't so much that I expected her to be there, it's just that it was the kind of thing she would make a point of attending. At the time, I really didn't think too much about it. I just assumed she was busy and couldn't make it.

"Then, all the other things happened. Jack discovered Harry Hodges dead at the Auto Shop. I headed over there, as you know, Nate. And after that, well, I was just concerned about my grandfather."

"Why were you worried about your grandfather?" the Sergeant asked.

"He suffers a lot from a stress disorder from his war service. He has for most of his life, and one of the things that really sets it off is seeing blood. Finding Harry like that shook him up, as you can imagine. So, with all that, and the restaurant, the day flew by. The next day I called Elizabeth a couple of times at home, and then at her office. Jessie must have been at lunch because I wasn't able to reach her. Then later that same evening, I tried calling Elizabeth's house again, and again there was no answer. That's when I started to worry."

"Would she have let you know if she was going out of town for a few days?"

"I'm sure she would. We're very close. Elizabeth was my parents' closest friend, and since they died, she's been

like a mother to me. I'm sure she would have let me know."
Lucky felt tears springing to her eyes as she spoke. "I'm
sorry." She swiped her eyes. "I don't mean to get so upset,
I'm just worried sick."

"I understand. Normal reaction."

"And even if by some strange reason she didn't mention
anything to me or to Jack, she would never have left her
assistant Jessie up in the air, trying to field calls. That's not
Elizabeth. On top of that, she would never ever have left
her cat unattended. She dotes on Charlie."

"Does she have any health problems that you know of—
physical or mental?"

Lucky bristled. "Certainly not. She's very healthy, she's
strong for a woman of her age and she's not gaga."

"I'm sorry. We have to ask these questions." Sergeant
Woczinski tried to smooth her ruffled feathers. "A lot of
people do go missing because they're not able to take care
of themselves, or suffer from mental or emotional problems. We usually find them very quickly, but it's always
upsetting for the people close to them."

"You're right, you're right. I'm sorry." Lucky sighed.
"No, no heart disease, no diabetes, no history of depression. Nothing."

"Okay. That should do it. Do you mind if we speak to
your grandfather while we're here? He might have some
further information."

"Not at all. I'll cover the cash register and send him in."

"I understand you've been to her house and taken care
of her cat. Did you notice anything out of place?"

"Not a hair. I did go through her desk calendar to see if
she had an appointment to meet anyone. I looked in her filing cabinet to find her car license for Nate. Oh, and I listened
to the messages on her answering machine. There was
nothing unusual at all. Nothing to point to anyone she
might have been meeting or any place she might have
headed to."

"We'll check out her house this afternoon. You have a key?"

"No, but there's one hidden in the gardening cabinet inside the garage. The garage isn't locked. It's on a hook on the left inside the cabinet. Please be careful not to let Charlie out. She doesn't like him roaming around when she's not there."

"We'll take good care of everything."

"When I was there, it looked to me like she might have just had breakfast and gone to work as usual. There were a bowl and a cup in the dish strainer."

"And nothing looked out of place, or looked like there might have been a struggle?"

"Neat as a pin."

Nate spoke up. "Do you have a photo of Elizabeth that we can use?"

"We found a good photo from the mayoral election at the *Gazette*. I asked Sophie to have some flyers prepared. She's going over to Lincoln Falls this afternoon to a print shop and we'll have three thousand of those flyers by this evening."

"Make sure she lists the State Police hotline, the station here and my cell phone. Does she know about the websites for missing people?"

"Yes, she's found several. She's posting Elizabeth's photo on those today."

"I plan to make an official announcement tonight." He turned to Sergeant Woczinski. "There's a town meeting tonight at the Congregational Church. The people from the University want to update everyone about what they've found so far with the remains we discovered. I plan to make an announcement about Elizabeth there. The more people who are on the alert, the better." He turned back to Lucky. "You're sure the flyers will be ready by tonight?"

"Yes. Sophie's very efficient. I'm sure they will be. I'll

call her though to make sure she has all those numbers and websites listed."

"Well, that's it then." The Sergeant stood. "We'll canvas Elizabeth's neighborhood. You never know what people might have seen. And we'll examine her house and her office and her phone records. If there are no leads there, we'll be organizing ground searches and calling in the FBI."

Lucky gulped at the mention of the FBI. She was grateful Nate and the State Police were taking this very seriously, but with every step taken, the possibility of Elizabeth being dead or in real danger became more real. "Thanks. I'll send Jack in next to see you." She rose from the chair and moved to the office door. She turned back to the men. "I didn't mean to get so upset. I just wish I could spend my whole day searching for her."

"Any help you'll be able to give is greatly appreciated. Just so you know, Ms. Jamieson, we do sometimes find the missing."

Lucky couldn't think of a response. She took a shaky breath and slipped through the door.

Chapter 19

THE OLD CONGREGATIONAL Church had never hosted such an excited crowd. The air was electric with anticipation. The demonstration against the car wash that Harry had been instrumental in organizing had brought the town together. Now, with Harry's death, fear had brought people together again, to share gossip and information.

Lucky and Jack had once again agreed to provide drinks and half sandwiches for the crowd at their regular price, with a percentage going to the church. Pastor Wilson couldn't have been happier. Locals always frequented the Spoonful whenever they could, but a small sandwich board announcing the name of the By the Spoonful Soup Shop wouldn't hurt as an advertisement, particularly for summer visitors. Refreshments would be sold during the break, which would be followed by a question and answer session. Horace planned to chair tonight's presentation, since he was now as knowledgeable about the case as was anyone at the University. Lucky surveyed the crowd, attempting to count heads. She hoped their sandwiches wouldn't sell out too quickly.

Pastor Wilson raised his hand to gather everyone's attention. Horace introduced Professor Arnold, who had driven over from the University and now joined them on the small stage at the head of the room. Professor Arnold took the microphone, tapped it gently, and spoke. "Thank you, everyone, for inviting me." Several people murmured, "Thank you," in return. He took a breath and began to speak.

"As you know, a skeleton, a very old one, was found near the center of your town. We believe he—and we now know this individual was male—was buried in a relatively shallow grave, certainly not six feet deep. It also appears that this man was buried without religious ritual or casket. We can't be exactly certain, because the earth was disturbed by construction equipment before he was found, but we discovered no wooden remnants of a coffin to indicate otherwise. He was a young man, we believe under the age of twenty-five judging by the long bones. Based on the artifacts on his person at the time of his death, it is possible he died during a local battle of the Revolutionary War. If that's the case, it was not that uncommon for colonials or militiamen to be buried in such a manner. Many people died in battle and had to be hastily buried. Moreover, the British were known to treat rebels' bodies in a very undignified fashion."

"Are you saying the skeleton is as old as that?" asked a resident of Snowflake.

"Given the artifacts we've found and the condition of the bones, that is our working hypothesis. We plan to run several tests—a chemical analysis will tell us how much nitrogen is contained in the bony tissue. As bones deteriorate, nitrogen levels decrease. Also, different amino acids disappear from bones at different rates. Testing for those is another method of determining the age of bones."

"Was he a militiaman? An American?"

"It's a possibility. Assuming we're correct, and the skeleton dates from the same time period as the artifacts, he would not have worn a uniform. Most militiamen wore their everyday clothing—homespun, I might add. This type of fiber would break down and disappear very quickly. Fortunately, we were able to retrieve two very tiny fragments that we plan to test."

"Sounds like you don't know very much," one woman called out.

Professor Arnold smiled, not taking offense. "We will know a lot more in the near future. So I hope you will all be patient. We will keep you updated."

Another woman spoke. "I think it's very exciting. For all we know, he could be one of our ancestors!"

Cordelia Rank sat ramrod straight in the front pew, watching the proceedings avidly. She stood. "Sir, my name is Cordelia Rank and . . ."

Lucky spotted Hank and Barry, a few seats closer to the dais. Barry nudged Hank, and Hank shot him a look, shushing him from further remarks.

A voice from the rear said, "We know who you are." A few titters were heard throughout the room. Cordelia held her chin higher, ignoring the remark. ". . . and I am a Daughter of the American Revolution . . ."

Someone was heard to groan loudly. Lucky, standing next to Jack, stifled a laugh.

Cordelia continued, "I believe the Daughters of the American Revolution would be very interested in your findings. In fact, many of my sisters will be here soon to attend the Reenactment of the Battle of Bennington. I would like to suggest that the bones be donated to their museum."

Professor Arnold raised his eyebrows. "Well, uh . . ." He looked inquiringly at Horace. "I agree they should be preserved in a museum setting, but I imagine that will be up to the town of Snowflake and the Vermont Division for Historic Preservation. It's certainly not for me to say. In any case, we at the University would need a lot more time to continue our studies. A find like this is quite exciting."

"Sit down," an older man muttered in Cordelia's direction.

Cordelia turned, silencing him with a withering glance. She rearranged her skirts and sat down heavily in her chair.

When the Professor was finished, Horace took the microphone. "Why don't we have a little break for refreshments? Fifteen minutes. And then we can open the discussion to any other questions you might have."

Lucky slipped out of her seat and walked to the side of the hall, opening the doors to the adjoining room. The smell of freshly brewed coffee wafted into the large meeting room. Janie had volunteered her services this evening, and she and Jack had arranged four different types of half sandwiches, wrapped in plastic, on trays. Cold drinks and water were on ice in a large cooler. Lucky took over the coffee urn, filling cups and keeping the pitcher of cream and sugar bowl full.

She overheard two men she recognized from the demonstration. They were standing next to the long table while she poured coffee. One said, "What'd I tell you. Rowland's not here."

"Are you sure?" the second man asked.

"He wouldn't have the nerve to show up."

"Kinda odd in a way. You'd think he wouldn't pass up an opportunity to make trouble. After all, it was the discovery of the bones that brought his project to a halt. I woulda thought he'd try to make it a point to learn what he could about all this."

"I don't care if he does or he doesn't. But given a choice, I'd rather not see him or hear from him again." The man tossed his paper cup into the trash and turned away.

Lucky gave a signal to Janie, and slipped out from

behind the table. The break was almost over. In a vain hope that her fears about Elizabeth were unjustified, she walked back into the main meeting hall and, standing on tiptoe, scanned the crowd for Elizabeth's silver white bob. She knew it was a desperate hope but couldn't resist looking. She felt as if she had been searching for Elizabeth the last few nights in her dreams. There was no sign of her. Lucky took a deep breath and fought down the rising anxiety in her chest.

"Hey, give me a hand, Lucky." Sophie was holding the outside door open with her foot and trying to push a large cardboard box over the threshold.

"You made it." Lucky hurried over, secured the door and helped Sophie carry another heavy box into the rear of the meeting hall.

Sophie brushed her hands off on the back of her jeans. "No word? She's not here?"

Lucky shook her head. "I looked everywhere. I know it's crazy, but I was hoping against hope. She's definitely not here."

"Sorry it took me so long. I wanted to wait until the print shop finished the last batch."

"How do they look?" Lucky asked, dreading the moment when the flyers would make Elizabeth's disappearance all the more real.

"They did a good job." Sophie squeezed Lucky's hand for support. "I know you're scared. Your hands are shaking. Try to keep it together. We *will* find her."

The noise level had grown, but many people were settling back into their seats. "Sophie, you have a seat and I'll help Janie clean up." Sophie nodded and grabbed a chair near the rear of the room.

Lucky headed to the side room, but left the doors open so she could hear the rest of the presentation and Nate's announcement. When everyone had quieted down, Horace and Professor Arnold returned to the stage at the front of the room. Professor Arnold, microphone in hand, asked if there were any questions.

Barry raised his hand. "What does this mean for the construction site? You must know we want to close it down."

"Yes," Arnold answered. "I had heard about the dispute. This closure should only be temporary. I understand it must be difficult for the developer."

"Not as difficult as we're gonna make it for him!" a man shouted from the back. He was greeted with a murmuring of agreement.

"Our graduate students have been working hard, but we have not found any evidence that this might be a larger burial site. If it were, it would certainly be eligible for the State Registry. In the best of all possible worlds, the developer should do due diligence. In other words, find out about the site before any plans are drawn up. Unfortunately, in my experience, this never happens. So, as soon as we've finished our work, then, I assume, the construction will begin again."

The outside door to the meeting hall slammed open. Several heads turned. As if the name of the devil had been spoken, Richard Rowland marched from the back of the room and stood in the center aisle between the rows of chairs. At first there was silence and then a disapproving murmur grew throughout the hall.

"You better believe it'll begin again," Rowland announced angrily. "All you people be warned. I'm hiring my own guards, and if anybody tries to screw up my site you'll be sorry as hell." Rowland was less agitated than he had been during the demonstration but there was no mistaking his anger.

Norman Rank, Cordelia's husband and Lucky's landlord at the Spoonful, stood and pointed a finger in Rowland's direction. "You little weasel. What the hell do you think you're doing here? You weren't invited and no one wants to see your face." His voice was level and chilling. Norman's outburst was greeted with grumblings of approval throughout the room. Rowland stood his ground, facing Norman down.

"You may own a lot of this town, Mr. Norman Rank, but you don't own this building, and I'll damn well come here if I want. Maybe you oughta mind your own business before you lose some of your precious real estate." Rowland snickered coldly.

"Why you . . ." Norman struggled out of his row and stormed down the aisle toward Rowland.

Rowland smirked, his hands on his hips, calmly watching Rank approach. "Oh yeah, what are you gonna do about it, old man?" Rowland smiled wider, taking in the room. He was playing to the crowd, Lucky knew, and the tension was palpable.

Hank and another man moved quickly into the aisle to intercept Norman before he could reach Rowland. Hank grasped his arm, holding him back "Leave him be. It's not worth it, Norman."

Norman's face was red with fury. "You'll be sorry you ever showed your face in this town," Norman spat.

"Oh yeah? What does that mean?" A flicker of fear passed across Rowland's face. He was surprised for a moment at Norman's vehemence.

Cordelia rushed down the aisle and grasped her husband's other arm. She leaned close to him and whispered in his ear. Norman's shoulders finally relaxed and Hank released his firm grip. Cordelia took her husband by the arm and led him back to their seats.

Lucky, watching the exchange, realized she had been holding her breath, afraid that some form of violence would erupt. Professor Arnold was silent, taken aback at the animosity in the room.

Horace took the microphone from him and spoke in an effort to break the tension. Ignoring the exchange between

Norman Rank and Rowland, he said, "I'd just like to say a few words." He cleared his throat. "First of all, as many of you know, I am thrilled to be living in Snowflake. Even though I'm not a longtime resident, as most of you are, I can honestly say I've fallen in love with this town and am happy to be working on my research in a place that was so important during the Revolution."

"Get on with it, Horace. We love you too," one man called out. Several people laughed nervously. At the same moment, the outer door slammed shut. Richard Rowland had stormed out of the hall. Lucky breathed a sigh of relief.

Horace, ignoring Rowland's exit, smiled broadly at the jest. "So . . . let me just say, the tiny remnants we discovered were very exciting. We believe the fabric will be found to be homespun cloth and in colors created with native plants. Besides the skeleton and fabric fragments we uncovered some very astonishing articles. We came across silver shoe buckles and a powder horn. Now that doesn't necessarily mean he was a militiaman, since many of the colonists hunted for game, but he could have been. On the powder horn there were carvings. Very lovely, like scrimshaw. If anyone is interested, I will have some photos I can make available."

"What kind of carving?" a woman asked.

"It was a small carving of a house, a house in the colonial salt box style, most likely the home of this man. Underneath that was a date—1777. And that's not all—on the other side . . ." Horace paused for a moment, making sure he had everyone's attention. "On the other side was carved, '*This horn belongs to Nathanael Jared Cooper, may this powder kepe saf my home.*'"

Cordelia Rank stood, her face white. Her husband took her hand and urged her back into the seat.

"And," Horace continued, "lodged in the remains was the projectile that probably killed this poor man. We are having it analyzed to see if it is alloyed like the bullets made at home in the Colonies. You may know this already, but many people melted their household pewter—which is tin and lead—to make these lead balls during desperate times.

"More importantly—and this is the astounding fact—this lead piece showed evidence of scoring that indicates it was fired from a rifle. The colonists had been using rifles for some time, but British regulars shot only muskets. So, whatever killed this poor man, it was not a British bullet. Perhaps he was killed by friendly fire, as they say. Or perhaps he was killed because he was a traitor to the cause."

Cordelia stood, her lips pinched, her face ghastly white, and shouted, *"You are a liar and a fraud. My ancestor was a patriot!"*

Chapter 20

Nate Edgerton wasn't long on patience at the best of times, but before the meeting could erupt in shouts and chaos, he took over. Horace, stunned by Cordelia's outburst, relinquished the microphone to Nate immediately. Professor Arnold looked from one to the other for an explanation of Cordelia's shouted words.

"All right, everyone, that's enough. Settle down." Nate's voice held such authority that people were silenced immediately and resumed their seats.

"After I'm done, you're free to ask all the questions you like of Professors Arnold and Winthorpe, but before everyone disperses and heads home, I have a very urgent announcement to make." Nate surveyed the room. "It appears, unless someone here has evidence to the contrary, that Mayor Elizabeth Dove is missing."

One woman cried out in shock. Lucky heard several gasps. Nate continued. "Lucky Jamieson has brought it to my attention that Elizabeth hasn't been seen since the evening of August tenth. Her assistant at her office has not spoken with her, or heard from her."

"How do you know she just didn't go out of town for a few days, Nate?" a man called out.

Nate heaved a sigh. "There's always that possibility, but it doesn't seem to line up with what we all know of Elizabeth."

Lucky felt a hand grasp her arm. Startled, she turned to see Edward Embry, a look of shock on his face. "Is this true, Lucky? No one knows where Elizabeth is?"

"Yes. It's true. I haven't seen her or been able to reach her since the day of the demonstration—or since Harry was discovered. And she hadn't told Jessie, her assistant, that she'd be away."

"She definitely would have let someone in her office know if she was taking a few days off," he said thoughtfully.

Nate allowed the buzzing in the room to continue for a minute or so. Then he tapped the microphone to get everyone's attention. "We have to assume that she is officially a missing person and operate accordingly. I've contacted the State Police, who have already stepped in, and the FBI, who will be sending a team." He glanced at Sophie, who nodded affirmatively. "Flyers have been prepared and need to be distributed. Please, everyone. Please pick some flyers up on your way out, and post them wherever you can. Talk to everyone you know, and let them know about this. This will hit the news media tomorrow."

"Nate!" a woman called out. "Maybe she's had an accident."

"Could be, could be. But her car has not been reported. There have been no hospital or morgue admissions that match her description. We are putting this out on the web, as well. There are many organizations that do good work publicizing the missing and locating them nationwide. We plan to use all the resources at our disposal. What I want from all of you here tonight is to see me before you leave, and I emphasize this: Let me know if you have seen Elizabeth Dove in the last four days. She was seen publicly at the demonstration, and last seen leaving her office that evening. If you have any knowledge of her whereabouts after the evening of the tenth, make sure you talk to me before you go. My deputy Bradley is at the rear of the hall with Sergeant Steve Woczinski of the State Police." Nate nodded in his direction and several heads turned to stare at the Sergeant. "We are organizing a ground search of areas around the town and the woods and we desperately need volunteers. If you can help, please do so."

"You got it, Nate," Barry Sanders called out. He looked as shocked as the rest of the crowd. Lucky was heartened by Nate's quick response and the feeling of concern in the room for Elizabeth.

"Give Deputy Moffitt your name and contact information. We'll be starting early tomorrow morning with the help of the State Police, but again, we need all the volunteers we can get. We'll split people up into groups and organize searches by grids and by areas. Sad to say, people do go missing in Vermont and all across the country. Sometimes they're found. Let's hope this is one of those times." Nate turned and handed the microphone back to Horace. He looked toward the back of the room where Bradley waited. A small table had been set up with several pads of paper. Anyone who could meet at the designated time was to list their name and contact numbers to join a search party.

"Nate," a man in the rear called out. "What about Harry Hodges?"

Nate took the microphone from Horace. Before he could answer, a woman called out, "Have you arrested anyone?"

Nate cleared his throat. "This is an ongoing investigation. I can't comment on that as yet." Nate passed the microphone back to Horace and walked to the rear of the hall.

Horace spoke into the microphone. "Everyone, please, if you possibly can, fold up your chairs and place them against the side wall. Thank you."

Sophie stood next to Lucky, one of the cardboard boxes in her arms. "Let's make sure no one escapes without a bunch of these." Sophie hauled a batch of flyers out of the box and handed half the pile to Lucky. She took another stack and placed them on the table where Nate, Bradley and Sergeant Woczinski stood.

Most of the crowd headed in their direction. It seemed everyone was ready to volunteer whatever free time they had to join in the search. Lucky and Sophie blocked the exit door, checking that every person leaving had a small stack of flyers to take with them. Lucky glanced down. A photo of Elizabeth run by the *Snowflake Gazette* when she was elected Mayor filled one quarter of the page. The word MISSING was emblazoned across the top. Sophie had done a good job preparing the flyers. They read, "Police are asking for the public's help in finding a missing woman last seen on August 10. She is described as 58 years old, 5'5" weighing 130 pounds. She was last seen wearing a white blouse and navy skirt. If you have any information, please contact . . ." and then the flyer listed several numbers and e-mails, with websites for further information.

Lucky fought a wave of terror. A woman she had known all her life, summed up in one paragraph that conveyed such dread. There was simply no way to shut off the pictures that flashed through her mind of what might have happened to Elizabeth.

Marjorie and Cecily were the first to approach. "Oh, Lucky. This is just terrible. First Harry and now this. What's happening in Snowflake?"

Lucky wiped her eyes and took a deep breath. She could barely choke out the words. "I don't know, Cecily. I just don't know."

"Do you think this could have something to do with Harry's murder?" Cecily breathed.

"You know, it's strange. That's what I've been wondering. It was the news of Harry's murder that first made me worry. Elizabeth would have certainly called us or come to see us. That's when I really started to worry—the fact that we didn't hear from her at all after that was just too strange." Several groups had collected behind Marjorie and Cecily. "I'm sorry. I don't mean to cut this short. I just want to make sure no one leaves without several of these to post around town."

"Of course," Cecily said, taking a batch of the flyers. "We'll stop in at the Spoonful tomorrow to see you and we'll sign up with Nate. Whatever we can do, we will."

"Thank you."

Janie and Jack had packed up leftovers and washed out the coffee urn. Jack had returned to the hall and with Horace's help was busy folding up the remaining chairs, stacking them at the side of the room.

Professor Arnold, carrying his briefcase, approached Lucky. "Why don't I take some with me, back to the University. I can have some of my students post them at school and around town." He didn't say it, but Lucky thought his tone implied it was a long shot that any news of Elizabeth could come from another town.

"Thank you. I really appreciate that. Anything you can do."

"I'll talk to my students. Maybe they'll have some time to volunteer in the search. Tough business. I'm really sorry." Horace followed Professor Arnold to the door and shook his hand. He returned to offer help packing up.

"Thanks, Horace. I think Jack has everything loaded on carts, but we'd love a hand back to the Spoonful."

"Be glad to. And I'll be going out with Nate and Bradley first thing tomorrow. Happy to do all I can for Elizabeth. I'm sure we'll find her."

Lucky nodded, unable to speak. "I'll just check on Jack and see what he needs." The first box of flyers was empty. The second box, half full. "Sophie, do you want to bring these back to the Spoonful?"

"Sure, and I'll take a pile up to the Resort and post them everywhere I can." Sophie reached out and pulled her close in a hug. Then she pulled away, grasping Lucky's shoulders and looking in her eyes. "She's not dead."

Lucky nodded in response.

"She's not. I just know it."

Chapter 21

THE NEXT MORNING, Lucky and Sophie stood in the entry hall of Elizabeth's home watching another police officer as he moved carefully around the first floor, checking windows and door locks. Charlie had bounded down the stairs, his bell jingling when he heard voices. At the sight of two strange men, he trotted to the dining room cabinet and hunkered underneath it.

Sergeant Woczinski was questioning them again. Lucky reiterated her movements. "The only thing I found out of place was the mail on the floor right here and two magazines and a flyer on the porch swing."

"Where did you put them?"

Lucky pointed to the hallway table. "Right there. The magazines and the flyer were too big to fit through the slot, so the mailman had to leave those on the swing outside."

The other officer returned to the entry hall. "Doesn't look like anything was disturbed here. No sign at all of a break-in. Whatever happened, I'm inclined to think she left home voluntarily."

"Sophie and I thought we'd take another look through her desk and cabinet if that's okay. Just on the off chance there's something that might give us an idea."

"Go right ahead. We've already searched but maybe you'd notice something that we missed. If so, let us know. Make sure no one else enters or knows about that spare key. We're going to canvas the neighbors now and then get back to the ground search. Here's my number." He pulled two cards out of his pocket and handed one to each of them. "Call me if you come up with anything, anything at all."

Lucky followed the men to the front door and locked it behind them. She walked into the dining room and knelt in front of the china cabinet, calling to Charlie, "Come out, Charlie. Come on, big guy. The scary men are gone." Charlie trilled and rushed into Lucky's arms. "Let's get you some fresh food."

Sophie followed Lucky into the kitchen. "That cat loves you. Listen to him purr."

"He's so sweet natured. Elizabeth's doted on him his whole life." Lucky gently lowered Charlie to the floor and opened the refrigerator. Charlie rubbed against her legs, knowing his dish would soon be full of food.

"This is such a nice room," Sophie said, gazing around. Elizabeth's kitchen walls were painted a soft coral color. Pots and pans hung on a rack near the stove. Everything was well used but spotless. Custom shades and curtains in pillow ticking, white background with thin blue stripes, hung at the windows, and place mats and plaid napkins echoed the coral and blue colors of the room. "It's so cheerful and orderly."

"It is, isn't it?" Lucky responded. She filled a small watering can half full and pulled a step stool close to the sink. She climbed up and watered the trailing ivy that hung in the window. "When Elizabeth comes home, I want her to feel that everything is in its place and has been cared for."

"She will," Sophie replied, watching as Lucky rearranged the trails of ivy leaves. "Let's go upstairs and start going through the filing cabinet."

Lucky climbed down and put the small watering can under the sink. "This may be a complete waste of time and there's no time to waste, but I'd hate to think there was something here that could help us find her." Lucky folded the step stool away and replaced it in the pantry.

They climbed upstairs and went straight to the small office. Lucky opened the top drawer of the three-drawer filing cabinet. She pulled out a stack of files and handed them to Sophie. "We just have to remember to put these back in order."

"That's easy. She's labeled them all alphabetically." Sophie flopped to the floor and leaned against the daybed. She laid the folders next to her, and after opening the first one, started to go through its contents methodically.

"Where was Elias last night? I didn't see him at the meeting." Sophie focused on the papers in front of her, carefully turning each page over.

"He went to Lincoln Falls. One of his patients had surgery early today, and another's been admitted. He'll be back late afternoon probably."

"I feel awful going through her things like this. I hope she'll forgive me whenever she turns up."

"I'll feel more awful if there's something here that I've missed." Lucky rubbed her forehead. "I should have sounded the alarm sooner. That's what I keep kicking myself about. I should have known when I didn't see her at the Pastor's ceremony or the dress rehearsal on the Green."

"Stop that!" Sophie said sternly. "You couldn't have known. You're not a mind reader. Stop beating yourself up." Charlie had followed them into the room and now jumped on the daybed, purring loudly. Sophie reached up to pet him. He meowed and rolled onto his back, enjoying the attention. Sophie gently pulled on Charlie's ears. "Maybe we should take him to your apartment. What do you think?"

"I've thought about that, but I don't know. Cats are so territorial. It might freak him out. Besides, he'd be just as lonely there. I'm never home."

"Guess so."

"I'll just stop by every morning and make sure he's okay." Something in Lucky's voice made Sophie look up. "What do we do if we can't find her in the next day or so? Oh, Sophie! People do disappear, just like my parents disappeared."

Sophie climbed out of her sitting position and grasped Lucky's hands. "I know they did. And it was terrible. And this is bringing all that up again. You're not wrong to be worried about her, but your perspective might be a little bit skewed," Sophie said, carefully gauging Lucky's reaction.

"I don't want to lose anybody ever again in my life, Sophie. I know that's crazy, but that's what I want." Lucky grabbed a tissue from the desk and wiped her eyes. "It's the worst thing in the world."

Sophie waited patiently for Lucky's outburst to subside. "It is. Nothing's worse. But we haven't lost her yet, have we? We'll find her. Nate's doing all the right things. He's called in the right people who are organizing everything. It's gone public as of today and the State Police are making sure it's plastered all over the media."

Lucky was still for a moment. "I know they've organized ground searches, but instead of joining one of those groups, why don't we drive around, go up and down every street in town, all around the Resort and every turnoff from here to the main highway. If she drove away, and she must have because her car is gone, then her car is somewhere— somewhere it hasn't been spotted yet. Somewhere in the woods or off the road. Otherwise, it would have been reported by now."

"It could take days to cover all the roads and paths into the woods, but we could do it early in the morning as soon as it's light out."

"Let's split it up. I'll get a map and we'll divide the whole area into sections. I know Nate's had Bradley try to do that, but they're not gonna have the time, especially with Harry's murder investigation. Let's start tomorrow. You up for that?"

"Absolutely," Sophie agreed. "I guess it's something we can do until we have a better idea."

Lucky and Sophie waded patiently through every folder in Elizabeth's filing cabinet, every drawer in the desk and every drawer in the bedroom bureau. Time had passed and nothing remarkable had been found. "Well, that's it," Lucky said as she gently closed the last bureau drawer. "All this time wasted. We could have been searching with one of the groups for the past two hours."

Sophie heaved a sigh, replacing the last of the folders. She gave a rub to Charlie's stomach. "Does he have enough food?" she asked as they headed down the stairs.

"He's fine. I'll check on him tomorrow on a break."

"Set your alarm. I'll be at your apartment door at five o'clock tomorrow morning with maps. Take pity on me and have some coffee ready. We can easily get in a few hours' searching."

Lucky locked the kitchen door behind them and returned the key to its hiding place in the garage. They walked slowly down the driveway. When they reached the sidewalk, Lucky looked up and down the street. "I know you and the police have already done it, but do you think it's worth talking to some of the neighbors again?"

"You need to get back to the Spoonful. Why don't I do that? I can just say I'm checking back with them and I can pass out flyers. They may remember something they didn't think to tell the police. They may not know what they know."

"Thank you, Sophie. I can't thank you enough."

"Don't thank me. I just want Elizabeth back. I can't bear to see you in this state."

Chapter 22

ELIZABETH GRASPED THE handle of the door that imprisoned her. It opened outward from the small room. The doorknob turned, but when she pushed against it, it refused to budge. It was held solidly in place. But by what? Was it barred? There was no lock on the doorknob itself. With all her strength, she pushed against the door to no avail. She pounded on the wood with her fists, shouting Maggie's name until her voice was hoarse. No one answered.

Elizabeth collapsed on the sleeping bag and reached for the jug of water. At this rate, the water wouldn't last long. Fear had made her thirsty. She needed to fight the panic and think. Surely there was a way to escape. She had hoped when Maggie returned to the cellar and opened the door, she might be able to overpower her. Elizabeth wasn't a big woman, but she was strong. That hope had been dashed once her wrists had been untied. Now Maggie never opened the door. She would only shove a small plate of food through the ragged hole at the bottom, just large enough to allow a dinner plate, but not large enough to reach out to whatever lock was on the outside of the door.

Unless Maggie grew careless, the window was now the only possible hope of escape. Elizabeth dragged the chair to the wall under the window and climbed up. She could reach the narrow window. It was locked with only a small catch and opened inward. Chicken wire mesh was nailed to the outer frame, no doubt to keep small creatures out of the cellar. And on the exterior of the house, two planks nailed across the opening allowed a thin sliver of light to filter through. Elizabeth reached up and, bruising her fingers, managed to turn the latch a quarter inch. She pulled at the window frame, but it refused to open. Peering closely she could see that thick eightpenny nails had been driven through the framing to secure the window. If she had a crowbar or heavy hammer, she might be able to release the frame. She sighed in frustration, staring at the window. She might not be able to open it, but nothing prevented her from breaking the glass.

She climbed down from the chair and picked her cardigan up from the sleeping bag. She wrapped it carefully around her elbow. She didn't want Maggie to hear the sound of glass breaking. Who knew what she might do. She had been so frightened when she saw the kitchen knife in Maggie's hands. If she were truly insane what might she be capable of? Once the sweater was wound tightly around her elbow, she climbed on the chair and stood on her tiptoes. The chair creaked suddenly and threatened to collapse. She grasped the edge of the window frame to keep her balance and made a quick, sharp blow to the glass with her elbow. It cracked and a large chunk of glass fell between the frame and the outer planks. She stopped and listened carefully for a minute but heard no footsteps approaching. A breath of fresh, warm summer air caressed her face as she stood balanced on the chair. She breathed in deeply. A bird sang in a nearby tree. Her current situation seemed all the more painful. Outside this house the world continued, people went about their business, and even if her friends and loved ones realized she was missing, how would they ever know where to look? Tears came to her eyes and she quickly brushed them away. Mental discipline was essential. If she broke down, she could never hope to be free. There had to be a way out of this cellar.

She carefully picked a few small shards of glass from her sweater and, wrapping it tightly around her elbow again, made another jab at the window glass. Half of the glass fell away. With two fingers, she gingerly moved aside the larger pieces and reached out to the planks covering the outside of the window. These boards were relatively new. She pushed hard against them. They were nailed in solidly. If only she had some kind of tool, but there was nothing in the room she could use. She remembered the sliver of light when she had first descended the stairs. It was the opening of a wooden hatch that would lead outside. There had been a workbench next to the hatch. If she could escape from this room, the workbench might hold tools she could use. In the meantime, the only possibility was this one window. Her shoe. Perhaps her shoe was strong enough to dislodge the boards. She reached down and slipped off one shoe. Using the heel, she struck a solid blow against the lower board. She didn't care any longer if Maggie heard her. If Maggie returned and opened the door, she would shove her way out, even if Maggie held a knife in her hand. She was desperate. She was no longer concerned about the consequences of being heard. Her one goal was to escape. Angry now, she banged steadily away at one of the planks. If she had a ladder she could gain more leverage and make better progress. Reaching up from the rickety chair didn't give her much purchase. Using all her strength, she hammered at the board, ignoring the creaking chair. She was sure one corner of the plank had moved slightly. Hopeful, she landed one more powerful blow against the plank. As she did so, the chair gave a loud squeak and collapsed under her. She fell to the floor, and cried out in pain as her ankle twisted under her.

THE LUNCH RUSH was over by the time Lucky reached the Spoonful. Janie and Meg were taking a break at a corner table. Sage was laying out utensils on his work space in the kitchen, and Jack was counting out bills from the cash register. It was a lull in what would later be a busy afternoon and evening. The flyers Sophie had prepared were displayed in several spots in the large front window where they would be seen by passersby. Jack had refreshed the stack next to the cash register. Lucky slipped on an apron and went out to the front room to talk to him. He looked up expectantly.

She indicated the front window. "I see you've put them up."

"Yep. Some of the tourists have taken an interest too. A few told me they'd volunteer with the State Police."

"Really? That's awfully good of them."

"Something will break. Just wait and see." Jack put his arm around her shoulder and gave her an encouraging hug. "What have you been up to?"

"We were at Elizabeth's with Sergeant Woczinski. The police were just finishing their search of the house. Sophie and I went through Elizabeth's files and drawers just to be thorough and leave no stone unturned, but no luck. We decided to focus on searching for Elizabeth's car. We'll check all the roads in and out of town and paths into the woods," Lucky continued. "Then whenever I can get away from the Spoonful, I'll volunteer for a walking search— Sophie will too."

"That'll be a tough schedule."

"That's all right. I'd rather be up at the crack of dawn

doing something than wandering around in a state of anxiety."

"I'm joining a search tomorrow morning. They're gonna start around seven bells. You think you can manage with me gone for a few hours?"

"We'll be fine. You feel up to it?"

"I feel the same way you do. I'd rather be doing something than nothing. I'm sorry about the other night, my girl."

"The other night? What do you mean?" Lucky was confused.

"You were worried about Elizabeth that night and I joked about it. I should have listened to you. I don't blame you for being worried sick, especially after Harry being . . ." He trailed off and shook his head. "Who would do such a thing? Harry never bothered a soul. He wasn't the friendliest cuss, but he was all right."

Lucky squeezed his hand. "Nate's got help in that quarter now. They'll figure it out."

Jack shot her a quick look.

Lucky blushed. "I didn't mean that the way it came out. I didn't mean to sound cavalier about Harry, not at all, but he's gone. There's nothing we can do about that. Elizabeth could still be alive."

"Of course she's alive. I feel it in my bones."

A family approached with their bill in hand. Jack smiled at them and rang up their charges. Lucky went to the counter and glanced at the blackboard where Sage had listed his specials for the day. There were three different soups, one hot and two chilled, in deference to the heat. Her favorite salad was on the menu today too—romaine with thinly sliced red onions, small cubes of sweet potato and apple with caramelized walnuts, served with a sun-dried tomato vinaigrette dressing. Her stomach growled in response.

Jack must have read her mind. He called over to her, "Have you eaten anything today?"

Lucky had to think a minute before she replied. "Just a piece of toast this morning, I guess."

"And to think you try to baby me! Sit right over there at the counter. I'll bring you one of those salads."

Janie finished her break and took over the cash register while Jack put together a salad for Lucky. He served it to her at the counter with a flourish and slipped another CD into the player. It was soothing music, a new age kind of synthesizer. She dove into the salad, eating ravenously. Jack returned to his seat by the cash register and Janie slipped onto the stool next to Lucky.

"I'm going on one of the search parties tomorrow, as soon as Jack's back. No news?"

Lucky shook her head. "Charlie's been taken care of. Flyers are posted everywhere. It's on the web. The news media is picking it up. Sophie and I are starting very early tomorrow by car. We're going to search every street, road, dirt path and byway we can find for Elizabeth's car. And we'll just keep searching. I can't think what else to do."

"You're right. But try to stay calm. We're all on edge now after what happened to Harry. I just want Nate to catch whoever did that to him." Janie placed a comforting hand on Lucky's shoulder and rose from her stool. She walked around the room, checking each table to make sure everything was set for the next wave of customers.

Lucky picked up her dishes and carried them into the kitchen, rinsed them off and put them in the dishwasher. The bell over the front door rang. She peeked through the hatch. She groaned when she saw the bright strawberry blonde hair—Rowena.

"Hey, Lucky!" Rowena waved at her through the opening. "Hi, Jack," she called out and grabbed a stool at the counter.

Lucky returned to the counter. "What can I get you,

Rowena?" Rowena had been devastated and close to tears a few days ago when Lucky had run into her at the rehearsal. Today, Rowena was fully recovered and bursting with energy.

"I heard there's a new chilled cherry soup with cream. Is it good?"

"Fantastic. I'll get you a bowl." Lucky placed the order on the hatch and a minute later Sage had filled it.

She carried the bowl to Rowena. "Anything to drink?"

"Love some iced coffee. Thanks, Lucky."

Lucky placed the tall glass and a small pitcher of cream at the side of the place mat and started to turn away. The bell jingled again. Guy Bessette walked in. Like an imprinted duck, he headed straight to the counter. He only had eyes for Rowena.

Rowena leaned closer over the counter. "Lucky, you know I had no luck with that developer. But . . ." Rowena trailed off. Lucky had a sneaky suspicion what Rowena was leading up to and kept silent. "Maybe I could talk to Jack about the discovery of Harry's body. A real crime story."

"Hi, Rowena. How are you?" Rowena turned and stared at Guy as if an insect had just appeared in her soup. "Oh, hi," she said flatly.

Lucky suppressed a grimace at Rowena's treatment of Guy. "You're welcome to ask Jack yourself. He's right there."

Guy remained silent, listening to the back-and-forth conversation. He was screwing his courage to the sticking point and finally said, "Rowena, maybe we could . . . uh . . . get together some night."

Rowena stared coldly at him for a long moment. "Get together?"

"Uh . . . yeah, you know, maybe we could have dinner or go out somewhere."

Rowena regarded him blankly and said, "I don't think so, Guy."

"Oh." Guy's face fell. He looked down at the counter, blushing bright red. Lucky had watched the exchange, cringing at Guy's embarrassment.

Rowena turned back to her. "You don't mind if I talk to Jack?"

"I don't mind. I can't say he'll talk to you, but why don't you ask him?"

Jack was close enough that he had caught the drift of the conversation, but ignored it. Rowena finished her soup and trotted over to the cash register. As she paid for her lunch, she said, "Jack, I wonder if I could interview you?"

Jack pretended to look surprised. "Me? Why would you want to interview me?" Lucky turned away. She didn't want Rowena to see her grinning.

"I'd like to write a piece—kinda human interest about how you found the body."

"Rowena, how can you ask that? It isn't something I can talk about. Besides, Nate's warned me not to speak about anything I saw there."

"What?" Rowena's voice went a few decibels higher.

"Just what I said. I was warned not to talk about anything," he replied innocently.

Lucky poured an iced coffee for Guy and leaned closer. "Don't feel too bad, Guy," she said. What she wanted to say and didn't was that Rowena was a self-absorbed twit and he wasn't missing a thing.

"I've been trying to work up my nerve for a long time, hoping she'd give me the time of day, but I guess I don't stand a chance."

"When the right person comes along, she'll really appreciate you."

"Maybe," Guy said uncertainly. "Listen, Lucky, can I talk to you about something?"

"Sure." Lucky laid a stack of place mats on the counter and moved closer.

"The night Harry died . . ." Guy took a deep breath.

"Norman Rank had called and said he was gonna pick up his car later that evening. Harry said he'd wait there for Norman. So Norman had to have been the last person who saw Harry alive."

"I do remember seeing two cars in the shop when I was there, right after Jack. One car I know was Jack's. You say the other was Norman's? Maybe Norman didn't stop by that night after all. You told this to Nate, didn't you?"

"I did. But all the same. I don't want Nate to think that Norman might have hurt Harry? I don't want Norman to be mad at me about telling Nate."

"Don't worry about all that. Nate would have figured out pretty quick that it was Norman's car. And I'm sure Nate's already talked to him by now."

"There's something else." Guy leaned closer and whispered, "I got a call this morning from a lawyer over in Lincoln Falls. He told me . . ." Guy struggled to find the words. "He told me Harry made a will." Guy paused and looked over his shoulder to make sure no one could overhear their conversation. He turned back to Lucky and whispered, "Harry left everything to me." Guy looked more frightened than excited about his news.

"Really! Why, Guy, that's wonderful. He must have thought the world of you to do that."

"I just can't believe it. I can't get my head around it. Why would he do that? Make a will, I mean? He wasn't that old. He left me his house, the business, some money too . . ." Guy shook his head in disbelief. "But I'm really worried."

"Worried? Why?"

"What if people think I had something to do with Harry's murder? I'm really scared about that."

Lucky heaved a sigh. "Guy, please don't worry. Anybody that knows you knows how hard you worked for Harry, how much he liked you. Besides, who was Harry going to leave anything to anyway? He had no relatives and no children and who else could run that business besides you?"

"Lucky, you're the only person I've told. I just don't know who I can talk to."

Lucky was taken aback. Guy was so terribly shy and quiet. It surprised her that he valued her opinion and that he had no one else to talk to. She leaned closer to him. "Listen to me—if you want my advice, keep this under your hat for now. Don't tell *anyone* what you've told me. Other than Nate. You can tell Nate. Eventually, the lawyer will sort things out and it will be public knowledge, but I'm sure by that time, Nate will know who was responsible for what happened to Harry. Just keep quiet about all this for now and don't let your business become part of the rumor mill around town. You deserve this and obviously Harry wanted you to have it."

Guy nodded shakily. "You think?"

"Yes, I do. The smartest thing for you to do is keep quiet until the dust settles. After that, it doesn't matter what envious people might say."

"Okay. Okay." Guy swallowed nervously. "Thanks, Lucky. I feel better already. It's good advice."

Lucky hesitated, but finally couldn't stop herself. "And Guy . . ."

"Yes?"

"Whatever you do . . . do not tell Rowena." She stared at him intently.

"Oh!" Guy rattled that around for a moment. "Why?"

Lucky wondered how best to convey to Guy that Rowena was a selfish narcissist, but couldn't seem to find the right words. Finally, she said, "Because she works for the *Gazette* and she'll want to write about it so that everyone in town will know. If you're smart, you'll keep your mouth shut."

Guy swiveled slightly on his stool and stared at Rowena, now leaning across the counter at the cash register. Lucky wondered if perhaps a bit of the veil might have been torn away. Guy looked back and nodded. "Okay. I won't say a word."

"Trust me—it's the smartest thing to do."

Rowena had been so intent on coercing Jack into an interview she hadn't overheard Guy's whispered conversation at the counter. Lucky hated to think Rowena might suddenly develop an interest in Guy for all the wrong reasons.

Rowena's voice rose even higher, but Jack stood his ground. "That's ridiculous. Nate can't order you to do that."

"'Fraid he can, Rowena. He's the Chief of Police, and I don't want any hassle from him."

"Fine," Rowena responded. "Have it your way." Rowena huffed loudly and stomped toward the door just as Horace Winthorpe, outside, reached for the door handle. In spite of Horace's bulk, he was almost knocked off balance as Rowena flounced out. She stormed away, a cranky expression on her face. Lucky started to laugh, but stopped, afraid Horace might think she was laughing at him. He stepped into the Spoonful, mopping his brow from the heat.

"Hello, everyone," he called. Jack, Hank and Barry greeted him in unison as he approached the counter.

"What can I get you, Horace?"

"Something cool. I've been thinking about fresh lemonade over ice all the way here."

"Not a problem," Lucky replied. "Something to eat?"

"How about one of those little sandwiches with cream cheese and watercress on brown bread. That would be lovely."

"Coming right up."

Horace swung around on his stool and surveyed the group. "Did I arrive at a bad time?"

"No," Hank replied, tilting his head back to view Horace through his pince-nez glasses. "We were just talking about Harry."

Horace nodded sadly. "Of course. Does Nate have any leads?"

Barry shrugged his shoulders. "That I don't know, but it must have happened the night before the demonstration, after he closed his shop." Barry looked across the room at Guy, who was hunched over his drink at the other end of the counter. He called out to him. "Guy, you were probably the last person to see Harry—other than whoever killed him. Any ideas?"

Guy swallowed nervously, his Adam's apple bouncing in his throat. "No. No. Sorry." Guy jumped from the stool and rushed out the door.

Barry looked around the restaurant. "What did I say? He's as nervous as a cat."

Lucky realized her advice was the best thing she could have said to Guy. No wonder he was nervous.

Horace moved to the table to sit with Hank and Barry. "I must apologize to you all." He turned to include Lucky in his comment.

"About what, Horace?" Hank asked.

"It was very careless of me to openly imply . . . no, to state, in fact, that the young man in the grave could have been a traitor. I had no idea Cordelia Rank had an ancestor named Cooper and that I was opening a can of worms. It's a fairly common name and I was just so excited by our find."

"Aw, don't worry about it. You couldn't have known," Barry replied. "Cordelia Cooper Rank—serves her right, that uppity cow. She's always lording it over everyone in town that she's a Daughter of the American Revolution. Such nonsense. As if half of the people in Snowflake can't count an ancestor who was here two hundred years ago. Tiresome woman."

Lucky took Horace's order off the hatch and placed it on the counter as he returned to his stool.

"Lucky, if you have any interest in seeing the artifacts we found, I'd love to show them to you."

"You still have them?"

He leaned across the counter and whispered, "Just for a few days. They've allowed me to borrow them so I can take some pictures for my research."

"That's fantastic." Lucky smiled indulgently. Horace was like a very large boy with new toys.

"Why don't you stop over and I can show you?"

"I'd love to. I would like to see the powder horn up close."

"It's amazing—that carving was done just like the scrimshaw that sailors have done for centuries. But the lead ball is far more interesting."

"I gather that's what set Cordelia off. I didn't hear the whole thing. I was busy cleaning up and running around."

"Well, you see, we know it was a projectile shot from a rifle. Now, that's not to say this poor young man was definitely shot by another colonist. The gun could have come into the possession of someone other than a British soldier, but it couldn't possibly have been fired from a British gun. The colonials used rifles and they can take the credit for developing a gun with grooves in the barrel—the kind of gun that would have scored the lead ball the way it did. Well, that's not quite accurate. I think originally the rifle was invented by the Germans to allow for better aim, but it was refined in the Colonies and used widely. It was a much better gun for a straighter shot, especially for longer distances in hunting."

"I didn't know that." Lucky leaned on an elbow and listened, fascinated. "No wonder Cordelia was so upset."

"I'm afraid she'll never forgive me."

"Horace, don't worry your head about it. She is rather insufferable most of the time."

"Her status as a Daughter of the American Revolution seems to be terribly important to her."

Lucky shook her head and refilled Horace's lemonade. "If it wasn't the DAR, it would be something else, I'm sure—the Junior League, the size of her bank account, whatever. Maybe I'll take you up on your offer and come by for a visit this evening."

Horace smiled. "I would be delighted. See you then."

Chapter 23

THE SMALL AMOUNT of light filtering through the cellar window was fading. Elizabeth felt she was losing all sense of time and day. It was afternoon, but why wasn't it brighter outside? Was a summer storm on the way? How many days had elapsed since she'd been locked in? She should have been doing her best to mark the days. Anything that would offer a sense of order was important. She thought she had been locked in this room for five days, and now it seemed this fifth day was ending. If she didn't have someone to talk to, she'd lose her mind. With the chair in pieces, reaching the window was impossible. Unless she was strong enough to tear the toilet from its mounting, there was absolutely nothing to stand on to reach that one window. The only possibility of escape was to get Maggie to open the door and force her way out.

She lay on the sleeping bag willing herself not to scream in frustration. Perhaps if she left the food untouched for a day or so, Maggie would become concerned, open the door

and enter the room. She had once not returned a dirty plate
to the opening at the bottom of the door to see if Maggie
might unlock it. Maggie had only slipped a fresh plate of
vegetables under the door later that day. But what if she
could hold out and lie on the floor as if unconscious or
dead. Would Maggie be fooled into coming closer? It was
a thought. If only she could last without any food. It
was the one plan she could think of. If it worked she'd be
able to overpower Maggie and escape.

She heard a heavy footstep above her. It couldn't be
Maggie. Maggie was quiet and light on her feet, afraid to
disturb anything around her. Elizabeth lay quite still in the
fading light. Had the dark enhanced her hearing? Someone
else must be in the house. Someone was with Maggie. A
voice that was low but deeper. She couldn't hear a response
from Maggie, but it sounded as if a two-way conversation
were taking place on the floor above her. She didn't care if
there really was someone Maggie feared. She had to
escape. She had to get help.

Elizabeth struggled to her feet. She was stiff from lack
of activity. She grabbed a shoe and rushed to the washroom. With all her strength, she began to bang on the pipes
that ran up the wall to the ceiling. The clanging sound
echoed through the walls. She shouted for help. If someone
else was there, they would hear and come down to the cellar to investigate. She screamed and banged for what felt
like an hour and finally, exhausted, stopped to catch her
breath.

It was completely quiet above her. Had it been only her
imagination? Was Maggie alone? Was it merely a voice on
the radio? She dropped the shoe and sank to her knees,
sobbing.

LUCKY PULLED UP in front of Elizabeth's house, wishing
by some miracle that Elizabeth's car would be parked in

the drive. The sky was a wash of pink and purple as evening approached. The lamp in the parlor was already on, the one that was on a timer, but nothing else had changed. The driveway was empty and she knew there would be no car in the garage. Charlie had been alone all day. She felt slightly guilty that she hadn't done more for him today, but tonight she'd spend some time brushing and petting him before she headed down the road to Horace's. A curtain moved at a side window of the house next door. A woman peered out at her suspiciously. Lucky held up a hand in greeting, not wanting to alarm Elizabeth's neighbor. The woman waved in return and lifted her window. Inside, Lucky saw an antique hutch and a colonial style brass chandelier in a room very similar to Elizabeth's dining room. The neighbor leaned out.

"Hello. Any news about Elizabeth? You're Lucky, aren't you? Elizabeth often mentions you."

Lucky walked across the drive, closer to the neighbor's window. "Yes, I am. Sorry, but there's no news. I'm just here to keep Charlie company for a little while. You're Enid, right?"

"Yes, that's me."

"Elizabeth has spoken of you too. Nice to meet you."

"Same here, just wish it were under different circumstances. The police were here yesterday and today, and a woman who said she was a friend of yours knocked on my door—pretty girl, dark hair. They were all asking me if I had seen Elizabeth or seen anything unusual."

"That was Sophie. And did you? See anything?"

Enid shook her head. "No. I almost wish I had because then they might have something to go on. I did see her back out of her driveway. That was the morning of the eleventh, I told the police. She was all alone in the car. I have a clear view from my kitchen and dining room windows, but other than that, just looked like a normal day. I wish there were something more I could do."

Lucky nodded. "We all feel that way."

"It's just terrifying, I'll tell you. First, poor Harry Hodges. And now this. Elizabeth, of all people! That's all anyone on our street can talk about."

"If there's anything you think of, anything at all, you call Nate Edgerton, or call me at the Spoonful."

"I will, dear. My feet aren't what they used to be, but I'm volunteering to go with a search party, starting tomorrow. I'll walk until I can't walk anymore, and then maybe I can man the phones or do something useful until we find her."

"That would be great. We have to do everything we can."

Enid waved good-bye and shut her dining room window. Lucky walked slowly down the drive and opened the garage door, just as she had earlier that day. Removing the key from its hook in the cabinet, she let herself in through the kitchen door. A small night-light over the kitchen sink lit her way, and she reached out to turn on the overhead light.

Charlie meowed and came running to greet her, his bell tinkling. The cat made deep purring sounds and pushed his face against her legs. She dropped her purse and reached down to pick him up, crooning soft words to him and rubbing his belly. When he tried to wriggle away, she put him down gently on the floor. "I know you're lonely. I'm sorry, Charlie. Let me get you some food." She dished out a generous helping of cat food in a fresh dish, added some dry pellets to his other bowl and refreshed his water.

After cleaning his litter box, she opened and closed kitchen drawers until she found his brush. She sat on a kitchen chair and pulled Charlie up on her lap. As she brushed his coat, he purred, exposing one side and the other until he had had enough. He jumped off her lap and lay on his back on the kitchen floor, exposing his white fur belly. But when Lucky tried to brush his stomach, he grabbed the brush with both paws and wouldn't let go.

She laughed. "Charlie. If you do that, I can't brush you."

The radio still played soothing music. She considered opening the kitty door but decided against it. She felt guilty about leaving him inside alone, but she didn't want to let him out of the house when there was no one here to keep an eye out for him. Charlie was middle-aged now, almost a house cat. He'd be safer inside.

"I'm sorry, Charlie. I'll be back tomorrow afternoon and maybe she'll be home by then. Please God," she prayed. She mentally reviewed the possibilities in her mind. If Elizabeth had had an accident on the road, someone would have reported it. The car would have been seen, either with Elizabeth in it, or abandoned. She was sure Nate and the police had alerted all hospitals in the state, in case Elizabeth had been in an accident and couldn't talk. She tried to picture Elizabeth stopping for a hitchhiker, but quickly dismissed that possibility. If she had been heading to her office, she'd be within the town. No one would be hitchhiking within a small community. If some errand had taken her to a road outside of town, someone looking for a ride might be a possibility. But Elizabeth was always sensible and cautious. She would never have picked up a stranger on the road. She might stop for someone she knew very well, but never a stranger. Had she driven out of town and broken down somewhere? Had someone accosted her on the road and harmed her, and driven away in her car? The possibilities were endless. She had to stay centered or she'd lose her mind. The longer this went on, the more her panicky feelings threatened to overwhelm her. She felt a desperately anxious need to do something—anything—but what more could she do, other than search the roads in the early morning or join a search party when she could get time away from the Spoonful?

She moved slowly through the first floor, checking everything. Nothing had changed. The windows were all locked. She peered at the thermostat. The air-conditioning was on low. The house was cool and comfortable. Charlie had curled into a ball on top of his cushion in the living room. The latest post sat on the floor by the front door. She picked it up and sorted through it—a bill from the power company, a long white envelope with the State Bar insignia in the corner and an advertising flyer. Nothing to indicate where Elizabeth might be. She dropped it on the hallway table and noticed a very light smattering of dust on the surface. How long since Elizabeth had been at home? She cast her mind back. Five days. It had been five days since Enid her neighbor had seen her. Well, that was something she could do. She returned to the kitchen closet and found a duster. Moving through the living room, dining room and hallway, she wiped off every surface. When Elizabeth came home it would look as if she hadn't been gone more than an hour. She found a dust mop and repeated her actions, picking up really nothing more than Charlie's hairs deposited in various spots.

She tucked the mail under her arm and climbed the stairs with her housecleaning tools. Methodically, she dusted the desk and file cabinets in the office and finally the bedroom furniture. A photo in a silver frame stood on the bureau. It was one of her mother and Elizabeth. There were other framed snapshots of friends and even one of Lucky herself. Lucky looked closer at the photo of the two women. They wore shorts and sat on a pier at the lake dangling their legs in the water. Elizabeth squinted in the sun while Martha Jamieson, wearing sunglasses, smiled widely. Perhaps her father had taken this very picture. A moment captured in time. Two friends enjoying a sun-filled day before one was gone and the other went missing. Lucky held the photo to her cheek and closed her eyes. If only she could bring them both back. She sighed and replaced the picture on top of the bureau.

She returned to the office and plopped down in the desk chair. No new messages on the answering machine. Charlie had followed her up the stairs and jumped into her lap as she sat at the desk. He curled into a ball. She reached down and gently pulled on his ears, a thing she knew he loved. "I'm sorry, Charlie. I don't know where she is. I wish I did."

She dropped the new mail on the desk, glancing at it. The State Bar Association. Why would the State Bar be writing to Elizabeth? She picked up the envelope and looked closer. A series of six numbers followed by letters, 572639THIBEA, was typed in the upper left-hand corner of the envelope, under the logo. *THIBEA?* Was it a legal case designation of some sort? Elizabeth wasn't an attorney. Why would she receive correspondence like this? THIBEA. The beginning of a name? Curiosity took over. If she had to, she'd explain herself later, but a question started to form in her mind. She neatly sliced the envelope open with Elizabeth's letter opener. Unfolding the letter, she read it through twice. Rod Thibeault was under investigation for improper conduct. A hearing was scheduled for later in the month. Elizabeth Dove's testimony was required and she was to appear at the disciplinary hearing on August 25. Rod? Why was he being called before a disciplinary board? This sounded quite serious. And why was Elizabeth called as a witness at this hearing? The letter raised more questions than it answered.

She picked up the phone and dialed the police station. It was after hours, but Nate answered the phone on the second ring.

"Nate, it's me. Lucky. I'm at Elizabeth's. Any news?"

She heard Nate's sigh at the other end of the line. "Nothing, Lucky. Sorry. We haven't found her or her car. A few calls came in, and the State Police are checking them, but they're probably nothing. The good news is there haven't been any hospital admissions or accident reports that match her car or her description."

"I don't know if that's good news or not. As horrible as that would be, at least we'd know where she is."

"I know this is rough for you, but try to stay calm. I'm sure there'll ultimately be an explanation. We'll find her." Lucky was certain she detected a note of uncertainty in Nate's voice. He was a cop, after all. He'd seen his share of bad things, and even he couldn't deny that a missing person was a very bad thing.

"I'm at Elizabeth's. I came by to take care of Charlie and I found something that might be important." Nate waited silently on the other end of the phone while she relayed the information in the letter from the State Bar.

"You just found this tonight?"

"Yes. On the floor under the mail slot. It must have come in the post today."

"Is there a contact person or number on that letter?"

"It's signed by a Sarah Atkinson, Case Manager. Her number is . . ." Lucky glanced at the top of the letter and recited the telephone number to Nate.

"I'll call that woman first thing tomorrow and find out what kind of difficulty Rod is in. More importantly, how does this concern Elizabeth?"

"That's what I'm wondering too."

"When you go, just leave it on the desk. I'll stop over tomorrow and pick it up."

"Okay. Just be careful not to let Charlie out."

"Will do," Nate grumbled.

Lucky clicked the button and dialed Sophie's cell phone next.

"Where are you?"

"At Elizabeth's. Taking care of Charlie and just

checking around. Found something kind of interesting. I'll fill you in later. Did you have any luck with the neighbors?"

"Not much. A woman two houses away thought she saw Elizabeth four or five days ago, driving away. She couldn't remember the exact day. That was about eight thirty in the morning. It could have been the morning of the demonstration but she's not entirely sure. Elizabeth must have been on her way to the office."

"I saw her next-door neighbor as I was coming down the drive—Enid. She says she saw Elizabeth pull out of the driveway the morning she didn't arrive at the office."

"Oh yes. I spoke to her too. She was sure Elizabeth was alone. She didn't see anybody with her, or anybody in her car."

"She never got there, Sophie. And her office is less than five minutes away. What could have possibly happened between here and there?"

"Maybe she wasn't going there right away. She must have taken a detour to do an errand."

"I've thought about that, but where could she have been going that early in the morning?"

"Maybe she stopped at the market to pick up groceries, or the pharmacy?"

"The market's right in the center of town. Somebody would have seen her. And Flagg's Pharmacy doesn't open till nine thirty anyway."

"Listen, is there anything I can do tonight? I'm at Sage's, soaking my feet. I've been walking the woods with a group of searchers, but we can come over to your place if you'd like some company."

"No, that's all right. I'm stopping over at Horace's next. He wants to show me his finds. I'm just hanging out a little while to keep poor Charlie company."

"Okay. Call me if you need anything at all. Sage and

I can take turns with Charlie too. I'm sure Elizabeth wouldn't mind if we were at her house."

"She wouldn't at all. Especially if you're taking care of Charlie. He's her baby."

She clicked off the call and sat for a moment petting Charlie. She pushed away the thought that Elizabeth might be beyond caring about her house or her cat.

Chapter 24

HALF AN HOUR later, Lucky pulled into the driveway of her parents' home, Horace's home now, only a half mile from Elizabeth's. She turned off the engine and listened to the chirping of crickets. A car engine came to life somewhere on the road. She breathed in the cool, humid night air. Several lights were on inside the house. She grabbed the bottle of wine she had brought along for the visit and rang the front doorbell. A strange feeling to be a visitor in the home she had always known, once so familiar, and now no longer hers.

Horace had fallen in love with the house the minute he had seen it. In a former life, it had been a barn, and was still painted deep red. A center peak and high window betrayed its origins, and the wings of the house extended from either side. After her parents' death, she wasn't able to return there to live. The shock had been too great and too many fresh memories haunted her. Besides which, living here had been out of the question. She couldn't afford it, not with the Spoonful being hit hard financially, and she couldn't have sold the house for what it would have taken to pay the mortgages. When Horace came to town and wanted to rent it on a long-term lease she was thrilled. The house had found the right person.

She rang the bell once again but didn't hear Horace's footsteps approaching. She knocked loudly and waited. No one came. Strange, she thought. Horace had specifically said this evening and she had agreed. It wasn't like him to forget. She turned away and walked to the side of the house. Stepping carefully in the dark, she peeked in a few of the windows but couldn't see Horace. Could he have stepped out for a few minutes? But where would he go? His car was parked outside. Surely he wouldn't have gone into the woods after dark. She continued to the rear of the house. She reached a window that allowed her a view of the spare room next to the kitchen. Horace had converted this space to an office. She couldn't see the desk from where she stood, but papers were strewn all over the floor. That wasn't like Horace. He was obsessively neat and organized when he worked.

She stepped away from the window and looked behind her. The familiar woods now loomed dark and foreboding. At the back, the light over the door was lit, as was the kitchen light. She peeked through the window of the door. The kitchen was deserted. She was certain Horace wasn't inside. She left the bottle of wine on a back stair and walked to the edge of the grass nearest the trees. She called Horace's name, her voice carrying on the warm night air, and peered into the woods. Either her eyes were playing tricks or there was a flicker of light deep within the trees. Something was very wrong.

She called Horace's name again and slipped through the trees heading to the spot where the light shone. Twigs and dry leaves crunched under her sandals. Her foot caught on a tree root and she almost stumbled. She reached a small clearing that she knew well and found the source of the light. A flashlight lay on the ground, its beam aimed at a tree trunk. She picked it up and turned slowly, aiming at the dark spaces, afraid that someone could be lurking in the shadows. The moon was only a thin sliver in the sky. Inside the trees it was pitch-dark. She shivered, suddenly aware of how alone she was. An owl hooted in the distance and a small creature scampered through the undergrowth. She whipped around, aiming the flashlight at the sound. Her eye caught something out of place. She moved closer. It was cloth, a dark cloth, and something brighter. She aimed the flashlight. Plaid material—a shirt. Horace's shirt. He was behind a large pine tree, splayed on the dead leaves and pine needles. Her heart leaped to her throat. The image of Harry Hodges lying in a pool of blood flashed before her eyes.

Lucky knelt and placed a hand on his neck. His skin was warm. She shook his shoulder gently. "Horace."

He groaned and his eyes fluttered open.

"Horace, what happened?"

"I . . ." He tried to roll to his side but winced in pain. Lucky dropped the flashlight and guided him slowly into a sitting position.

"I don't know. Someone was calling . . ." He touched his head and winced in pain again. "I went to see what was wrong."

"Let's get you back to the house. Can you stand up?"

"I think so." He struggled to his feet and reached out to a tree trunk for balance.

Lucky took his arm to guide him, shining the flashlight on the path before them. When they reached the house, she picked up the bottle of wine she had left on the step and led Horace inside to a kitchen chair. She locked the kitchen door. "Let's have a look at you."

Horace held a hand to the back of his head.

"Does that hurt?"

He nodded. "Yes. A bit."

"Did you fall and hit your head?"

"I think I must have. I tripped over a tree root and went flying."

"Horace, what were you thinking to go into the woods at night?" she asked gently.

Horace took a deep, shaky breath. "I heard someone calling. It was faint but it sounded like a woman. I'm not sure now but I thought she was saying, '*Help me, help me.*'" Horace looked up. "Lucky, I didn't imagine it."

"The song of the siren." Lucky shivered. "No, I don't think you imagined it. Too many weird things have been happening lately. But all the same, if you ever need anything or you're worried about anything, just call me or call Jack. We'd come out immediately to help you."

"You're right. I guess it was foolish. But I thought someone was in trouble."

Lucky nodded. "After what happened to Harry, I think we should report this to Nate."

"Oh," Horace groaned. "I really don't want to bother Nate. He has enough to deal with."

"Horace, listen to me. What if this is connected to Harry's murder?"

Horace's eyes widened. She was getting through to him. "I see what you mean. All right. If you insist, I'll call Nate tomorrow—first thing."

"Let's call him right now. If we don't, we'll have to listen to a lecture about not calling him immediately."

Horace sighed and nodded slowly. "You're probably right."

Lucky picked up the phone on the kitchen wall and dialed Nate's cell phone. He answered on the first ring. She quickly filled him in on Horace's condition.

"You did the right thing. I'll be there in twenty," Nate replied and hung up. In the background, she heard Susanna

Edgerton, Nate's wife, questioning him about the call. She was sure Susanna, like everyone else in town, was on edge.

"I don't think you should be alone out here, Horace. Not after this. If it's okay with you, I'd like to stay here tonight. I can sleep on the sofa, or even better, you could stay at Jack's. He wouldn't mind at all. In fact, he'd enjoy the company."

"Oh, there's no need to put your grandfather out. I'll be fine. You're certainly welcome to stay if you like but there's no need to worry about me. Maybe it was just kids fooling around in the woods."

"I hope that's all it was." Lucky doubted the explanation was that simple. This house was a mile outside of town. All the years that she had lived in her parents' home, she had felt isolated from the teenage hangouts in town until she was allowed to drive. Now Horace was here all alone. "I'd feel better if you had a dog."

"Me? A dog?"

"Sure. Why not? They're wonderful company and a dog would be sure to alert you if someone was prowling around. Sit still. I'm going to check your scalp." Lucky carefully examined Horace's head but could find no blood. The skin wasn't broken but a large egg was starting to form on the back of his head. "Can you look up? I just want to check your pupils." Flashlight in hand, she aimed the light at Horace's eyes, first right and then left. "Try not to blink." Horace obediently complied. "Okay, your pupils are normal. But since that's the extent of my nursing skills, you might still have a concussion. Ask Elias to check you tomorrow."

She found a dish towel in the drawer and soaked it in cold water. Then she broke open a tray of ice cubes, wrapped them inside the towel and banged the bundle against the old porcelain sink until the cubes were smashed. "Here, hold this at the back of your head. It will help. And I'll pour us some wine." She uncorked the wine and poured a small glass for herself and a much larger one for Horace.

"Thank you, my dear. If you hadn't found me . . ." he trailed off.

"You most likely would have come to and found your way back, but all the same, I'm so glad I happened to come by. I think you need to have a look around as soon as you can. I peeked through the window and someone's made a big mess in your office."

"What? Oh no. All my work." Horace stood quickly and swayed a bit. He grabbed onto the back of the chair for balance. Spotting Lucky's concerned look, he managed a smile. "I'm all right. Really I am."

"I think the goal was to lure you away from the house."

"Oh my. I hadn't thought of that. But why? I don't have any valuables, and only a little bit of cash in the house. I can't imagine why I would be a target."

He walked somewhat unsteadily toward the office. Lucky followed, watching him carefully for any sign of imbalance.

"Look at this!" Horace surveyed the disarray. "Why would anybody do this?" He started to bend down to reach papers on the floor and stopped midway.

Lucky took his arm and led him to an armchair. "You sit here. Keep holding the ice to your head. It must be throbbing."

He followed her direction and watched as Lucky moved around the room, picking up books and papers and laying them in neat piles on the desk. One of the desk drawers was slightly open. "Horace, what do you keep in here?"

"Why, nothing, just supplies. Except . . ." Horace's face turned gray. He stood and moved quickly to the desk. He opened a deep drawer on the left side of the desk and pulled out a cardboard box. He lifted the lid and breathed a sigh of relief. "Thank heavens this is safe."

Lucky looked over his shoulder. Horace very carefully picked up the bundle of cloth inside. He gently laid the contents on top of his desk and unwrapped the covering to reveal a powder horn, the one found with the skeletal remains. "Look at this. Isn't it amazing? It has some damage but you can see the beautiful, smooth patina. They very carefully cleaned this at the University. See? Here is Nathanael's name and the carving of his family's home." Horace's finger traced the pattern in the air above the horn. "This one is about eleven inches in length and its base is just under three inches. It would have held perhaps three quarters of a pound of black powder. Here is Nathanael's prayer—'*may this powder kepe saf my home.*'"

"So sad, to think these men died so young."

"What's sad is that nothing at all has changed. Young men and women are still dying. We can't seem to keep peace on our planet." Horace sat down heavily in the desk chair. "But . . ." He smiled broadly. "Here's the really interesting bit—the one that so upset Cordelia Rank." Horace pulled the center drawer open and retrieved a small box. A delicate velvet box that a jeweler might use. He placed it next to the powder horn and looked up at Lucky. "Wait till you see this." He gently pulled the lid open. Lucky stared at Horace's stricken face.

The lead ball was gone.

Chapter 25

LUCKY AWOKE TO a vibration at her hip. Her phone was buzzing in her skirt pocket. For a moment she couldn't remember where she was, and then the events of the previous night came rushing back. She was in her parents' home. She hadn't wanted to leave Horace alone in the house, afraid that whoever had attacked him might come back. She had slept in her clothes, wrapping herself in a blanket and falling heavily asleep on the sofa. She was exhausted to begin with, and the glass of wine had helped put her to sleep. Horace's snores could be heard even now through the closed door of the bedroom, while outside noisy birds were making a cacophony in a nearby maple tree.

She reached down and fished her phone out of her pocket. Sophie. She had overslept.

"Where are you?"

"Sophie! Sorry. I meant to set my alarm. I'm at my Mom's house—Horace's. I'll explain when I see you. I'll be there in fifteen minutes."

"Hurry up then. I brought coffee today."

Lucky clicked off and rubbed sleep from her eyes. She folded the blanket and laid it neatly on the sofa, then used the bathroom, splashing water on her face to help her wake up. She found a pad of paper in the office and quickly wrote Horace a note. Leaving it on the kitchen table, she slung her purse over her shoulder and slipped out the back door, making sure it locked behind her.

The night before, Nate had arrived within minutes of Horace discovering the loss of the lead ball. Nate was of the opinion that if someone had rummaged through the desk and found the box, they might have opened it, thinking it could be a valuable piece of jewelry. It was possible the lead ball could have fallen out and rolled away into a corner. They had all searched the room, but found nothing. Nate theorized that perhaps someone had been in the house and Lucky's arrival frightened them off. She recalled hearing a car engine start when she had pulled into the driveway. Had that been someone escaping the scene? Perhaps this was nothing more than a simple robbery. If someone had wanted to steal the lead ball, then why hadn't they taken the powder horn and shoe buckles found with the remains? Lucky couldn't argue with Nate's logic. He might be right. But who would choose this house when it was so obviously occupied? And who lured Horace into the woods in order to enter the house? That didn't sound like a simple robbery. Whoever broke in must have known what they were after.

She climbed into her car and drove as fast as possible back to town and her apartment. Sophie was waiting in her car outside Lucky's apartment building, leaning against the headrest with her eyes closed. Lucky tapped on the window. Sophie's eyes flew open. She glanced over and hit the door lock. Lucky climbed into the passenger seat.

"Here." Sophie passed her a warm thermos.

"Thanks." Lucky poured coffee into the small plastic top of the thermos and sipped.

"Why were you at Horace's?" Lucky filled Sophie in on the events of the night before.

"Whoa. That's weird." Sophie shuddered.

"I think someone wanted to lure him out of the house. It could even have been more than one person. One to call to him and another to get into the house."

"And the only thing missing was the bullet?"

"Seems that way. Nate thinks it might have just rolled away, it was so small. The office was a real mess when we got there."

"Too many strange things are going on."

"I agree. That's why I felt better staying there with him last night."

"Oh, great protection you'd be in an attack. What do you weigh? One hundred and fifteen pounds?"

"What do you mean? I could call the police, I could grab a fireplace poker. It'd be a lot safer than leaving Horace alone after hitting his head like that. Besides, I can be tough when I want to be," Lucky retorted.

"Oh, speaking of tough, I ran into Elias the other day and we stopped to chat. Don't know how he managed it, but he brought the conversation around to your name— your nickname, I should say."

"Oh?" Lucky cringed.

"What's that about?"

"You didn't tell him did you?" Lucky squinted her eyes, glaring at Sophie. "Did you?"

"Noooo." Sophie drew out the word. "He knows your real name is Letitia, but I figured if he didn't know about your nickname, it wasn't me who should tell him."

"I appreciate that. I'm trying to be feminine, remember?"

Sophie burst out in a belly laugh. "Give me a swig of that coffee." She held out her hand and Lucky passed her the plastic cup. "You didn't want to tell him about Jimmy Pratt?" She laughed again. "Why not?"

Elias had been nagging her for months to know the secret of her nickname. All Lucky would tell him was that Jack had named her. What she didn't want him to know was that Jack had named her after Virgil Luckorski, a middleweight champion and one of Jack's wartime shipmates. When Lucky lost her temper and broke the nose of an elementary school bully, her parents were horrified. But Jack was extremely proud of her. *"You gave him what for, my girl,"* was all he said. And from that day on, he called her Lucky, after his favorite fighter. She basked in the compliment and insisted that everyone call her just that—Lucky. She did sometimes feel rather bad that Jimmy Pratt's nose had never healed right. Once in a great while, their paths would cross in the town, but Jimmy always walked to the other side of the street and pretended he didn't see her. Obviously he hadn't forgiven her.

"Did you bring the maps?" she asked.

"Yes. And I'll ignore the fact that you're changing the subject." Sophie reached behind her seat and spread a map of the town and surrounding roads out on her lap. "I thought maybe we should work the roads west of town today. All the way up to the Resort."

"Okay. I'll take this area here." Lucky pointed to a two-lane road that angled just south of the Resort. "You should maybe take this part up here, and all around the Resort, since you know that area better than I do."

"Sounds good. We'll check in with each other every half hour by phone."

Lucky took a last swallow of coffee. "We could lose reception in this area, so don't panic if we can't reach each other."

"If that happens, I'll keep going as long as I can and I'll see you at the Spoonful later this morning."

"I'll keep driving till eight thirty and then I've got to get cleaned up and off to work. Can you give Sage a call and let him know I might be a little late? Jack's volunteering for a ground search this morning."

"Catch you later." Sophie turned the key and her engine came to life.

Lucky clambered out. "Thanks for the coffee. I could use another bucket of it." Sophie smiled and, waving, made a U-turn and drove away.

There were only so many roads into and out of town, but they were winding, separated by acres of woodland, and many dirt tracks and fire roads led into the woods. Lucky couldn't imagine why Elizabeth would take a detour off a main road, but if she had stopped to help someone, she could have been attacked. It was possible her car was many miles or even many states away—perhaps even over the border in Canada. Although that would be difficult with a stolen car. Passports were required for U.S. citizens to enter Canada. She was sure the Canada Border Services Agency would also require proof of vehicle registration and insurance. But if her car was still anywhere in this area, near Snowflake, then hopefully Elizabeth was too.

She started her engine and, following in Sophie's general direction, took the road that angled south of the Resort. She drove slowly, scanning the sides of the two-lane highway, searching for any path that would allow a car through. It was very early and there was only the occasional car that passed in the opposite direction. For that she was grateful. There were few spots where she could pull over if cars came up fast behind her.

She had driven about three miles when she spotted a dirt road. It led off the road at a very sharp angle. She had almost missed it. If she hadn't been looking very carefully, she might never have seen it. She hit the brakes and backed up slowly, checking her rearview mirror. She turned the wheel sharply, making a turn onto the dirt path. She drove several more feet and stopped, turning off the engine. It made clicking sounds as it cooled. She climbed out of the car and examined the path in front of her. Tire tracks were clear in the dust, wider than a car's tires. Someone had driven here recently. It hadn't rained in a while but the dirt was soft and the tires had made a good impression.

She climbed back in and turned the key, continuing on very slowly up the dirt road. It rose slightly and widened. Through the trees she caught a glint of something bright. Could it possibly be a car hidden in the woods? Elizabeth's car? She stopped and stared. The early sunlight was shining on a metallic object. She'd need to move closer to see. Quickly, she dialed Sophie's phone, but a steady beep-beep-beep warned her there was no cell service.

She turned the engine off once again. She climbed out and followed the track through the trees for another twenty yards or so. At the top of the rise, the path dropped down to a large clearing with a small cabin in the center. A black flatbed truck was parked nearby. Disappointed, she heaved a sigh. She hadn't realized she was holding her breath. It wasn't Elizabeth's car. Fishing rods were propped against the roof of the cab. The door to the cabin creaked as it slowly opened. Ducking behind a tree, she watched from her hideout. A man stepped out. He carried a large bundle wrapped in a tarp. He wore a T-shirt and a baseball cap. Struggling with the awkward bundle, he placed it on the bed of the truck. He pulled off his cap and wiped his brow. The red hair was unmistakable. It was Rod Thibeault.

What was Rod doing in the woods with fishing gear on a day when he said he had a court appearance? And more importantly, what was inside that large bundle? He was obviously packing up the truck to leave. Lucky knew she had no choice. Her stomach lurched at the thought of what could be under that tarp. She had to confront him before he drove away. There didn't appear to be another exit. He'd see her parked car blocking the exit. Rod wouldn't be able to drive away unless she backed out. She waited until Rod closed the door behind him for the last time and locked it. He leaned down and slipped something under a rock, then returned to the truck and slammed the back panel shut.

She stepped out of the trees and walked slowly down the rise, her heart thumping heavily in her chest.

"What have you got there, Rod?"

"Huh?" Startled, Rod turned in her direction. Lucky moved closer. "Lucky? What are you doing here?"

"I could ask you the same question."

"It's my place. Or rather my Dad's. We use it when we go fishing."

"I thought you had a court appearance today."

"I do. But it's this afternoon." Rod's face darkened. "Why all the questions, Lucky? And you didn't answer mine. What are you doing here?"

"Sophie and I are checking all the side roads around the town."

"Oh yeah? Where's Sophie now?"

Lucky felt a jolt of fear. She was all alone and had nothing to protect herself with. Who knew that Rod had a cabin in the woods? Probably no one. "She's right behind me. She's just parking her car on the road."

"Okay. Well, if there isn't anything else . . ." He jiggled his keys in his pocket. "I'll be on my way."

"What's under that tarp, Rod?" Lucky could feel her legs start to shake. Could Rod have been responsible for abducting Elizabeth? Elizabeth had correspondence about the complaints against him. Had she reported him to the State Bar? Or was she just being copied on the investigation? Did he have a motive to abduct or harm her?

"What? Why, my camping gear. My Dad and I are heading up north at the end of the month—fishing."

Lucky kept a safe distance. "Would you mind pulling the tarp off? I'd like to see." The color had drained from her face. She had to know. If Rod was guilty of something and tried to attack, she knew she could run faster than he could. She'd fly to her car and lock herself in.

Rod looked confused, then the meaning of her request hit him. His face paled under his freckles. "You can't think . . ." Then he blushed furiously. Obviously angry, he turned back to the flatbed and opened the back panel. He pulled the tarp away in a violent gesture. Underneath was an assortment of tents, cooking gear and two lanterns. Lucky breathed a sigh of relief.

"Satisfied?" Rod replied sarcastically. "Jeez, Lucky, how could you even think anything like that?"

"Sorry, Rod. I had to be sure."

Rod closed his eyes and took a deep breath. "So you know, don't you?" Lucky remained silent, watching him carefully. "You know that Elizabeth was a witness to what happened." It was a statement, not a question.

"Yes." Lucky knew nothing in truth, but silence seemed the best way to draw Rod out.

"Well, I'd be willing to bet you don't know the circumstances. The guy I confronted at the courthouse got on the stand and flat-out lied about my client. I don't know why he did it. I lost my temper. It was completely stupid. I never should have spoken to him, much less gotten into a shoving match with the creep. So now I have to go before a disciplinary board. Isn't that just great? I just hope to hell I'm not disbarred because of it. Look, I lost it that day. I had worked so hard on that case and I just lost my temper. I did a very wrong thing, and hopefully I'll just get a slap on the wrist. But I would never hurt Elizabeth. I like her very much, and even though she has to make a statement because she was a witness to it, she's been very supportive. She's told me she plans to speak up on my behalf at the hearing. Believe me, I want her found just as much as you do."

"Sorry I was suspicious."

"It's been a tough year for me, Lucky. I just don't need

any more accusations. Let's let bygones be bygones, all right?"

"Fine with me." Lucky turned away and climbed to the top of the road. She trudged back to her car and reversed down the drive. She checked both directions and backed out onto the road. Before she could put her car in forward gear, Rod's truck charged out to the road and roared away. He didn't give her a second look.

Lucky sat in the car for a few minutes more mulling over her options. She turned on the engine and drove back up the dirt road all the way to the top of the rise. Once there, she turned off the motor and climbed out. She walked slowly down into the clearing toward the cabin. She was willing to bet there was a key to the cabin hidden under the rock that Rod had moved. Fearful that he might return and catch her entering his cabin, she hesitated. She weighed the guilty feeling against the possibility that Rod might have something to hide in the cabin, and that any doubts about him would eat away at her. She made her decision. She rolled over the rock near the front door and grabbed the shiny key that lay in the dirt.

The door opened easily. She stepped inside, key in hand, and surveyed the tiny cabin. It consisted of a small living room with a rock-encrusted fireplace, an opening to a kitchen area and a bedroom on the left. There was a bare minimum of furniture—a sofa, kitchen table, three chairs, a floor lamp and twin beds and a bureau in the next room. The smell of recently cooked bacon hung in the air.

Lucky checked the bedroom closet, the bath, the bureau drawers, the kitchen cupboards and the alcove that housed the water heater. She found a few mismatched dishes and cups, a frying pan and a large pot. She locked the door behind her and replaced the key under the rock. The cabin had no cellar but rested on a raised foundation. She walked to the back of the building and, kneeling on the ground, peered under the structure. She could see all the way to the front of the little house. She stood and brushed her hands off, relieved there was nothing suspicious, but disappointed she still had no idea where to search.

If Rod had anything to hide, it wasn't here.

Chapter 26

ELIZABETH FORCED HERSELF to keep walking. It didn't matter that she walked in a circle; it was simply important to keep moving, otherwise her muscles would atrophy. Every day the stiffness increased. She was terrified she'd be in too weakened a state if an opportunity to escape ever did come. She touched the wall where she had started to mark each day as best she could, judging by the light filtering into her small prison cell. Some days torpidness overcame her. On those days, she slept. Had Maggie been drugging her food? No, that couldn't be. If so, she wouldn't have moments when all she wanted to do was scream. She must maintain control. Control and mental discipline would get her through this experience. Maggie never opened the door now, never gave her a chance to talk, to reason with her. The water was almost gone. She had to be careful. She had to conserve. It was a blessing that it was so cool in the cellar. The heat of the day never reached this place and caused thirst. But when the water ran out, would

Maggie bring more? A person could die much quicker of thirst than of hunger.

She stopped. And listened. Had she been talking to herself as she completed the circuit of the room? No, there were voices. Voices above her head. Unmistakable. Someone had come to Maggie's house. A heavy footstep walked across the floor. It wasn't Maggie. It was a man's footsteps, moving heavily back and forth, as if pacing. She waited, her ear pressed to the pipes.

Was Maggie telling the truth? Was there someone here—the "he" that Maggie had referred to—who would hurt her? She heard an enraged deep voice. *"You . . . stay away from . . . keep her . . . cellar . . ."* Then a higher pitched whimpering voice responded. Elizabeth, horrified, clasped a hand over her mouth. She tried to recognize the speaker. Distorted by the metal pipes and muffled by the floorboards, it was impossible to identify him. Someone was ordering Maggie to keep her locked away. But why? A loud crash came from above followed by a woman's scream. After that only silence. Terrified, Elizabeth huddled on the sleeping bag. She drew her legs up, wrapping her arms around her knees, fearful those heavy footsteps would descend the cellar stairs.

THE CROWD GREW steadily as everyone who could attend the Reenactment gathered at the edges of the Village Green. A special seating section had been set up in front of the steps of the white-steepled church for the town council members, the Mayor, Cordelia Cooper Rank and several other women. These important personages had to be the visiting Daughters of the American Revolution in Snowflake for the festivities. Elizabeth's chair was empty.

The noontime sun beat down upon the crowd and the noise level rose. One of the local vendors sold cold drinks from a cart across the street. Lucky knew he'd make a small fortune on a day like this. All the same, she and Jack were glad they had closed the Spoonful for a few hours to allow everyone—Sage, Janie and Meg—to attend the festivities. Lucky and Elias, along with Jack, had found a good viewpoint under a spreading elm tree. Sophie and Sage were a short distance away, Sage's arm thrown over Sophie's shoulder. Sage looked exhausted. He had worked late every night preparing food so he could be out early in the morning with the search parties. Janie and Meg had covered for him until he could arrive at work a little later in the day. The girls would be joining another group this afternoon that Nate was leading, so only she, Jack and Sage would be at the Spoonful the rest of the day. It seemed every streetlamp and tree were papered with missing flyers. What more could they do? She had wasted precious time that morning snooping in Rod's cabin. If she hadn't been so suspicious of his actions, she could have covered a lot more territory. The news of Snowflake's Mayor's disappearance had played on every TV and radio news station for the past two days. A truck from WVMT with a satellite dish was parked farther up Water Street to film the Reenactment. Undoubtedly their reporters would be covering Elizabeth's disappearance as well.

Lucky couldn't help but stare at the empty chair on the dais. She couldn't decide which would be worse—to have Elizabeth's chair there and vacant, or neglect to place a chair for her? Elias followed her gaze and squeezed her shoulder protectively. She leaned her head against his chest. There was no need for any words. He knew what she was feeling and there wasn't anything he could say to comfort her. He hoped this short break from the Spoonful would raise her spirits.

Jack checked his watch. "It's just gone one bell. Time for me to be at my station. Gotta make sure everyone has their armaments. I'll be back to the Spoonful in time for reopening."

"See you in a little bit, Jack." A large tent had been set up on Water Street to house the players, costumes and props. Lucky watched Jack as he maneuvered through the crowd. The local men taking part in the Battle were milling about at the edge of the Green waiting for their cue. Hank, scarecrow thin and taller than the rest of his group, fussed with his loose pants and linen vest. Barry readjusted his long braided wig and headband.

Lucky heard her name called and turned to see Horace in his Hessian outfit pushing through the crowd to reach her. He wore his long skirted dark blue coat and carried a knapsack and an enormous wooden sword. He was sweating profusely in the heat. "How in heaven's name did those soldiers of yore manage to do any fighting in these outfits?" he asked rhetorically.

Lucky smiled. "I think you look quite dashing."

Horace did his best to smile. "I was so looking forward to taking part in the Battle until . . ." he trailed off.

"Until last night," Lucky stated.

"Yes. I just don't know what I'm going to do or how I'll break this loss to the people at the University. They trusted me and I let them down."

"Horace, you didn't let anybody down. You were robbed."

Elias watched the exchange quietly, but Lucky could tell he was paying particular attention. "What happened last night?"

"Oh, sorry, Elias. I haven't had a chance to tell you." Lucky gave him a summation of the events of the previous evening.

Elias shook his head. "There's only one person I can think of who had an interest in that piece of lead, and she's sitting right up there." Elias nodded in the direction of the roped-off special section where Cordelia Rank sat.

"I follow your logic," Horace replied, "but somehow I can't imagine Mrs. Rank hiding in the woods in the middle of the night. I'd be more inclined to suspect a summer visitor who collects Revolutionary weapons and artifacts." Horace turned to Lucky, a concerned look on his face. "You look rather worn-out. It's all my fault, embroiling you in my little drama last night."

"It's certainly not your fault, Horace, and it was no little drama. I'm just glad I was there. If I look tired it's just that Sophie and I were out early this morning to search the roads for Elizabeth's car."

"That's exactly what I mean," Horace responded. "What happened to me pales in comparison to recent events."

A bugle blew on the other side of the Green. "Oh, my cue! I must get back in place or I'll be fighting on the wrong side." He wiped his dripping brow with a handkerchief. "Wish me luck."

"Break a leg, Horace, as they say in the theatre," Elias called after him. Horace hurried off and Lucky saw several other men scurrying away from family and friends to be in place for the commencement of the Battle.

A festive feeling was in the air. The temperature was soaring and the Village Green was awash in color— banners, balloons and masses of yellow and gold marigolds swarming with bees were everywhere, in flower beds and planters and around the perimeter of the Green. Other vendors had set up barbeque grills at the corner of Broadway and Spruce, blocked off for the event. They were roasting beef, chicken, hot dogs and hamburgers for a crowd that would be very hungry soon. The sizzling aroma wafted their way on the breeze. Lucky took a deep breath to savor the smells of grilled food and freshly cut grass—the smells of summer.

Elias shook his head. "I can't think of anyone who'd wish Harry or Horace or Elizabeth any harm. They're the last people in the world you'd figure had any enemies. Hey, before all the commotion starts, and before I forget, are you free for dinner tonight?"

Lucky nodded affirmatively and graced him with a huge smile. "I'd love that, but I warn you, I may fall asleep over my dinner plate."

"I'll forgive you." He squeezed her shoulder tighter. "See you at eight?"

Lucky nodded. "Anything I can bring?"

"Nope, just yourself." He leaned down and kissed her lightly on the lips.

A bugle blew again. The British—that is, townsmen playing British soldiers in the Reenactment—were waiting up the hill on the other side of the Green for their cue to begin their march on Snowflake. With them were a large group of actors dressed as loyalist colonials, Canadians, Hessians and Native Americans. A muted and steady drumbeat caused the onlookers to become still as the "militiamen" in small groups converged on the Green from all directions. They carried their weapons, most of which were made of wood. A few men, collectors of artifacts, carried the genuine article—unloaded per the town rules. A sound system nearby had been set up to mimic gunfire at the time of the attack. Its operator waited patiently for his cue. The militiamen carried thick branches and crouched on the Green, holding their foliage in front of them to represent the forest that would conceal them from the approaching British troops.

Lucky was very familiar with the details of the Battle thanks to a former teacher who was a history buff. The actual battle, she knew, took place not in Vermont, but in New York State approximately ten miles northwest of Bennington. British General John Burgoyne had ordered a detachment of troops consisting of Hessians, French, Loyalists, Canadians and Native Americans under the command of Lieutenant Colonel Friedrich Baum, a Hessian, to move south, ahead of Burgoyne's main army. Burgoyne was in desperate need of food for his army, and Baum was ordered to take what was needed from the colonists.

Baum's ultimate mission was to reach the supply depot at Bennington and confiscate the guns and ammunition the colonists had managed to accumulate. Burgoyne held a very low opinion of the colonial militia, and since the stores at Bennington were guarded by a small contingent, he was sure Baum would be successful in his mission.

Vermont's Council of Safety, well aware of Baum's approach, sent to New Hampshire for aid. The local rebels were joined by General John Stark, commanding fifteen hundred militiamen. It was Stark who made the decision to attack Baum's troops before they could reach Bennington. When the attack began on the afternoon of August 16, 1777, Baum's less disciplined allies fled, abandoning him. The Hessians fought bravely but were outnumbered. Baum was mortally wounded and soon his troops surrendered. As the battle finished, and the militia celebrated, Lieutenant Colonel Heinrich von Breymann, another Hessian, arrived with a second unit of Burgoyne's army. The battle began again. The militiamen were exhausted from their earlier struggle and might have been vanquished if it were not for Seth Warner and his Green Mountain Boys, who arrived in the nick of time and joined the fighting. The scales were tipped once again in the colonists' favor.

The decision to intercept and attack Baum's raiding party was a brilliant maneuver. Not only did Burgoyne lose almost a thousand men, he was abandoned by the Indian tribes who had previously supported him. The colonists' victory helped to galvanize support for the independence movement. Denied his needed supplies and food, Burgoyne surrendered in New York a mere two months later, on October 17, 1777.

The British contingent began a ragged march down the hill and onto the Green. The drumbeat continued, louder now and more insistent. When the British line was completely in view, the drumbeats became more rapid. The militiamen shouted, dropping their branches, and began to fire. The Hessians and loyalists struggled to load their muskets and fire back. Many of the British troops fell "dead" on the Green. Over the soundtrack of muskets and rifles, the militiamen shouted war cries and attacked the enemy from all sides while the Hessians regrouped and moved to another corner of the Green, hunkering down in a defensive position. The crowd began to cheer and clap in unison with the rhythm of the drums.

Next, the militiamen fired upon the Hessians in their leafy redoubt, and slowly, one by one, they fell and died. The effect was nearly deafening—the loud cracks of the gunshots, the wailing cries of the wounded and the battle cries of the colonists, sensing victory. An enormous roar erupted from the crowd. One young boy beat out a victory rhythm on his drum. The soundtrack began to fade as the cheering subsided and was replaced by another young boy playing a victory march on his flute. The battle had been won.

As the drumming ceased and the flutist finished his tune, a scream sliced through the air. Not the scream or war cry of an actor, but a chilling blade of sound that cut through the hot summer atmosphere. It came from the construction site beyond the Village Green.

Lucky had been aware of the heavy odor of smoke but assumed it came from the outdoor grills at the edge of the Green. She realized with a shock it was the smell of real smoke and fire. A hush ran through the crowd. People stood and looked around, not sure from which direction the cry had come. Slowly everyone realized that something terrible was happening. More shouts came from the construction site and several men ran across the road.

Elias squeezed her hand. "Something's wrong. I'm going over there." He took off running and Lucky followed him. When they reached the chain-link fence, flames were licking the sides of the construction trailer. Nate and two other men rushed to the trailer door where a metal bar had been jammed through the handle. Edward Embry was on the site as well. He had located a fire extinguisher and aimed it at the door handle while another man attempted to break a window in the trailer with a heavy wrench.

Lucky spotted Jack standing next to Nate. Jack tried to grasp the end of the bar lodged in the trailer door but quickly pulled his hand away. Nate pulled him back and slipped off his jacket.. Wrapping it around his hand, he was able to dislodge the metal piece that was keeping the door secured. Another man had broken through the glass of the high window, but as soon as he did, flames shot out and the man jumped back. Nate yanked open the door of the trailer and, spraying the contents of a fire extinguisher in front of him, attempted to enter the trailer. He was driven back by the heat and flames. Two of the construction workers carried a heavy hose and another brought a larger extinguisher to the blaze. Working furiously, they finally managed to control the inferno. Elias had rushed through the break in the chain-link fence and, following Nate, entered the trailer. They retreated immediately and Lucky saw Nate shaking his head. They were too late to save Richard Rowland.

Chapter 27

LUCKY, JACK AND Elias sat quietly at a table by the window. The Spoonful was closed and all but one of the lamps had been turned off. Elias had spent the day arranging for the transport of Rowland's body to the morgue in Lincoln Falls and was forced to juggle several appointments at the Clinic. He smiled apologetically when he arrived at the Spoonful, but Lucky assured him it wasn't too late to eat. Their dinner date would not happen tonight. She prepared a sandwich for Elias and two bowls of soup, one for herself and one for Jack.

Jack muttered to himself as he struggled to use a spoon with his left hand.

Elias looked at Jack. "I hope that's not too painful."

"Nah, I'll live. Just awkward. Thanks for fixing me up though."

Lucky shook a napkin out on her lap. "I hope this is enough. Sage has gone home and we just finished putting everything away."

"It's great and thank you. I didn't have a chance to eat at all today. Never expected to be sending anyone else to the morgue."

"I doubt anyone in town woulda had much sympathy for Rowland, but doing that to him . . ." Jack shook his head. "Just damn gruesome. Burning to death like that—with the whole town right there."

"I'm sure he was gone before we got the door open—smoke inhalation, which in a way is a blessing. It would be very doubtful he would have pulled through anyway."

Lucky shivered. "Let's not talk about that anymore. I'm losing my appetite."

"You're absolutely right. I apologize."

"Hard to push it out of your mind though. Whatever happened to Harry was bad enough. He was one of us. But this . . ." Jack trailed off.

"Nate's sure it was premeditated. An accelerant was used. Everyone disliked Rowland and his car wash, but to kill him like that?" Elias shook his head.

Lucky took a sip of her soup. "I do know Norman Rank threatened him at the town meeting. And Edward Embry had a nasty exchange with him at the construction site too, but maybe that was because Embry was the one person on the town council to buck him. It's strange that two men have been killed within days of each other, but I can't imagine what the connection between them could be, or if there even is one. The only link I can think of was the dispute over the car wash. And now, with Horace being robbed and Elizabeth missing . . . are all these events related in some way? I've had Elizabeth on my mind so much, I haven't been able to think about anything else."

"Still no word from Nate?" Jack asked.

Lucky pushed her bowl away. The thought of Elizabeth still missing had killed her appetite. "Nothing. Absolutely nothing. I wasted a lot of time this morning talking to Rod Thibeault."

"Where did you see Rod?" Elias asked.

"I found a dirt track into the woods about three miles out of town. I pulled in. I could tell a truck had driven through recently, so I followed the tracks."

Jack's face darkened. "You be careful. I don't like that one bit. You're a slip of a thing and you're out there all alone. You don't know what you could run into."

"Jack, believe me, I thought of that. If it hadn't been Rod, I don't think I would have approached. He was coming out of a cabin with a large bundle."

"Whose cabin?"

"His, apparently—or his Dad's. He says they use it to go fishing. When I saw it was Rod, I walked down to the cabin. We had a bit of a . . . misunderstanding."

"What do you mean by that?" Elias asked.

"He was dumping a huge bundle in the back of his truck. I made him pull off the tarp. I had this awful thought . . ."

"That he was dumping a body?" Jack's eyebrows shot up.

"I didn't really think so, but I had to confront him. I didn't want him to drive off with that thought in my mind, especially after . . ."

"After what?" Elias stopped with his fork in midair.

"I picked up some mail at Elizabeth's house yesterday. There was a letter from the State Bar addressed to Elizabeth. I saw what might have been a case number—or maybe a bar number. I don't know what it was, but it was some kind of code typed in the corner, and the first six letters of Rod's name—THIBEA. So I opened it. The police had told us to let them know if we found anything suspicious or different or out of place. I shouldn't have opened Elizabeth's mail, but curiosity got the better of me."

"Elizabeth wouldn't mind. Not under the circumstances," Elias remarked.

"Turns out Rod has to go before a disciplinary board and Elizabeth has been called as a witness."

Jack whistled in response. "That's not sounding good."

"I think Rod realized that I might have found out about it, so he insisted on telling me his side of the story. He said he got into an argument with a witness he thought had lied on the stand. It got out of control and turned into a shoving match. Rod claims he lost his temper because he knew the witness was lying."

"Can't say I blame him." Jack was listening closely.

"Well, he certainly wouldn't be allowed to talk to someone else's witness, much less accuse him of anything. He claims it just got out of control—at least that's Rod's side of the story. He said Elizabeth just happened to be there at the time. She saw the whole thing and that's why she's been called in as a witness."

"Before the State Bar?" Elias asked. "That sounds serious. I wonder if that would be enough of a motive for him to want Elizabeth out of the way."

"He claims Elizabeth had offered to be a character witness for him and he wants Elizabeth found as much as we do."

"I'm sure she wasn't the only witness. There could have been a lot of people milling about who saw the argument or fight or whatever it was," Elias said.

"Yes, but Elizabeth, as Mayor, would be an extremely credible witness."

"What was in the back of his truck?" Jack asked.

"Camping gear. Just a huge bundle of camping gear."

"Funny day for him to be out fishing, don't ya think?"

"I thought so too. He said he just likes to get away sometimes. I asked him about the court hearing that he claimed to have. He said the hearing was in the afternoon and he had the morning off."

"Well, if he likes Elizabeth so much, he shoulda been volunteering with the police, not thinking about fishing!" Jack declared angrily. "But you two—you and Sophie— oughta stick together, not go traipsing all over hell on your own. There's safety in numbers. Today you ran into Rod, but who knows what's out there. I don't want you to go missing too. It's no time to be foolish—not now."

Lucky shivered. "You have a point, Jack. Maybe we should do this together. I tried to call Sophie when I spotted that truck through the trees, but I couldn't get a signal."

"Jack's right," Elias said. "Don't go out searching on your own. That's exactly why the police organize these things in groups—groups that stick together, I might add."

"I've been browsing the websites that Sophie listed on the flyers." Lucky sighed. "It's so frightening. Do you have any idea how many people go missing in this country?"

"It's not something I've ever given much thought to." Elias reached across the table and squeezed her hand. "But I'm sure quite a lot of people are found, and maybe many go missing voluntarily."

"Why would someone do that?" Lucky asked.

"Who knows? Pressures they can't handle. Desire to change their lives, but they don't know how. Temporary insanity." Elias shrugged his shoulders. "But that doesn't minimize one bit the people who are kidnapped or harmed or worse."

"Something awful's happened, I can feel it." Lucky bit her lip to hold back the tears, frightened that one more connection would be taken from her, terrified that Elizabeth could be lying in a ditch needing help or, worse yet, dead, like her parents, and there was no one there who could help her. Jack quietly passed her a paper napkin. She sniffed back the tears and angrily swiped her nose.

"We need to stay calm, my girl. Something has happened but we don't know what. The smoking lamp is out for now but we'll know more soon." Jack ate the last spoonful of his soup. "It's Harry's death that bothers me most. Rowland—I can understand somewhat—not the way he died, I don't mean that; we were all pretty disgusted with him. We all wanted him and his project out of town. But Harry . . . who the hell would want to hurt poor Harry?" Jack shook his head.

Lucky tucked her damp napkin into a pocket. "I over-heard Barry and a couple of men making comments about Harry when he wasn't at the demonstration—along the lines of wondering if he was really committed—and then I think somebody said they'd seen him talking to Rowland, which struck them as strange."

"Harry was committed to the whole thing. He was defi-nite about not wanting a car wash in the middle of town," Jack grumbled. "Besides, if they were gonna put it any-where, why not behind Harry's shop? Be the perfect place for it. Out of sight—it's zoned right there, no neighbors real close."

Elias looked thoughtful. "Could Harry have been trying to work out some kind of deal with Rowland?"

Jack shrugged. "Anything's possible. But it was a little late in the day for that. The bulldozers were already at work. Construction had started."

"I heard Norman Rank made some heavy-handed com-ments to Rowland at the demonstration—and you say they almost came to blows at the town meeting?" Elias asked.

"That's true," Lucky replied. "It was very tense for a few minutes. Then there's Ed Embry. It's obvious he had no use for Rowland and he took a lot of flack because he wouldn't go along with the rest of the town council."

"Good for him," Jack said. "Good to know one man couldn't be bought off."

Lucky heaved a sigh and gathered up the empty dishes. "Two murders in Snowflake. That can't be a coincidence. There has to be a connection, but those men led totally different lives. They were completely different people."

"Until last winter when that woman's body was found, if

anyone had told me a murder could happen in Snowflake, I would've told them they were crazy," Elias remarked. "Now? I don't know what to say. This time it was a local . . . two, I guess, if you count Rowland. And neither one was an accident. Somebody locked Rowland in that trailer and doused the thing with gasoline. He didn't stand a chance. And no one noticed or heard anything; we were all focused on the Reenactment."

"Nate'll have a hell of a time trying to figure out who could have been around the trailer. There were mobs of people," Jack said. "And a lot of people made threats to Rowland." Jack chuckled. "Norman Rank threatened to bury him in his own concrete. And Ed Embry told him he'd drown him in his car wash."

"Where was Rod Thibeault when the Reenactment was going on? Was he in town? Did anyone see him there or talk to him?" Elias asked.

"I didn't," Lucky replied. "But that doesn't mean he wasn't there. He said he would try to make it, but he could have changed his mind."

"We have no way of knowing when the door handle was jammed. Rowland could have been in there for a while before the fire started," Elias said.

"He would have smelled the gasoline though, wouldn't he? And started yelling?" Lucky asked.

"Would we have heard him? Between everyone yelling and cheering and the drums and sound effects, he might not have been heard. No one sounded the alarm until they saw the fire."

"And what about the break-in at Horace's? Could that be connected to the murders?"

"I'd vote for Cordelia Rank on that one," Jack said.

"Maybe, but why? She wanted the artifacts to go to a museum. If she stole them, that could never happen. Any museum would investigate. And if she did want to steal them, why not take the powder horn and the shoe buckles? Why go to all that trouble and break in and just take the lead ball?"

"What did Nate have to say about all this?" Elias asked, sipping his iced tea.

"He isn't convinced it was stolen. He thinks it could just as easily have rolled out of the little jewelry box and fallen into a crack."

"Did you search for it?"

Lucky nodded. "We all did. But it was dark and it was late. We were pretty tired. We could have missed it. If she did steal that lead ball, it's because, as Horace says, it has rifling marks."

"Oh, I heard all about that," Elias said. "She had a conniption at the town meeting."

"She certainly didn't want anyone accusing her ancestor of being a traitor. She'd do anything to maintain her DAR status." Lucky giggled. Both Jack and Elias stared at her. She wiped her eyes. "I'm sorry. That's just too funny. Two murders and a robbery at Horace's and she's worried about the DAR. How relevant is that?"

"Well, it's late. Almost four bells. I'll be on my way." Jack stood and pushed his chair away. "You okay on your own?"

"Sure, Jack. You go ahead. I'll close up." Lucky gathered their dishes and carried them into the kitchen. Jack waved good-bye at the front door and headed home.

Elias waited while Lucky turned off the lamps and the neon sign. She locked the door behind them. He placed an arm around her shoulder, and she smiled up at him. "You're too tired. There's no need to walk me home. I'm a big girl."

"I don't want to let you out of my sight until whoever's behind these attacks is caught. Humor me. I'll feel better if I know you're safely home."

"Yes, sir." Lucky smiled.

They walked slowly down Broadway, turning the corner

on Maple Street. The Snowflake Clinic was closed. They could see a small night-light burning at the front desk as they passed and reached the stairway to Lucky's apartment building next door.

"What did Jack mean earlier? He said something about the . . . smoking lamp?" Elias asked.

Lucky smiled. "It's an old Navy expression. He's saying that we can't be too careful. On a ship, fire is always a terrible danger, so when the smoking lamp is out, it's not safe to relax and have a smoke. The ship must stay on alert and every man needs to be at his post."

"Interesting," Elias remarked. "I'll have to remember that one."

"I'm a regular encyclopedia of nautical trivia." Lucky hesitated. "Elias . . . there's something else I meant to mention at the Spoonful. I guess with all the other things that have been going on, it slipped my mind. Sophie and I were at the church the day before the demonstration and I accidentally overheard a conversation between Harry and Pastor Wilson. It sounded as if Harry was very upset and they were discussing something serious."

"Like what?"

"That's just it. I don't know. I could have sworn I heard Harry crying. Then, Harry came out of the Pastor's office and the door was partially open. I don't know if I can recall the exact words. Harry was saying something like . . ." Lucky trailed off, recalling the incident. "Harry said, *'I had to tell someone.'* And then Pastor Wilson was encouraging him, telling him he was doing the right thing, and then said that he and Harry could talk again whenever Harry was ready.

"I really didn't mean to eavesdrop. I never expected that they would be talking about a personal matter—but that's what it sounded like. Harry looked startled when he saw me standing in the corridor. I had such a strong feeling about the whole thing, as though Harry wanted to . . ." She struggled for the word that would best explain. "Confess, I guess. As if he had something quite terrible on his mind and had to talk to someone about it, but it also sounded like Pastor Wilson was telling him that when he was ready he should come back and talk to him. That's the best way I can put it."

Elias stopped. "Maybe there's something you should know, but you must keep this to yourself at least for now." Lucky looked up at him silently. "Harry was dying. He didn't have a lot of time." Elias's face looked gaunt in the light from the streetlamp.

"What? Oh!" Lucky breathed.

Elias could see the shifting realization on her face. "It's true. Sad but true."

"I had no idea. Did anyone else know?"

"That I couldn't say. Other than his specialist in Lincoln Falls, I really don't know who he was close to, who he might have confided in."

"Maybe that's what he was talking to Pastor Wilson about. It would make sense that he'd want to get something off his chest. That definitely puts another color on the whole thing."

"Quite possibly. I sent a copy of his medical file to the pathologist, so it will be in the police report, and since he had no living relatives, well, I'm not hurting him or anyone else in telling you." Elias followed her up the stairs to the front door and continued until they reached her apartment on the second floor. Lucky turned to say good night, and Elias pushed her gently against the door frame.

"Why, sir, are you assaulting me?"

"Yes." He breathed, holding her close. He pulled back and looked at her. "If anything ever happened to you. I don't know what . . ."

"Nothing's going to happen to me. I'm as safe as houses here. Now stop worrying. You're a worse worrywart than I am."

"Sorry about that dinner I promised you. How about tomorrow night?"

"Tomorrow it is." Elias kissed her long and passionately and finally let go. He remained standing in the hallway until he heard the lock click on her front door.

Chapter 28

LUCKY LOOKED UP as the bell jingled over the front door. Two groups entered—a family of five and another group of young summer tourists. She recognized the couple she had seen at the demonstration. Janie and Meg were still on their break, so she grabbed menus and distributed them around the tables, taking orders for cold drinks. Jack rose from his stool at the cash register to help her and carried trays of drinks to their tables. By the time Janie and Meg returned from their break, Sage had filled most of the orders.

Lucky slipped off her apron and called Janie over. "I'm going to stop by Elizabeth's office to talk to her assistant. Can you and Meg handle everything for about a half an hour?"

"Sure, Lucky. We'll be fine. You hoping Jessie's heard something?"

Lucky shrugged. "I think she would have let me know

if she had. But I want to see if she has Elizabeth's calendar. Maybe there's something there or on her desk that might give us some ideas. I'm sure the police have looked at everything, but I'll feel better if I go myself."

"Good idea." Janie smiled in encouragement and nodded to a customer attempting to get her attention.

"Can you let Jack know where I've gone when you get a chance?"

"Will do." Janie smiled encouragingly.

Lucky exited by the front door and hurried down Broadway, past the Village Green, and cut down Spruce Street to the municipal offices. The heat was even more intense today, made worse by high humidity. She glanced at the sky and spotted clouds gathering above the mountain. Maybe a blessed thunderstorm would alleviate this heat. Her blouse was sticking to her skin by the time she arrived, and a trickle of perspiration rolled down her back.

Inside the town hall the air-conditioning system was working full blast. Goose bumps formed on her arms from the chill when she entered. She climbed the stairs to Elizabeth's office. The door was open and Jessie sat at the front desk, a crossword puzzle in front of her. She looked up expectantly.

"Hi, Lucky." She closed the magazine and pushed it to the side of her desk. "I'd be working if I had something to do, but I've done everything I can think of, filed everything away, reorganized the supply closet, straightened up Elizabeth's desk. Having nothing to do is driving me crazy and I'm worried sick."

"Me too. I thought I'd take a walk over and maybe have a look at her appointment book if you don't mind."

"Sure. You're welcome to it. I've gone through it and I showed it to Nate. He stopped by yesterday again." She rose and followed Lucky into the inner office. "Here it is." She passed it across the desk.

Lucky sat in the same chair she had sat in so many times before when visiting Elizabeth in her office and leafed through the pages. "There are two meetings listed."

"Yes. But they were both here. She had no appointments outside the office. Everyone she was supposed to meet with called or came by expecting her to be here." Jessie sank into Elizabeth's chair and leaned back. "I can't think of anything. I've wracked my brain trying to remember if she mentioned having to go out of town. I'm sure I'd remember if she did, but she didn't say anything to me at all."

"No strange phone calls?"

"Nope. Nothing like that. I know everyone here and all the people who do call her. I feel absolutely horrible now that I was trying to cover for her. I'm an idiot. I should have sounded the alarm immediately when she didn't come in. Nate gave me a funny look when I tried to explain. At first, I thought it was my fault. That Elizabeth had mentioned she'd be somewhere and I forgot and didn't write it down. I mean Elizabeth's probably the last person on earth you'd think would be in some kind of trouble. She's so organized! After that, I didn't want her to look bad to anyone, so I just kept stalling anyone who asked for her. I know Nate and that state cop think I'm nuts or stupid or both." Jessie rubbed her temples.

"I can understand why you reacted that way. In a way, maybe I did too. I kept making excuses to myself. First, I expected her to be at Pastor Wilson's ceremony when they were getting ready to unearth the skeleton. I just assumed she was busy and couldn't attend. Then after we discovered Harry, I still didn't hear a thing from her. She knows Jack has flashbacks to the war when he gets upset and she worries about him too. I kept calling her and leaving messages and didn't hear back. So, it was a couple of days before I decided something was really wrong and I finally reached you. And you know the rest."

Jessie nodded sadly. "She's such a nice lady. I really

hope . . ." Jessie trailed off. There was no need to continue the thought. Both she and Lucky were doing their best to push the worst-case scenario out of their heads.

Jessie sighed. "It's just so weird. There's been nothing out of the ordinary. Elizabeth was here as usual. She left a minute before I did, and said, "Night, Jessie. See you tomorrow.' I definitely should have freaked sooner. She's always very methodical. She never would have told me she'd see me the next day if she had another appointment or had to go out of town. I am a total idiot!" Jessie stifled a sob.

Lucky's heart sank. How many times do we say those very words to loved ones, coworkers, friends, never suspecting there might not be a tomorrow. She remembered the last phone conversation she had had with her mother, just before the holidays. Remembered how excited her mother had been that they would be together soon, and her description of the holiday dinner she was planning. A dinner that never happened.

"Have you searched her desk?"

"Yes. There's nothing there. Elizabeth is very organized. All of it just pertained to the office. She didn't keep any personal papers here at all."

Lucky heard a footstep behind her and Jessie looked up. Lucky turned to see Edward Embry standing on the threshold.

"Any news, Jessie?"

"Nothing, Ed. Sorry. Have you met Lucky Jamieson?" Jessie stood and came around the desk to stand next to Lucky's chair.

Edward Embry smiled and moved closer to shake Lucky's hand. "Yes, we've met. Nice to see you again. Elizabeth introduced us at the demonstration." He leaned against the large desk. "I've been worried sick about her."

"Jessie mentioned Nate was here yesterday," Lucky offered.

"He stopped in to see me too. I have a little cubicle I use down the hall. There was nothing more I could tell him. He did say her car hadn't been reported, so it doesn't seem as if she had an accident. No hospital admissions. I was thinking she might have had an accident on the road and was injured, but that doesn't seem to be the case."

They sat quietly for a few minutes, brooding about Elizabeth, as if she were an invisible presence in the room with them. Lucky finally broke the silence. "Jessie, thank you. It was just a thought that I might find something here. I better get back to the Spoonful. Janie and Meg are in charge, but it'll be getting busy."

"Stop by anytime. I just show up every day and hope she calls. That's why I haven't been volunteering. I figure it's better for me to stay here and man the phones if nothing else."

"You're probably right." She turned to Edward. "Let's all stay in touch in case any of us hears anything— anything at all."

Edward straightened up and walked Lucky down the corridor. "Elizabeth's a wonderful woman and a dear friend. I've been on the ground searches every day since the town meeting but if there's anything you can think of that might be of use, please let me know."

"I will." Lucky turned and headed down the long stairway. She turned back to see Edward Embry standing at the top of the stairs, a very worried look on his face.

Chapter 29

"WHAT DID YOU finally come up with?" Lucky asked, peering over Sage's shoulder.

"I think I've got it. Look—if you add cayenne pepper to the broth at the beginning, then the peanut butter won't be too cloying, kind of like an African dish with chicken and hot pepper." Sage scribbled a few more notes in the margin of the notebook for his new recipe.

"I've never even heard of peanut butter soup."

"I think it's popular in the south. They're fairly simple soups. Chicken based, celery, onions and peanut butter, maybe chopped peanuts sprinkled on top. I was just thinking that red pepper would give it a little kick and you'd still get the creamy taste of peanuts."

The bell over the front door rang. Lucky peeked through the hatch. "It's Sophie." Lucky watched as her friend made a beeline for the kitchen.

"Hey, guys!" Sophie announced as she dragged a stool

closer and climbed on it. She dumped her large satchel on the floor. "What are you up to?" she asked.

"Sage is working on a new soup—peanut butter."

"Yum. Sounds great." She blew Sage a kiss and, turning to Lucky, remarked, "He's a genius, isn't he?"

Sage rolled his eyes. "Or something."

"By the way, I'm starving. I could eat an elephant."

"That's an idea," Sage remarked.

"No way," Lucky replied. "They're endangered. Plus they're almost human. They remember one another and people they've met. You can't even think about killing an elephant and making soup."

Sage held up his hands in surrender. "Hey, calm down. Just a joke. I was letting my mind wander."

Lucky slipped off her stool. "I'll fix you something," she said to Sophie. She mixed together cubes of chicken, shredded lettuce, almonds, a few bits of arugula, chopped tomatoes and red onions, and added a light creamy dressing. When it was thoroughly mixed, she wrapped it up in a large spinach tortilla and placed a few baked chips on the side.

"Thanks, Lucky. This is just what I need. My feet are killing me and I'm ready to die from the heat."

"You need something cool." Lucky filled a glass with ice cubes and lemonade, adding a sprig of mint. She handed it to Sophie.

"Mmmm. Fanks," she replied with a full mouth.

The bell over the front door jangled. "Customers?" Sage asked.

"So much for a break." Lucky peeked through the hatch. "It's Rod Thibeault. I'll take care of it." Sage nodded and returned to his notebook.

Lucky felt a mixture of embarrassment and suspicion at the same time. She didn't entirely trust Rod after what she had learned about his disciplinary hearing. But on the other hand, he enjoyed a good reputation as a lawyer. Was he being completely honest when he recounted his argument outside the courtroom? Or was he painting a benign picture and there was a darker side to him? She couldn't avoid him now. She'd just have to face him.

Rod joined Jack, Hank and Barry at their table. "An oasis. An oasis in the storm," he announced as he sat.

"What's up, Rod?" Barry asked him.

"Nate's been on my case. If he out and out accused me of something I could handle it, but the questions . . . for God's sake, what's he thinking? I'm a lawyer. I'm not gonna kill anybody just 'cause I lost a case."

"What can I get you, Rod?" Lucky asked as she approached the table.

Rod looked up, a disarming smile on his face. She really hoped he didn't mention their meeting in the woods in front of Hank and Barry. "Iced tea would be great. Thanks, Lucky."

She nodded and walked behind the counter to prepare the drink. Rod hopped out of his chair and joined her at the counter. He leaned closer as she poured the iced tea. "Look, I hope you're not still harboring suspicions about me."

"Of course not," Lucky replied carefully. "I'm sorry if you thought I was accusing you of something."

Rod raised his eyebrows. "Well, you were, but it's okay with me. Friends?" he asked.

"Sure." Lucky nodded and smiled in a way she hoped looked sincere. She couldn't help it. Rod had done nothing to earn her distrust, but she had only his word about the State Bar hearing and Elizabeth's role in it. And Jack had made a good point. If Rod were so concerned about finding Elizabeth, why wasn't he on a search team? She handed Rod his iced tea and he carried it back to the table.

Hank pushed his glasses up on the bridge of his nose. "There were plenty of other people with a much better motive to kill Rowland than you," he said to Rod.

Rod's eyes widened. "Tell that to Nate. He keeps harping

on that. Why wasn't I there? I told him I had a court appearance that afternoon." Rod heaved a sigh. "Worst of it is, I
just didn't feel like watching the Reenactment. I didn't
want to be in town no matter what. I think a lot of people
feel I dropped the ball not getting that injunction.

"We don't think you dropped the ball," Hank replied.
"They can blame those idiots on the council—all except
for Ed Embry. The only man with the you-know-whats to
stand up to Rowland."

Rod leaned over the table and spoke quietly to the men.
Lucky remained at the counter, eavesdropping on their
conversation now that the restaurant was nearly empty.
"This is just between us, but it's no joke about the town
council. I know for a fact there was talk about taking some
parcels of Norman Rank's land by eminent domain."

"Eminent domain?" Hank asked. "What for?"

"For some other dumb project Rowland had in mind.
Norman Rank's the one Nate should be talking to."

Barry and Hank exchanged a look across the table.
Hank turned to Rod. "Too bad you weren't at the town
meeting."

"Why?" Rod asked.

"Rowland showed up and he and Norman almost came
to blows. Rowland made a remark about Norman needing
to watch out before he lost some of his precious real estate."

"Whew!" Rod whistled. "Norman must have gone bal-
listic. Sounds like maybe he's heard the rumors."

"Who told you?" Hank asked.

"I can't say. The person who told me didn't care if the
word got around, just didn't want anyone to know where it
came from." Rod took a long swallow of his iced tea.
"Now, don't get me wrong. I'm not accusing Norman of
murdering Rowland—not at all—but if anybody had a
motive it was him. There's another strange thing . . ."

Hank tilted his head back and looked quizzically at Rod
over his pince-nez glasses. "What's that?"

"Well, it may mean nothing at all, but I saw Harry Hodges talking to Rowland the day before Hodges was murdered. I had come into town to meet with a new client and parked my car on the other side of Water Street. When I came back to my car, I saw them on the Green. They looked like they were discussing something pretty serious."

"I've heard that before," Barry said. "Some people thought Harry was making a backdoor deal with Rowland."

Rod shrugged. "Maybe he was. Maybe he was making a last-ditch effort to talk Rowland into putting it behind his shop. Would have been good for both of them."

"And now they're both dead," Jack replied. "It seems the car wash was the thing they had in common. I just hope Nate gets to the bottom of this soon."

Chapter 30

ELIAS DEFTLY MIXED the grated cheese, nutmeg and cream with the steaming fettuccini. Then he stirred the contents of the bowl until the hot noodles blended the cream and cheese into a delicious, thick sauce. When he was satisfied with his efforts, he scooped generous servings onto their two warmed dinner plates.

"Pepper?" He smiled holding a large wooden grinder over her plate.

"Yes, lots." Lucky breathed in the delicious aroma as Elias grated hunks of fresh black peppercorns over the plate of steaming fettuccini. "I'm so glad you cook. The last thing I want to do when I leave the Spoonful is think about making food."

"Are you saying I'd make a wonderful wife? I'm no expert, but I'm good at simple things." He shook out his linen napkin and spread it over his lap. "So tell me. Any news? Anything at all?"

"Nothing." Lucky felt a clutch in her stomach and

wondered if she'd be able to eat her meal. "I'm worried sick, but I don't know what more I can possibly do. I keep thinking her car will turn up, but we haven't found anything, except running into Rod Thibeault."

"The more I think about that, the more it gives me the creeps. Jack's right. Neither you nor Sophie should do this alone."

"We just thought we could cover more ground if we split up and stayed in touch by phone."

"That's terrific, but as you learned, there are lots of spots where you can't get service." Elias looked as if he were about to launch into a lecture.

"Are you upset with me?"

"Upset? No, I'm worried. You shouldn't be trawling the woods alone. There have been two murders in this town. We have no idea why . . . or who might have done them. The whole community is in a state of panic but you don't seem to have an ounce of fear."

"That's not true. I am afraid. Just like everyone else. And I'm terrified for Elizabeth," Lucky retorted angrily.

Elias sighed. "I'm sorry. I don't mean to get on a soapbox about it, but I really think if you're going to do this, you do it with someone—Sophie, Sage, anyone. And make sure you let somebody know what area you're searching."

Lucky took a deep breath. "You're right. I know you're right. I had a moment when I was scared to confront Rod." Lucky stirred a fettuccini noodle around in the creamy sauce.

"So now he thinks you suspected him of disposing of a body. How did he take all that?" Elias spoke quietly. "You could have been in a serious bind. Maybe Rod isn't guilty of anything, but what if he did have something to hide? What if something happened to you? I couldn't live with myself if something happened to you."

Lucky reached across the table and grasped his hand.

"I feel the same way about you. I promise I won't go out alone anymore. Sophie and I will stick together."

"I'd feel a lot better." Elias finally smiled.

Lucky twirled a length of fettuccini noodle around her fork and took a bite. It was heavenly. "What is happening, Elias? First Harry—of all people. Everybody liked him; he never caused anyone any trouble. Not to mention that he kept everyone's cars running. That's the one I can't get my head around. Rowland . . . well, I'm not saying he deserved to be murdered like that, but at least there are plenty of people who won't be crying at his funeral."

"Harry was the main organizer of the demonstration against the car wash. And Rowland certainly had a motive to get Harry out of the way. Whether Rowland was capable of murder, I don't know."

"Harry was the main guy, yes, but he was just one of the organizers, certainly not the only one. Edward Embry had far more influence in town than Harry. He had voted against building the car wash. And he had been very outspoken about it. If it's about the car wash then Ed Embry might be the logical target."

"Nobody really wanted Rowland dead, just gone."

"A lot of the men were criticizing Harry for not being at the demonstration. Of course, we had no way of knowing he was already dead. And there were a lot of really angry people—not just Ed Embry, but Rod Thibeault and Norman Rank. Maybe we should look at it from another direction. What if the attack on Harry had nothing to do with the construction of the car wash?" Lucky speared a piece of arugula with her fork. "I'm sorry, Elias. I don't think I can eat all this. It's delicious but my stomach's in knots."

"Eat whatever you can. It'll keep." He swirled a long noodle on his fork. "Okay. What if it didn't? What if, as you said, Harry had something he wanted to get off his chest—a confession, a secret? Who would know?"

Lucky shook her head. "Pastor Wilson might have a

clue. Maybe Harry gave him some idea what he wanted to talk about. And even if we knew, how does that connect with Elizabeth going missing?"

Elias reached across the table and grasped her hand. "I'm not saying you're wrong to be worried about Elizabeth, and you're not overreacting, but it must bring up feelings about your parents."

Lucky shivered. Her first reaction was to hotly deny that she was influenced by the shock of her parents' sudden death. When she opened her mouth to retort, stinging tears came to her eyes. Her voice shook when she answered. "It's the cruelest . . . to have loved ones ripped away with no warning. I've had so many dreams and so many nights when I woke up convinced it hadn't really happened. When I look around me, I know it did happen. I'm not in Madison. I'm not in my mother's house. I'm in a small apartment and my past is gone."

Elias came around the table and took her in his arms. "You're not alone. I'm here and so is Jack. And Elizabeth will be found. I feel sure she will be."

Lucky felt her shoulders relax in the comfort of his arms. She touched the warm skin of his neck and breathed in a scent of aftershave. "I'm turning into a blubbering idiot." She quickly wiped her tears away with her napkin.

"Don't apologize. It's normal to feel that way. There's no magic formula—except time. Time always softens the hurt. Don't forget, it hasn't even been a year."

"I know." She took a shaky breath. "I know you're right."

"Eat a little more, miss, or I'll think you really hate my cooking." His comment elicited a smile from Lucky. He returned to his chair and poured more wine for both of them.

"Oh, another thing I meant to tell you. Rod Thibeault stopped in at the Spoonful earlier today. He mentioned something interesting. You know Norman Rank owns a lot of property all around, not just in town. In fact, he's our landlord."

"He owns the Spoonful building too?" Elias asked.

Lucky nodded. "Rod said Rowland had the town council in his pocket . . ."

"Meaning what? Bribed?"

"That was the implication. Apparently there is, or was, a plan brewing to take some of Norman Rank's real estate by eminent domain."

Elias chuckled mirthlessly. "I'm sure Norman would consider that grounds for justifiable homicide. Taken for what purpose? There has to be some benefit to the community as a whole, doesn't there?"

"We both know if there's enough money floating around, developers get what they want. Just look at that stupid car wash—case in point. But beyond that, there's got to be some connection between those two men— between Harry Hodges and Rowland. And maybe it's somehow connected to Elizabeth and to the attack on Horace." Lucky put her fork down and took a sip of wine. "Those two couldn't have been more different. They led totally different lives in different places. I keep replaying the conversation I overheard between Harry and Pastor Wilson."

"Maybe Harry was seeking some kind of spiritual help."

"Completely understandable, given what you've told me. If Harry was dying, maybe he did want to confess to something. And then he looked like he could jump out of his skin when he saw me. He bolted away. The Pastor wasn't forcing him into anything, just letting him know the door was open when he was ready to talk about whatever was bothering him."

Elias was lost in thought. "Harry's condition was terminal, as I told you. At the most, he had maybe a few months. You suspect something criminal?"

Lucky shook her head. "I don't know. I can't imagine Harry Hodges doing anything criminal. But what if he had knowledge of a crime and kept it to himself?"

"That could be what got him killed." Elias stared at Lucky's plate. "You've barely eaten anything."

"It's delicious but I lost my appetite. Can I have a doggie bag?"

Elias smiled. "Only if you promise to spend the night."

Lucky sighed. "I want to, believe me. It's just . . . there are so many wagging tongues in town. I have a business to run and so do you. You know how people talk." There was nothing she wanted more than to wake up in Elias's arms, but she wasn't sure what judgments would come their way in a town as small as Snowflake, what comments would be made about them behind their backs. It was especially true for Elias. As the only doctor in town, he was in a far more vulnerable position. In reality, she didn't give a hoot what people thought, but she didn't want anything hurting her business or Elias's position.

Elias reached across the table and took her hand. "I'm serious about this, Letitia Jamieson. I want us to be together. I don't want to wait much longer."

She was sure a deep blush was creeping up her cheeks. "I feel the same way about you."

"Then what's holding you back?"

"It's just not great timing right now, Elias. I have the restaurant to worry about and Jack."

"Jack would be thrilled."

"He would. He's really happy we're seeing each other. But it hasn't even been a year since my parents died." She detected a flicker of disappointment in his eyes. As soon as the words were out of her mouth she realized she had used Elias's own words against him. Was she an idiot or what? What was keeping her from making such a commitment? It was fear of course, but not a lack of feeling or trust in Elias. What fear though? Fear of loss? Fear of being totally at risk? Fear of losing her independence? She needed more time before she could give Elias a whole-hearted "yes."

He nodded. "There's that, of course." He pulled her from the chair. He grasped her hair and wove his fingers through it. Smiling, he lifted her chin and kissed her slowly. Without another word, he led her toward the staircase.

Chapter 31

A COOL EARLY morning breeze blew through the open windows of Lucky's bedroom. The flowered drapes billowed into the room bringing the heavy scent of roses from the garden below. Lucky stretched and reluctantly came awake remembering the evening with Elias, after which he had gallantly walked her home to her apartment door.

She was overcome with a sense of loneliness when he left to return home. She listened to his footsteps descend the stairs, angry with herself for once again shying away from an obvious proposal. She was overwhelmed with physical feelings she had never experienced before. And now she was pathetically head over heels in love with him. So what was holding her back? Elias had worked hard to achieve what he had and was ready to settle down. But was she? Once Elias had gone, she had fallen into bed and slept deeply for several hours until the alarm woke her.

She and Sophie went out together at first light and continued searching the smaller roads on the same route she

had undertaken the day she met Rod Thibeault. Sophie
agreed that they would stick together, particularly since
cell phone service was sketchy around the mountain. They
found nothing. By the time Sophie dropped her back at her
apartment, she felt as if she had been driving for days. She
set her alarm once again and fell across her bed, falling
into a deep, dreamless sleep for one more blessed hour. But
there was a heaviness in her muscles that even sleep would
not cure. If only her anxiety would abate. If only this feeling of dread would leave her. If only her mood could match
the sweetness of the world outside her windows. She
pushed back the covers and stumbled into the kitchen of
her small apartment. She turned the burner on under the
kettle and sat in a kitchen chair by the window. She rubbed
her temples, feeling a low-grade headache as she waited
for the kettle to come to a boil. When it started to shriek,
she turned off the burner and spooned two helpings of
strong coffee into a filter. She poured boiling water through
and dropped a piece of bread into the toaster.

Hugging the fragrant mug of coffee, she dragged her
chair closer to the window. She pushed the window halfway up, pressing her knees against the windowsill. She had
a clear view of the Victory Garden that abutted the fence
behind her apartment building. Next door, early risers were
already tending their rows of vegetables. It was Elizabeth
who had been instrumental in making sure the small plots
in the Garden were safeguarded and not bulldozed by a
developer. Those fortunate enough to have a few rows of
vegetables could keep what they grew. But if they har-
vested food in excess, they would deposit it in baskets by
the gate at the end of each day for anyone in town who
might need a few fresh vegetables. If only Elizabeth had
been in a position to control Richard Rowland's ambitions.
Now that he had been murdered, she wondered what would
happen to his construction project. Hopefully it would be

abandoned and forgotten. At least one major problem for the town would be solved.

The toasted bread popped up and Lucky grabbed the slice, dropping it onto a small plate. She broke off a corner of the bread and sprinkled crumbs on her windowsill. She sat back and waited, until finally the two gray doves approached. They were her favorites. She held her breath. Staying completely still, she watched them as they pecked at the crumbs. The larger dove she was sure was the male. He displayed bluish coloring on the top of his head. The other bird was female, her coloring more delicate, a soft grayish brown and tan. The male dove raised his head and scanned her sideways, his beady eye watching carefully for any threat or sign of danger. When he was sure that he and his mate were safe, he returned to his pickings. When the two birds had eaten most of the crumbs, they flew away, heading for a large maple tree on the other side of the Victory Garden. Doves mated for life, Lucky knew, as did many kinds of birds. Was that what Elias wanted? A mate for life? What did she want and why did she find the thought of a lifetime with someone frightening? Her parents had been childhood sweethearts and lived a full and happy life. Were they blessed to have died together? Never having to continue on in life without their mate? She smiled fondly, thinking of Elizabeth—Elizabeth Dove—a woman who had never married. She was sure Elizabeth must have had many opportunities throughout her life. Had she regretted turning suitors away? She'd have to ask Elizabeth about that. But first she'd have to find her.

She mulled over Elias's information from the night before. It made perfect sense that Harry might seek counseling or feel the need to confess a secret he had held. It seemed to fit. If he knew he was ill and close to death, did he need to confess to a sin, or perhaps just a terrible secret? She half remembered her dream of the night before. She

was stumbling desperately through the woods when a flash
of light hit her eyes. It was the sun glinting off a metallic
object, a car bumper. Twigs struck at her face as she tried
to push through the woods to reach the car. In her dream
she was sure it was Elizabeth's car. When she reached it,
she knew with an overwhelming sense of dread that something terrible was inside the car. She walked step by step,
frightened to look but unable to turn away. As she reached
the window to peer inside, she awoke in a cold sweat, her
heart pounding.

She glanced at the clock again. She had told Jack she
might be late this morning and not to worry, but still, she
wanted to reach the Spoonful before the first heavy rush
of customers. She slid the screen closed and left the window open for fresh air. She downed the rest of her coffee
and rinsed out her cup. After her shower she dressed
quickly in a summer skirt and top, brushing her long fair
hair into a ponytail. She glanced in the mirror over the
bureau and hesitated. She decided on a light lipstick and a
touch of eye pencil to accentuate her eyes. A year ago, it
wouldn't have occurred to her to wear makeup, but now
she was far more conscious of her appearance since Elias
was in her life.

As a kid, she would often come home with bruises and
covered with dirt. She had far more interest in capturing
spiders and eels than playing with dolls. Her parents had
assumed their little girl would be feminine. She knew her
mother had been terribly disappointed when she refused
to wear dresses with ruffles and little socks with embroi-
dery around the edges. She hadn't understood but had
handled it gracefully and with love. Even when she insisted
on being called Lucky, her mother went along with it and
only used Letitia when she was in trouble. In college, her
long-suffering roommate had insisted she take an interest
in fashion and makeup. She twisted Lucky's arm until she
agreed to go on shopping excursions and regaled her with

pictures from fashion magazines. She felt as if she were being forced to learn a foreign language. She was still a tomboy at heart, but at least now she could dress herself better and apply makeup without looking like a circus freak.

She grabbed her purse and keys and touched the nose of her folk art witch for good luck. Elizabeth had given her the New England kitchen witch, carved of wood with a black hat and straw dress, as a housewarming present when she moved into the apartment—in an apartment building owned by Elizabeth herself. Everything that had gone right for her had come from Elizabeth—an apartment, odds and ends of furniture, even a car. If it hadn't been for her mother's best friend, things would have been so much harder, if not impossible, when she had returned to Snowflake. She closed her eyes and said a prayer that Elizabeth, wherever she was, would soon be found. She didn't know what else she could possibly do except to nag Nate, continue to search for Elizabeth's car and take good care of Charlie.

She rushed down the stairs and out to Maple Street, passing by the Snowflake Clinic where Elias was seeing patients this morning. She glanced through the glass door as she passed and saw Rosemary, the receptionist, at the front desk with a room full of waiting patients. She waved to Rosemary through the glass and Rosemary returned the greeting. Elias was managing to handle the patient load, but his days were difficult. He had been casting about for another doctor to join the practice and take some of the load off his shoulders, but so far, either no one wanted to practice in such a small community, or many of the applicants hadn't been qualified. Hopefully, it wouldn't take too much longer for him to find someone. Her reasons were partly selfish. If Elias were able to free up his schedule they could definitely have more time together.

She took the side alley to the Spoonful and entered through the back door. She dumped her purse in the office and grabbed a fresh apron from the closet. "Hi, Sage," she called as she passed the kitchen. Sage smiled and held up a slotted spoon in response. Jack was at the cash register organizing the drawer for the day. She reached up and kissed him on the cheek.

"How are you, Jack?"

"Couldn't be better." He slammed the drawer shut. "Been quiet and easy so far."

The sun was shining through the checkered café curtains, bathing the whole room in a golden glow. Lucky loved this room with its photographs of ski slopes and local residents, its polished wide pine floors and now in the summer, hanging plants by the windows.

"That's good. Sorry I'm late. I just had to get a bit more sleep."

"I hear you. It's taken its toll on everyone. We just all have to keep going and volunteer as much time as we can manage."

Something in the kitchen smelled absolutely wonderful. Janie was at the counter. Lucky joined her. "What am I smelling?"

"Sage won't tell me, but I think it smells like peanut butter, don't you? He wants us to sample it later."

"Ah, he's been working on that one. I'll take over here, Janie. Can you set the tables?" Janie nodded and bustled off with a stack of woven place mats, napkins and silverware.

Jack moved to the counter and, grumbling, held up the front page of the *Snowflake Gazette*. "Have you seen this?"

"No. Why?"

"Such nonsense. You'd think this town was on the FBI's most wanted list. Good thing I told her I couldn't talk to her."

"Rowena's article?"

"She should be writing soap operas if you ask me."

"Don't let it upset you. She's just doing her best to be sensational."

"Hmph," Jack responded. "Bad enough what's happened, but advertising it like this isn't very good for business," he complained, returning to his stool behind the cash register.

The bell over the door announced the arrival of three groups of customers. Lucky grabbed a tray and poured several glasses of water. Janie took the tray and quickly dispensed water and menus at each table. She passed an order slip to Lucky for drinks, and Lucky filled orders for three glasses of iced tea, four coffees and two glasses of orange juice for the new customers. Janie continued setting each table and then returned to the first table to take orders.

Hank and Barry stepped in and waved to Jack and Lucky, nabbing their favorite corner. Lucky poured two cups of coffee, adding a small pitcher of cream and a bowl of sugar to a tray that she carried to Hank and Barry.

"Thanks, Lucky. We'll order in a little bit. We're gonna go out at noon with another search party."

"Have they found anything? Anything at all?" Lucky struggled to keep the quaver out of her voice.

Hank shook his head. "Nothing at all. I heard you and Sophie have been searching the roads. You think you might find Elizabeth's car?"

"It's a long shot but that's what we've been hoping. I'd join the ground search if I had more time away from the restaurant, but at least searching for her car is something I can do that no one else seems to be doing."

"Manpower's always a problem with these things, but I gotta say, everyone's been terrific, donating their time. Not easy to do, especially with this heat."

Barry started to line up chess pieces on the board. "Jack's getting pretty good at this game. Maybe I can teach him some more opening moves if he has a minute."

"I'll tell him." She returned to the counter, wiped off the tray and slipped it onto a shelf.

The bell over the door rang again. Marjorie and Cecily

bustled in. Cecily waved to her and hurried over to the counter.

"How are you doing, dear? You don't look like you're sleeping at all."

"I am, just not very well."

"I understand. I went out yesterday with Nate and his deputy. And Marjorie's going tomorrow. We can spell each other at the shop, but I know it's hard for you with the restaurant and all."

"It's unbelievable," Marjorie said. "That someone can just disappear into thin air. This has been a terrible summer for Snowflake. First Harry, then that dreadful developer man and now worst of all—Elizabeth."

Lucky didn't trust herself to speak. She quickly prepared the croissants with jam and two cups of tea for the sisters.

Janie approached. "Lucky, have you seen my watch anywhere? I can't find it."

"Haven't. Where was the last place you remember it?"

"The night we were at the church—at the meeting. I took if off to wash my hands, I think. At least that's the last place I remember seeing it."

"Tell you what, when the lunch rush has finished, I'll zip over there. I'll see if I can find it."

"Would you?" Janie breathed a sigh of relief. "I'm lost without it."

"No worries. I'm sure it's still there." What better excuse did she need to try to talk to Pastor Wilson about Harry?

Chapter 32

WHEN THE LAST of their lunchtime customers had paid and gone, Lucky pulled off her apron and hung it on a hook in the kitchen. "Sage, I'm taking a break. I'll be back in half an hour."

She headed up Broadway and cut across the Village Green, entering the front door of the white-steepled church. Cutting across the pews, she headed for the large meeting room and kitchen. She pushed open the swinging door and flicked on the light switch. She checked all the counters and the windowsills. She opened drawers and peeked inside. She was just about to give up the search for Janie's watch when something on a tall shelf above the sink caught her eye. There it was. She slipped the watch into the pocket of her skirt, flicked off the light and closed the door to the kitchen. She walked back along the corridor to the main part of the church. The door to Pastor Wilson's office was closed but she heard stirrings inside. She knocked on the door.

"Come in," the familiar voice called out. Lucky opened

the door and stepped into a slightly messy but comfortable chamber. Bookshelves lined the walls and piles of papers were littered across the desk. She breathed deeply, soaking up the residual aroma of mothballs, a comforting, homey smell, even if only for her.

Pastor Wilson looked up. "Hello, Lucky. Good to see you. What can I do for you?"

"I hope I'm not interrupting."

"Not at all, just struggling with next Sunday's sermon. I thought something along the lines of guilt and the wages of sin might be appropriate, given all that's been going on in town."

"I hope the right person hears it."

"Please, sit down." He waved a hand in the direction of one of the high-backed leather wing chairs.

Lucky looked down. An unstable stack of books and folders was piled on the seat.

"Oh, so sorry, let me give you a hand." Pastor Wilson rose from his chair and moved around the side of his desk. "Sorry. I haven't had a chance to straighten up for a while." He picked up the stack of files and books and turned in a circle, hunting for a place to deposit them. He finally dropped them on the floor behind his chair. "Now, what did you want to talk to me about?"

"Harry Hodges." Lucky knew she had never known Harry very well. Now, given all that she had heard, she wondered if anyone in town did. In the years she had lived with her parents, she had met Harry a few times. Each time she had been with her father when he needed to discuss a car repair. It seemed that no matter how many years went by, Harry never aged. He always appeared the same grumpy, grizzled man she remembered when she was younger. What was strange about overhearing his conversation with Pastor Wilson at the church was that Harry had never struck her as someone who doubted his place in the world or someone tortured by uncertainty.

"Oh." Pastor Wilson pushed his glasses up on his head. "Poor Harry. Yes. What about him?"

"The day before the demonstration, you remember, Sophie and I were here unloading drinks. I came down the hall to see you, just as Harry Hodges was leaving your office."

"That's right. Yes," he replied slowly.

"I didn't mean to, but as Harry was leaving . . . And I'm very sorry, I didn't intend to eavesdrop but I couldn't help but hear you talking and it sounded as if Harry was discussing something very serious."

Pastor Wilson took off his glasses and polished them carefully before putting them back on. "Well, I don't know if it would be quite proper for me to talk about that. It's not as though we have confession in our religious practice, but all the same, it would still be private."

"Pastor." Lucky leaned toward the desk. "Two people have been murdered. Elizabeth Dove is missing."

The Pastor cleared his throat. "Yes. Of course. My word. What's happening here? This is all too much." Pastor Wilson heaved a deep sigh.

"That's what I'd like to know. I'm asking you about this because Elizabeth disappeared right around the same time Harry was murdered. I am frantic with worry. Something has happened to her, and I'm terrified it might be connected with these two murders."

Pastor Wilson scratched his head, disturbing the few sandy hairs he had combed over his almost bald pate. "You really should talk to the police—to Nate Edgerton."

"I talk to Nate almost every day. I've told him about the conversation I overheard between you and Harry, and I'm sure he's spoken to you about that by now. There's nothing anyone can do for Harry, or for Richard Rowland, but we have to do everything possible to find Elizabeth."

"I agree and I appreciate how you feel, but to be honest, Harry really didn't say very much." He stared at the papers on his desk for a moment and finally heaved a sigh. "I guess nothing I say can hurt Harry any longer." Pastor Wilson leaned his elbows on his desk and wove his fingers together, his index fingers pointing heavenward. It reminded Lucky of the game children played with their hands. *Here's the church and here's the steeple*—then, opening their hands with fingers still entwined—*Open the doors and see all the people.*

"Harry came to me because he had made a decision. He told me he had kept a secret and that secret had burdened him his entire life. But he didn't tell me what it was. He was simply asking my advice in a very general way. But . . . he said there was something he needed to do first, someone who would be affected. Someone he needed to talk to." Pastor Wilson pulled his eyeglasses off his forehead and wiped them carefully once more. "I'm sorry, Lucky. That's all I know. I have spoken to Nate about this. He had no idea what Harry could have been talking about, nor do I. I know it's not very enlightening, but that's all I know."

Lucky leaned back in the large armchair, listening closely. Nothing in Pastor Wilson's response indicated he had any knowledge of Harry's failing health. He was either a very good liar, which she doubted, or he really had no idea Harry was terminally ill. "I'm grasping at straws, I guess. I just don't know what else to do. Tell me, did you feel it was something Harry had done or something he knew?"

"That's a good question, but I couldn't say." Pastor Wilson shook his head. "I have been praying for Elizabeth Dove's safe return and I sincerely hope it has nothing to do with this terrible business."

"Thanks for your time."

"Not at all." Pastor Wilson rose from his chair and walked to the door of his office with her. "I'm here anytime you'd like to come by."

"Thank you." Dejected, Lucky left the church and walked back across the Village Green. The sun had disappeared behind murky cloud cover, the air heavy and stifling. She mentally reviewed what she was certain of. Harry was dying. He had made a will leaving everything to Guy Bessette. Pastor Wilson more than likely knew nothing of Harry's illness, but he did confirm that Harry had been burdened by a secret of some sort. He had come to a decision, but that decision affected someone else. Who was that someone else? And had that someone murdered Harry to prevent him from talking? Was Rowland the person he needed to speak to? Or had he confided in Rowland? And now Rowland was dead.

If both Harry and Rowland had been murdered, then someone else was involved—someone who knew the secret Harry kept. Or had Rowland been killed only because his construction was a hated project and it had nothing to do with Harry's murder?

She turned and looked back at the church. The white steeple rose to the sky, startling white against gathering black clouds. A cool wind blew at her skirt. This was the very spot where she and Sophie had met Rowena, the day they delivered refreshments to the church. Rowena had been excited, planning her interview with Rowland, and then on the day of the dress rehearsal, furious and upset that Rowland had cut her short and had her removed from the site.

A car horn tooted. Lucky looked across the Green to Broadway. Sophie was at the wheel of her car, waving to her. Lucky waved back and hurried across the Green to meet her.

"I was just heading over to the Spoonful to see you. What are you doing here?" Sophie looked at her more carefully. "You don't look very good."

"I know. Everyone keeps telling me that."

"Hop in. We can talk a bit." Sophie turned off the engine as Lucky walked around to the passenger side and climbed in.

"I took a break to come over to look for Janie's watch. She left it at the church the other night, but really I wanted to see Pastor Wilson." Lucky rubbed her temples. "I had very strange, confused dreams last night, and all morning I've felt as if there's something nagging at me. Something I know but can't quite remember. Something that's right in front of me but I can't see it."

"What did Reverend Mothballs have to say?"

Lucky smiled in spite of her mood. "Not much. Harry really didn't tell him anything definite. But it seems he did want to get something off his chest. He had come to a decision but told the Pastor he had to talk to someone else first."

"Like something bad Harry had done a long time ago?"

"Maybe. But whatever Harry knew affected another person. Something definitely haunted him. And that was the impression I had when I overheard them in the church. There's another thing—but you must not mention it to anyone. Elias confided in me. Harry was terminally ill. He had only a few months to live."

"And somebody killed him." Sophie shuddered. "How horrible."

Lucky leaned over and rested her forehead on her knees. Sophie placed a hand on Lucky's back. "You're completely stressed out."

"I'm exhausted from frustration, even though I slept like the dead all night. When you spotted me, I was thinking about Rowena and the day we met her here."

Sophie wrinkled her nose. "*Thinking* and *Rowena* don't belong in the same sentence."

"Seriously, it was something she said that day. She was all excited . . ."

"She was full of herself, you mean."

"That too. But she was planning an interview with

Richard Rowland, remember? I recall thinking that no one wanted to hear his side of the story. But then we ran into her again the day of the dress rehearsal and she was very upset."

"I don't remember that."

"Oh. That's right. I think you took off when you saw her heading over. Anyway, I'm trying to remember what she said. She was upset because Rowland cut short the interview. I guess she had pressed it and she was outraged that he had her thrown off the site. She said it was going very well until she mentioned the pictures."

"What pictures?" Sophie prompted.

"She told him the editor was planning to run old town pictures with the interview and that's when his mood changed. She said, 'He couldn't get me out of there fast enough—as soon as I mentioned the pictures.' "

"Where are you going with this? Do you think Rowland's murder is somehow connected to Rowena's interview?"

"Not with the interview. He was willing to be interviewed. It seems it was the mention of running pictures that brought it to a screeching halt. And to answer your question, I think it's all connected, but I don't see how."

"I'm just trying to understand your train of thought."

Lucky heaved a sigh. "That's just it. There is no train of thought. Elizabeth goes missing as these other things occur. Come on, Sophie. This is Snowflake. Nothing like this ever happens here!"

"A year ago, I would have agreed. Until last winter when I almost lost Sage. But now look where we are." Sophie fell silent, tapping her fingernails on the steering wheel. "I haven't had any luck today either. I've driven up and down every road in town and all around. I've followed dirt tracks into the woods, everything I can think of, but I haven't found anything unusual, much less Elizabeth's car. I know I shouldn't have gone out alone, but I just had to do something."

"I'm going over to the *Gazette*. It's the only thing I haven't had a chance to explore. Do you want to come with me?"

Sophie groaned. "Not if I have to talk to Rowena."

Lucky shook her head. "I'll do all the talking, okay?"

Chapter 33

IT WAS CLOSE to three o'clock by the time Lucky and Sophie climbed the stairs to the office of the *Gazette*. The *Gazette* wasn't quite a newspaper, more of a local gossip sheet that occasionally carried news of wider interest. It consisted of an editor, a typist and a reporter, namely Rowena Nash. Lucky doubted Rowena made much money, if any. Her position was probably more freelance, if not volunteer, in hopes of building a résumé so she could move on to greener pastures.

Lucky knocked on the glass window of the door at the top of the stairs. A voice called out, "Come in."

Lucky stepped inside with Sophie following. Rowena was seated in front of a computer monitor. "Lucky! What are you doing here?" She completely ignored Sophie.

"I stopped by to see you. I wanted to ask you something."

"Well, you'll have to make it quick. I have to finish this piece."

"Remember when we met at the dress rehearsal? You mentioned your editor wanted to run some old town photos with your interview of Richard Rowland," Lucky prompted.

"Oh, him," she sneered. "A very unpleasant man. No wonder someone did him in."

Sophie jabbed her elbow in Lucky's side. She knew what Sophie was thinking. No matter how obnoxious Richard Rowland had been, dying in a flaming construction trailer was extreme punishment for a man who was merely unpleasant.

Sophie cut to the chase. "We'd like to see those pictures."

"Why?"

"We're curious." Sophie smiled insincerely.

Rowena studied Sophie for a long moment. "Well, I don't have them anymore."

"What happened to them?"

Rowena heaved a sigh, indicating how valuable her time was. "I returned all that old junk to the library. I'm sure they've filed them away somewhere."

"Thanks, Rowena," Lucky said. "We'll try there." She pulled Sophie out the door and headed down the stairs before Sophie could deliver a parting shot. When they reached the outer door at the foot of the stairs, they heard Rowena's heels clattering across the office floor above them.

"Lucky!" Rowena called from the top of the stairs. "What's going on?"

"Nothing. Nothing at all. I was just curious and thought they might still be here."

Rowena's eyes narrowed suspiciously. "Do you know something I don't know?"

"Of course not," Lucky replied innocently. "If I did, I'd tell you. You know that." Sophie snickered quietly.

Rowena hesitated. "Okay then." She turned and stomped back to the office.

Sophie whispered, "Right. Like anything you tell her wouldn't be in the next edition of the *Gazette*."

"Exactly. I'm just satisfying my curiosity about Rowland and why he had such a violent reaction to those pictures Rowena's editor wanted to run."

"Sure you're not grasping at straws?"

"Nope. Not sure at all. I probably am grasping at straws. But what else can I do? I want to find Elizabeth, and if I can figure anything out at all, it might help. Harry's gone. There's nothing we can learn from him. Even Pastor Wilson didn't know what he had on his mind. Rowland's been murdered. If there's a reason Rowland got so worked up about those pictures, I want to know why. And you cannot tell me that Elizabeth's disappearance just happens to be a coincidence. I just pray that wherever she is, she's still alive."

"I wish you luck. Listen . . ." Sophie rummaged in her purse. "Take my car. I promised Sage I'd help him get some stuff ready for tomorrow. I'll walk back to the Spoonful and cover for you."

"Thanks," Lucky said, pocketing the keys. "This won't take long. I'll be back in a half hour. Can you let Jack know where I went? Oh," she said, reaching into her pocket. "Give Janie her watch."

"I will. And try not to worry too much in the meantime." Sophie reached over and enveloped her in a hug.

"Easier said than done."

LUCKY CLIMBED THE stairs to the small cottage that housed the Snowflake Library and town archives. It sat among tall pine trees at the end of Elm Street, and one could easily imagine it was exactly as it appeared, a charming family home. The house had been donated to the town on the condition it be used as a library. Emily Rathbone, a retired teacher like Elizabeth, was one of several volunteers who served as a librarian. One of Sophie's missing flyers was prominently displayed in a window on the front porch, and another on the glass window of the door. Inside, a small stack stood on a hallway table.

Lucky knocked on the door and entered. The temperature inside was as warm and humid as the outdoors. Several windows stood open to catch any possible breezes. The house was old and had never had central air-conditioning installed. Every wall was lined with bookshelves and filled with books, all organized and catalogued. The center of each room held a large table with displays of the most current offerings. The living room of the cottage was devoid of furniture except for a massive oak desk and a cabinet with many small drawers in which index cards were filed. The librarians also used an electronic database but were unwilling to eliminate the paper card catalog.

"Hello." Emily looked up and smiled. "You're Lucky Jamieson, aren't you!" she exclaimed. Emily was tall and thin and wore wire frame glasses similar to Hank Northcross. In fact, if they stood together they could have been mistaken for brother and sister. Emily's hair was long and gray, worn in a loose braid that hung halfway down her back. She wore several home-crafted beaded necklaces and a brightly colored long skirt paired with a peasant blouse.

"Yes, I am. I don't believe we've met."

"Not formally. I remember you at your parents' restaurant—before you went off to college. Can I help you with anything?"

"Actually, you can. I understand from Rowena Nash you had loaned her some old photos for an interview."

"Yes. That's right. She wanted to interview that dreadful man who was building the car wash. Whatever for, I can't imagine." Emily grimaced. "Of course, I wouldn't have wished that fate on him, but I'm awfully glad the construction's halted now—hopefully permanently. And that terrible business with Harry Hodges. I could hardly believe it!" She shook her head. "But you're in luck; I was just getting ready to put them away. Follow me."

Emily led Lucky down a hallway that stretched to the rear of the house. She pushed back a sliding door to reveal a large compartment of shelves, full of storage boxes all neatly labeled. "The school photos are on this side. Years and years of Snowflake students. We have all the 'official' ones. You know the kind. The entire class and teacher by grade. No one ever made a determined practice of taking candid shots, but we do have quite a few." Emily picked up a batch of photos that sat on a shelf next to one of the boxes of elementary school photos.

"Let's bring them out to the light so you can see better." Emily carried them to a table by the open front window. A short gust of cool wind blew the curtains back. Lucky looked out to see dark clouds scudding across the mountaintop.

Emily peered out. "Looks like a thunderstorm on the way. I always close and lock the cottage at night, but I sometimes forget to shut the windows. I better remember to do that tonight."

Lucky picked up the batch of photos and leafed through them. There were shots of young children playing in the schoolyard and ice-skating on the pond, several photos of children posing next to classroom art and the last one, three boys on a schoolyard bench.

"These are the ones I loaned Rowena. Or at least the ones she wanted to take. There are a lot more in that box if you'd like to see them. What exactly are you looking for?" Emily asked.

"I don't really know. Rowena told me Richard Rowland cut his interview short. Apparently, he changed his mind when Rowena mentioned that the editor planned to run old photos with his interview. I have nothing to back this up, but I'm suspicious that Elizabeth Dove's disappearance might somehow be connected."

"Oh yes," Emily gasped. "I was stunned when I heard about it. Poor Elizabeth. Is there any news?"

Lucky shook her head negatively. Emily's face fell. "For a moment, I thought . . . well, never mind. I've volunteered time to the searches almost every day since I heard. This is my first day back to the library. You know, I knew Elizabeth very well years ago. When we were both teaching. She was my mentor, more or less, when I first came to Snowflake. She had already been teaching several years when I first arrived. She was wonderful to me. She took me under her wing. I can't imagine why anyone would ever want to hurt her. She's never harmed a soul."

"Someone has taken her, Emily. Elizabeth would never voluntarily disappear." Lucky leafed through the photos a second time. "I was just hoping that these had something to do with the developer canceling his interview. At least it sounded that way. For whatever reason, he didn't want any pictures appearing in the *Gazette*."

The last snapshot of the three boys huddled on a school bench caught her eye again. They sat close together smiling at the camera. One of them had an arm around another boy's neck in jest. The boys appeared to be about eleven or twelve years old.

Emily followed Lucky's gaze. "Boys. Horsing around."

"Who are these three?" Lucky asked.

Emily plucked the photo from her hand. "I don't know. It should be on the back. Yes, here it is. That's Danny Harkins on the left; he has his arm around the center boy—Harry Hodges. Richard Rowland is at the end. Well, what do you know? There's Harry with Richard Rowland. Elizabeth knew all of them very well. They were in her class."

A chill ran up Lucky's spine. She remembered the gravestone with Danny Harkins's name at the cemetery.

And the other two boys—middle-aged men—were now dead within days of each other.

"Did you know the three of them then?"

"Oh no," Emily shook her head. "That was several years before my time. But I remember hearing about them."

"Danny Harkins. He was Maggie Harkins's son?"

"That's right. He died in a car accident. It was about oh . . . twenty-five years ago now? No, more . . . twenty-seven, maybe. Amazing, isn't it? How decades can go by in the blink of an eye? Danny was around twenty when he died. He had a bit of a . . ."—Emily leaned closer, whispering—". . . drinking problem, or so I've been told."

Lucky nodded encouragingly. She couldn't imagine why Emily felt it necessary to whisper. Danny was long gone and they were alone. Maybe she was superstitious about speaking ill of the dead.

"He crashed his car late one night. They found him the next day. Terrible. So sad for his mother. But the three of them as young boys were the best of friends, and then I think Rowland's family moved away."

"What happened? Why did they leave town?"

"Now this is thirdhand, so I might not have the facts straight. Elizabeth would remember much better than I. There was some trouble about a younger boy who used to follow the older ones around—trying to keep up with the older kids, I guess, even though they didn't want him around. They used to bully and try to scare the younger kid to get rid of him. Then the little boy died in a terrible accident. He was trapped in an abandoned house just outside of town and they think he was playing with matches. Anyway . . ." Emily trailed off. "He couldn't find a way out and he died in the fire."

"That's awful. But I'm confused. What did this have to do with these three?" Lucky held up the photo of Harkins, Hodges and Rowland.

Emily heaved a sigh. "There was a lot of talk at the

time—that the older boys might have caused the fire, or had something to do with that younger boy being trapped in that old, run-down building. They denied it. They admitted they sometimes played there but said they hadn't been there the day the boy died and didn't know anything about it."

"Who was the boy who died?"

Emily shook her head. "I have no idea. I only heard the story much later and no one really wanted to dredge that terrible thing up again. It was so long ago now. So that's why I'm not absolutely sure I have the facts straight."

"So people did suspect the older boys had something to do with it?"

"I don't really know. They wondered if the boys were sneaking cigarettes or playing with matches. Kids do dumb things like that sometimes. But nothing was ever proven."

Lucky flashed on a memory of walking across the Village Green with Elizabeth. She had turned and seen Maggie Harkins in the distance. Elizabeth had followed her gaze and remarked *"How strange . . . to see them all here again."*

"Are you all right?" Emily peered over her glasses.

"Oh yes. Sorry. I was just recalling something Elizabeth said. Thank you." Lucky passed the photos back to the librarian.

"Do you think that old story has something to do with the two murders . . . or Elizabeth's disappearance?"

"I don't know. But I'll bet Maggie Harkins is the one person who might know."

"Good luck there," Emily answered. "I'm not sure what information you'd be able to get from her. I've seen her walking along the road outside of town but either she doesn't want to talk to anyone, or she's not quite right in the head anymore. I just don't know." Emily shrugged and placed the photos at the side of her desk.

"You don't happen to know where she lives, do you?"

"Sure do. I went there with Elizabeth a few times after

Danny died. Just to pay our respects. Elizabeth was very concerned about Maggie and wanted to do her best to be helpful. You just continue down Elm Street and follow it until it turns into the old Colonial Road. Go about five miles and you'll see a row of mailboxes. After that, take your first right up a dirt road and that's her old farmhouse. It's hidden but it's not too far off the road."

"Thanks again."

"You're certainly welcome. You stop by anytime. I'm always glad of company here." Emily waved to her as she walked out the door.

Lucky sat in the car and glanced at the clock. Things would be quiet right now at the Spoonful. She could return and fill Sophie in, but something urged her on. She closed her eyes and leaned back against the headrest. Harry Hodges was murdered, and Elizabeth disappeared. Which came first? Or were those two events concurrent? She had tried to reach Elizabeth several times after Harry's death. That was what had alarmed her at first, the fact that Elizabeth hadn't contacted them after Harry's body had been discovered. Several days later, Richard Rowland burned to death in his construction trailer. Guilty or innocent of the little boy's death, the talk in the town must have been terrible enough to cause his family to move away. It was understandable that Rowland hadn't wanted old town pictures run with the interview. Were there more connections between Elizabeth and the three men who were now dead? Maybe Maggie Harkins would be willing to talk to her.

Chapter 34

ELIZABETH HEARD MAGGIE'S footsteps on the cellar stairs. Maggie mumbled to herself as she approached the door and slid a fresh plate of vegetables through the broken space. The house had been quiet since the day Elizabeth had heard the scream. She had listened carefully since then but had heard nothing more than Maggie's quiet steps above her.

Elizabeth rushed to the door and pressed her cheek against the wood. "Maggie, what happened? Did someone hurt you?" Elizabeth listened carefully, so carefully she could hear Maggie's breathing on the other side of the door. "Who was here?" Elizabeth waited. "Maggie, answer me!"

Elizabeth heard the sounds of Maggie shuffling away. A few minutes later she heard voices again, and a man's heavy footsteps. Was this the man who had caused Maggie to scream? She had to take a chance. Help might be within reach. She rushed to the bedding and grabbed her shoe. In the tiny washroom, she banged on the pipes and called out. She continued striking the pipes until her arm cramped. Elizabeth winced. She took a deep breath and massaged the taut muscles. In the few moments of silence, she heard Maggie cry out. Then nothing. Elizabeth leaned against the wall, exhausted. A strange smell filled the room, filtering through the floorboards above her head. She froze in fear when she recognized the odor. It was gasoline.

LUCKY MISSED THE turnoff on her first pass. She checked her odometer and realized she had gone too far. This very road was one she and Sophie had driven just two days ago. Why hadn't she seen the entrance to Maggie's house? She made a U-turn on the shoulder of the road and drove back two miles. Then she turned again and this time, driving slowly, scanned the side of the road. She spotted the mailboxes that Emily had described. Most were rusted and barely noticeable against the dark tree trunks. She finally found the dirt road. It was well hidden. Emily's directions had been good ones, but the drive was barely visible, half covered with encroaching trees. The sky had grown even darker and thunder rumbled close by.

She turned quickly off the road and drove up a short rise. Tree branches swatted at the sides of her car. In front of the house was a wide-open area. She pulled the car against a stand of trees away from the house and turned the engine off. The building itself was run-down, and for a moment Lucky thought Emily must have made a mistake. This house looked abandoned. The overhanging trees blocked out the diminishing light. Underneath the shade of the trees, a chill breeze blew. She shivered, suddenly fearful.

She had come this far. She wasn't going to let a crumbling

old house and a mumbling woman stop her now. She tossed her purse in the back and climbed out of the car. She called out, "Hello." A bird in the distance cawed a response—a crow. She walked slowly around to the side of the house. A late model dark sedan was parked at the side. Someone was here. But was Maggie still here? Did she have a visitor? Or did the house now belong to someone who planned to remodel the crumbling cottage? Lucky retraced her steps and climbed the rickety steps to the front porch. She called out once again but heard nothing. The front door stood open halfway. She knocked loudly but no one came.

There was an overwhelming smell of gasoline. It was unmistakable. She stepped inside and covered her nose. A moan came from a room to the left. It took a few seconds for her eyes to adjust to the dimness. A human bundle sat on the floor. It was Maggie Harkins. Her back was to the wall, her ankles were bound and her hands were behind her back, tied to a radiator. Lucky rushed to her side. Maggie was whimpering under her breath.

"Maggie, who did this to you?" Lucky asked as she struggled to untie the cord that bound the woman. Maggie shook her head violently, a frightened look in her eyes, but said nothing. The smell of gasoline was stronger here. Lucky spotted a trail of fluid across the wood floor leading to a puddle of fuel in the small dining area. A red can lay on its side. Whoever had tied Maggie up and poured gasoline through the house could still be here. Someone had planned to burn down the house with Maggie in it.

"Hold on. I'll get these untied," she spoke encouragingly. Maggie looked at her with watery, confused eyes. The cord was stiff and wouldn't move. Lucky's fingers were shaking. She had to release Maggie before whoever had done this to her came back. Or was someone here now, lurking, watching her? She ran to the kitchen and pulled one drawer after another open. Finally she found a large knife with a serrated edge. She ran back to Maggie and furiously sawed through the cord binding the woman's hands. Then she cut through the cord around her ankles.

A hollow clanging sound issued through the walls. Rhythmic. Too rhythmic to be old pipes acting up. Lucky stopped and listened. "Maggie, what is that?" Maggie shook her head violently, but didn't answer. Where were the metallic thuds coming from? Below. The sound was below. "Maggie, is someone down in the cellar?" Maggie shook her head again and began to croon to herself.

Lucky dragged the woman to her feet. "Get out of the house. Run, Maggie. It's not safe here." Once she was sure Maggie could stand on her own, she ran back to the entry hall. A small door was tucked under the rise of the stairway. She wrenched it open.

"Is someone down there?" she called. A faint cry came from below. Someone was trapped down there. Or was someone trying to trap her? Were they lying in wait? The same someone who had poured gasoline over the floorboards? She had to find out. And then she had to get far away from this house. She moved slowly down the stairs one step at a time. Her heart thumped heavily in her chest. It was pitch-black except for a thin sliver of light at the other end of the cellar. She called again, "Is someone here?"

"Here. In here," Elizabeth screamed and banged frantically on the door.

"Elizabeth?" Lucky, her hands in front of her to keep from bumping into strange objects, stepped carefully across the floor. She reached the door. Her eyes had adjusted somewhat and now she could see the outline of the opening.

"Elizabeth! It's me. It's Lucky."

"Lucky?" Elizabeth sobbed. "Oh, thank God. You have to get me out of here."

"I will. Hang on." Lucky felt the door with her fingertips. Some light came from the other side of the door through a break in the wood at the bottom. A board acted as a bar to the door. She grasped the heavy plank with both hands and lifted it up. The door creaked and gave way, opening to a tiny room. Elizabeth fell into her arms.

"Thank heavens I found you. The whole town's been searching for you. Are you all right?"

"It's hard to walk. I hurt my ankle. Please, Lucky, help me out of here." Elizabeth's clothes were streaked with dirt. Her feet were bare and her skin felt cold.

"Come on. I'll help you up the stairs." She reached an arm around Elizabeth's waist and led her slowly to the foot of the stairs. A loud, whooshing explosion reached their ears.

"What's that?" Elizabeth asked fearfully, clinging to her arm.

"Fire. The house is soaked with gasoline. Hold on to the railing. I want to make sure we have time to get out. Don't move." Lucky rushed up the stairs. She heard a crackling noise on the other side of the door and felt intense heat. The smell of old burning wood was unmistakable now. Lucky kicked the door open, hoping against hope they could make it out of the house—that the floor wouldn't collapse before they could reach the front door. The living room was engulfed in flames that licked at the walls. The air from the cellar fed the conflagration. A wall of flame rose up, blocking her path. An intense wave of heat almost knocked her down the stairs. She clung to the railing and backed down as quickly as she could.

Elizabeth moaned. "It's too late." The flames had caught the door and it crackled as old paint melted and peeled from the heat.

"We'll find a way." Lucky guided Elizabeth toward the thin sliver of light. "This has to be a hatch to the outside. I'll let go of you for a moment. Can you stand? This might be our only way out now." Elizabeth nodded and put a hand against the wall to keep her balance.

Lucky took the two steps up to the opening of the hatch and pushed with all her strength. It moved but wouldn't open. The cellar had taken on an eerie brightness from the flames upstairs and was quickly filling with smoke that curled above them, clinging to the floor joists. There was still air to breathe but it wouldn't last long. Desperate, she looked around and spotted the workbench. "It must be locked on the outside. Hang on. I'll find something to break through." She felt across the top of the workbench hoping to locate a tool. Her eyes were stinging. She looked up. An axe hung from a peg on the wall. She pulled it down and rushed back to the hatch, which she hoped would lead to fresh air and freedom.

Using the blunt head of the axe, she struck at the boards. They were old and half rotted. She continued to aim the axe at what she hoped was the weakest plank. She heard a crack, not the crack of burning wood that came from above, but the crack of old wood. A jagged square gave way and she could see light outside. The cellar was filling with smoke and fumes. Her eyes burned and each breath hurt. They heard a tremendous noise as the door at the top of the stairs gave way and crashed to the floor. Flames raged through the opening. They were looking up into the mouth of an inferno at the top of the stairs—an inferno that would rain down on them. They had to escape.

Using all her strength, Lucky struck at the partially broken wood. A large section cracked open. It was just enough space for them to crawl through one at a time. "Elizabeth. You first. Get out."

"No, Lucky. You should go."

"Don't argue. Go. Now." She grasped Elizabeth by the shoulders and pushed her up the steps to the opening in the boards. "Climb through." Elizabeth turned to the side and was able to get her head and shoulders through the opening, but it wasn't quite wide enough to allow her to climb through.

"I'm stuck." She sobbed.

"Hang on." Lucky turned around, pushing her back against the stubborn boards. She anchored herself on the cement stairs and pushed up with all her strength. Another large section of wood gave way. She felt it tear against her bare arm. Pain shot through her. But now there was a large, jagged opening. Elizabeth was free, stumbling out onto the grass at the side of the house. Lucky followed. She grasped Elizabeth's arm and pulled her away from the burning house. They took shelter in the trees several yards away and collapsed together on the ground, gasping and coughing. The windows of the house had exploded outward from the intense heat. The yard was littered with glass and burning debris.

Lucky reached over to Elizabeth and hugged her. "Thank heavens I found you. We need to get to the car and get out of here. We need to get help." She only hoped Sophie's car was far enough away from the house that it would be safe from the fire. And she hoped Maggie had escaped. A deafening crash of thunder sounded above them. Immediately a flash of lightning cut through the blackening sky.

"Can you stand up?" Elizabeth nodded and struggled to her feet.

"Let's stay among the trees—it's safer." Lucky put a protective arm around Elizabeth, guiding her, afraid she would collapse in her weakened state. Elizabeth could barely put weight on her ankle and was forced to move slowly. They reached the last barrier of trees. Sophie's car was just a few yards away. "We're here. Just a few more steps."

Elizabeth nodded. "I'm sorry. I can't move very fast."

"That's all right. Lean on me."

A branch snapped behind them. Lucky, startled, turned around. Edward Embry stood a few feet away. He was holding a gun and it was aimed at them.

Chapter 35

ELIZABETH TURNED TO follow Lucky's gaze. She gasped. "Edward?" She squeezed Lucky's hand tightly and a tremor ran through her body.

"I'm sorry, Elizabeth." He shook his head sadly. "It's too bad you had to go poking your nose into this. And you too, Lucky. I wish you both could have left well enough alone."

"What are you talking about Edward? Why do you have a gun? What are you doing?"

Lucky's blood ran cold. "It was you—you tied Maggie up and left her in that house. Why?"

Edward ignored her outburst and turned to Elizabeth. "You have to know it wasn't my plan to hurt you. You never should have come here. I needed to see this through."

"See what through, Edward? You're not making any sense." Elizabeth recalled Maggie's answer when she had pleaded with her in the cellar. "*He won't hurt me then.*"

Lucky tightened her grip on Elizabeth's shoulder. The

pieces of the puzzle had fallen into place. "You couldn't know, Elizabeth. Harry Hodges was murdered and so was Richard Rowland."

"Harry?" Elizabeth gasped. She turned to Edward. "Oh no. Oh no. Tell me you didn't, Edward." Tears rushed to her eyes.

"I wasn't responsible for Harry, Elizabeth, believe me. I didn't do that. If I had, he would never have gone so easily. He would have died screaming like my little Johnny, my sweet, innocent boy."

"And Richard Rowland?" Lucky asked.

Edward nodded. "Oh yes. Funny thing, though. You were right, Elizabeth. It didn't cheer me as much as I thought it would. In fact, I really didn't feel anything at all after all these years. But it was satisfying to know he died just like Johnny. I suspect Harry had an attack of conscience and decided to finally tell the truth about what they did that day. And I think that monster Rowland got to Harry first."

Elizabeth leaned against Lucky, unable to speak.

"I'm sorry, Elizabeth. I tried. For so many years, I tried to put it behind me. But it wasn't any good. It wouldn't go away. There were days I thought I had the rage conquered, but it would flare up again even stronger. It was tearing my brain apart. Harry knew. He could never look me in the eye. He knew how I felt. But Rowland . . . when he showed up in town again, it all came back. I really didn't think I had that kind of hate inside of me anymore." Edward shrugged, and the arm that held the gun relaxed slightly. "But then the opportunity presented itself and it was so very easy. And you know what I felt? I felt nothing. If anything, relief. Relief it was over. They were all dead. I had waited a very long time. There were so many nights I couldn't sleep. Nights I would lie awake planning what I wanted to do to them all, wondering if I had the stomach to do what needed to be done. And when the time came it was so simple, so easy. Like watching a film from a long distance away."

"Edward, there was a sworn statement that they weren't there." Elizabeth took a shaky breath. "There was never any proof they locked Johnny in that house or set fire to it. Everyone accepted it could have been an accident."

Edward started to shake with barely controlled emotion. His eyes darkened; his face twisted. "A sworn statement!" He spat. "Maggie Harkins was their alibi. She said they were with her that day. She lied. She lied to save her son."

"How long have you been torturing that poor woman?" Elizabeth demanded.

Edward smiled. "Not long. I just needed to keep her out of the way—until it was her turn. But I always kept an eye on her. She knew it too. She knew she was as guilty as those boys. Those three should have spent their lives in jail for killing my son. Everyone knew they hung around that old house, sneaking cigarettes, lighting matches. But the police let them go. Was that justice? Justice for my son or my wife?"

What little color was in Elizabeth's face drained. Lucky wondered if she might pass out from shock.

"I don't need proof. I know! For thirty-five years it's all I've dreamed about. I've been tortured by the memories. I've had a picture of my dead child in my head all this time. Can you blame me? When Rowland showed up, I knew it was time. The life I should have had was stolen from me. Why should they have been allowed to live?"

Lucky's mind was racing. Edward had grown increasingly unstable. She was sure any slight movement could set him off. She couldn't run and leave Elizabeth. Shaking or not, Edward could be capable of shooting her as she ran. Elizabeth wouldn't be able to move very fast if at all. And no one knew where they were. She hadn't told anyone where she was going—not even Sophie.

As if he could read her mind, Edward turned to Lucky.

"You know I can't let you or Elizabeth go free. My entire life has been a prison sentence. I have no intention of spending my last years in another sort of prison."

"A prison of your own making, Edward," Elizabeth said.

"That may be, but my only regret is that I didn't dispose of them all years ago. They weren't entitled to the years they had, the years they took from Johnny." Something in his face shifted. His eyes were grim. "Now walk." He indicated with the gun.

"Walk? Walk where?" Lucky croaked.

"Into the woods, follow that path." He indicated a well-worn path into the trees away from the house, away from the car, away from escape. Lucky felt her knees start to shake. He planned to march them into the woods and what? Shoot them? Had the man lost touch with all human feeling?

Elizabeth straightened up. A jolt of anger ran through her slight frame. "You'll never get away with this, Edward."

"Oh, but I have gotten away with it. For years I've gotten away with it." He laughed softly. "I made sure Danny Harkins died in that wreck twenty-seven years ago."

Elizabeth's eyes widened and a look of shock registered on her face. "What do you mean?"

Edward smiled at the memory. "It was quite by accident really. I was driving home and passed his car on the road. He had run off the road and hit a tree." He chuckled. "It's true you know, that old saying, 'God looks after fools and drunks.' Danny reeked of alcohol and yet there wasn't a scratch on him. The idiot had been drinking and missed the turn. His car was in the ditch, but he was conscious."

Edward barked a short, harsh laugh. "He actually thought I had stopped to help him. The gas tank was leaking. Fuel was everywhere. Killing him was so easy. But it was important to me that he was conscious and knew what was happening to him. And he knew I did it for Johnny. He

begged and screamed as I lit the match and watched him
die—die just like my Johnny."

Another scream, wild and primitive, came from the
trees. Maggie flew at Embry. She was like a beast of the
forest. Taken by surprise, he hadn't had time to even raise
his gun. She lunged at him, knocking him to the ground,
screaming, clawing at his face, his eyes. He shouted and
struggled, but Maggie had called upon superhuman
strength. Edward tried to get to his feet, to raise the gun
and aim it at Maggie. But she clung to him, fighting him
with all her strength, uncaring that she might cause her
own death. She grasped the weapon and, groaning with the
effort, turned it against his chest. The gun fired. Birds
screeched and flew from the trees. Lucky's ears rang and
finally all was quiet.

No one breathed. Time seemed to halt in the frozen
silence. Maggie slowly climbed off the body of Edward
Embry and stood, devoid of expression, staring at the dying
man. The gun dropped from her hand. Edward's mouth
opened and closed, but no words came. Blood bubbled
from his lips. Staring at the trees above him, his eyes
glazed over and his body was still. A sudden violent wind
bent the treetops. And then the rain came.

Lucky approached softly and, reaching down, picked
up the gun. It wasn't safe to leave it. She didn't know what
reaction if any Maggie might have to what she had just
done.

Lucky took Elizabeth's hand. "Let's go," she whispered.
They stumbled out of the clearing, leaving Maggie in the
rain still staring at Edward's body. They followed the path
out of the trees and reached Sophie's car. The heat from
the burning house was intense. By now, someone would
have seen smoke and reported a fire. Lucky only hoped the
downpour would quench the fire before it spread. When
they reached the car Lucky eased Elizabeth into the passenger seat. She climbed in on the driver's side, started the

engine and reversed down the drive. She backed up the road a good distance away and hit the brakes. Reaching behind her, she grabbed her purse and rummaged for her cell phone. She punched in the first few numbers, then heard the sirens. She grasped Elizabeth's hand, leaned her head back and waited for the cavalry.

Chapter 36

"I KNOW I said I wanted some time with you, but this is ridiculous." Elias chuckled as he threaded a suture through the fleshy part of Lucky's forearm. "This isn't quite what I had in mind."

"Just keep sewing, will you?" Lucky did her best to study the acoustic panels on the ceiling of the Snowflake Clinic. "It makes me sick if I look."

Elias looked up quickly. "Any pain?" His demeanor was immediately professional.

"Yes, you're a terrible seamstress . . . seamster . . . what's the right word?"

"Whoa there. Don't be casting aspersions on my abilities as a doctor. I'll have you know my mother taught me to sew!" Elias declared in mock indignation.

"Really? So did mine. Our mothers must have had a lot in common."

Lucky felt no pain after the anesthetic had been injected, but the tug on her skin was disconcerting. All things considered, she had no complaints. A jagged cut to her arm from the wooden boards of the hatch was minor compared to what could have happened.

The door from the waiting area flew open and Sophie marched into the examining room. "Hope you don't mind. This is taking way too long . . . visiting hours will be over soon." Sophie smiled. "How is she?"

"Worst patient I ever had," Elias mumbled without looking up. He tied off the last suture and covered the wound with an antiseptic ointment and a sterile bandage. "Come back to the Clinic in a few days. I want to check that there's no infection." He leaned over and planted a light kiss on Lucky's lips. "I know it's no good to tell you to stay out of trouble, but try to stay out of trouble."

"How did you know where to find me?" she asked Sophie.

"Well, you said you'd be back in a half hour. When more than an hour had gone by, Jack and I both got worried. Jack's in the waiting room by the way. I called Emily at the library and grilled her. She told me about the conversation you had with her and that she had given you directions to Maggie's house. I wasn't positive you had gone there first, without me. It was a long shot, but it was the only thing I could think of when you didn't come back. I got really worried. I finally managed to reach Nate and catch a ride with him. Nate got the report of a fire when we were headed out there. That's when he turned on the siren. And you know the rest. Oh, by the way, Nate found Elizabeth's car hidden way back in the woods behind Maggie's house. We never would have found it on our own."

"I guess our efforts were for nothing." Lucky shrugged and winced in pain from the movement. Once Nate had taken charge of the scene, Lucky handed the gun over to him and drove straight back to town with Sophie and Elizabeth. "Where's Nate now?"

"He's with the State Police at Maggie's house. They've

got quite a scene out there. More to the point, where is Elizabeth?" Sophie asked.

"She's right next door, getting her vitals checked."

"I'll go sit with her. Join us when you two are finished here." Sophie smiled suggestively at Elias. She breezed out and knocked on the door to Elizabeth's examining room. A minute or so later, Lucky and Elias heard gales of laughter. Lucky smiled. "Laughter's the best thing for her right now. Am I done? I'll go see Jack. I'm sure he's worried."

"Go ahead. I'll catch up. I need to see how Elizabeth's doing. It'll be a miracle if she isn't dehydrated. That'd be the most dangerous thing."

"She told me Maggie gave her a large jug of water and fed her every day. Elizabeth was worried though because the water was running out."

"Whatever possessed Maggie to go along with Embry?"

"I don't know. Maybe the shrinks can get something out of her. I doubt she's well-balanced so who knows what her mental or emotional competence is. Edward must have threatened her. He must have told her he'd kill her if she let Elizabeth go. She was the one he blamed for the boys not being charged with his son's death. Obviously he never told her what he did to Danny. He was sure she was still tied up in that burning house when he confessed to us."

"What was he doing in her house to begin with?"

"I think when he saw his opportunity to take revenge on Rowland, he didn't want anyone around to remember or rake up the past. After all, Maggie has done nothing but live in the past all these years. Apparently, it was Maggie who had given the boys their alibi. Edward said he had left her alone all this time, but always kept an eye on her. Her own guilt must have tortured her terribly. Perhaps she felt there was no one she could turn to for help. And of course he planned to kill her too. What he didn't anticipate was that Elizabeth would show up unexpectedly." Lucky shuddered.

"Elias, he had poured gasoline all over the house. If I had gotten there a few minutes later, it would have been too late."

Elias quickly wrapped his arms around her, careful not to touch the injured part of her arm. "If anything had happened to you . . ."

"I'm fine. I'll be fine. And Elizabeth too. Another thing . . . Embry said he didn't kill Harry. He said he was sure Rowland had done it, and I think he was right."

"Harry was dying. There are treatments, but it would have just prolonged his agony. And the information I had from his specialist was that he refused any treatment."

"Poor Harry. He must have felt the most important thing he had left to do was confess what really happened to Edward's little boy all those years ago. He must have told Rowland what he intended. It all makes sense now. Why he told Pastor Wilson he needed to speak to someone else first. He never got the chance to clear his conscience. Rowland took even that away from him."

Elias cleaned his instruments off the tray and pushed it out of the way. "Come on, bad patient. Off you go. Elizabeth is waiting for me." Lucky smiled and their eyes held. Elias reached for her as she hopped off the examining table. He pulled her tight in an enveloping embrace and buried his face in her hair. She could feel the beating of his heart. He was completely silent, but Lucky knew his thoughts and his fears without the need to say a word. She was so terribly grateful Elias was in her life.

Jack looked uncomfortable as he sat in one of the molded plastic chairs in the waiting room of the Clinic. Rosemary, one of the Clinic receptionists at the front desk today, was wonderful with patients and kept Jack chatting. When Lucky entered, Jack jumped up and rushed over to her, enveloping her in yet another bear hug.

"It's about time, my girl. You survived the rocks and shoals."

"I'm fine, Jack, no worries. Elizabeth is too. She'll be out in a minute."

"Who'd have thought . . ." He trailed off, unable to put into words the absurdity of Maggie Harkins keeping Elizabeth a prisoner in her cellar. He shook his head.

"I think it'll take everyone in town a while to process what's happened."

"If it weren't for you goin' out there, Elizabeth and Maggie Harkins would both be gone. And to think he held a gun on you. I would have killed him myself if he had hurt a hair on your head." Jack choked back a sob. ". . . and Elizabeth too. I just can't believe it. I can't believe Edward Embry of all people coulda been capable of something like this. Twisted. That's what it is. His head just got twisted, and we all thought he was doing fine."

"Have you heard anything about Maggie?"

Jack nodded. "Nate called a few minutes ago. He's been out there at Maggie's house the whole time. He just wanted to make sure you and Elizabeth were on the mend. He's gonna take Maggie over to the hospital in Lincoln Falls. They'll probably admit her. It was crazy what she did, but I guess she's been half crazy all this time. We should all be ashamed of ourselves that we didn't keep a better eye on her."

"You're right, Jack. Maybe it wouldn't have done any good, but all the same, it's like she slipped through the cracks, all alone with all that grief." Lucky shook her head. "You should have seen her. She was like a wild animal when she attacked Embry. She was in the woods watching us. When she heard what he did to her son—that Danny would still be alive if Embry hadn't set that gasoline alight—she went crazy, crazy with rage."

Chapter 37

NATE KNOCKED FIRMLY on the door. It was opened immediately by Cordelia Rank. Lucky had seen a curtain in the
front window move slightly. She was sure Cordelia
watched their progress up the path. Lucky squeezed Horace's hand to give him courage. She knew he was dreading
this moment, but it was something he had to see through.
Horace leaned over and secured Cicero's leash to the
column on the front porch. "Stay, Cicero." Cicero sat
obediently, his tail wagging. Lucky scratched the dog's
head, happy that Horace had agreed to adopt Edward's
orphaned pet.

Cordelia opened the door and turned a frosty gaze on
Nate. Her look swept over Lucky and Horace. "Nate," she
stated flatly. She was well aware why they were all on her
doorstep.

"May we come in?" Nate asked.

Cordelia said nothing, but stepped back and opened the
front door of her home. Without a word, she turned and

walked into the large front parlor taking a seat in a straight-backed armchair. The three of them, Nate, Lucky and Horace, trailed in after Cordelia and sat on the sofa facing her.

"Mrs. Rank, I have reason to believe that you lured Horace Winthorpe into the woods outside his home and that you or you your husband entered that home without permission to steal one of the artifacts found with the remains."

Cordelia stared at Nate stonily. "How dare you . . ."

"I'm here to ask you nicely to hand it over. It does not belong to you, and should be kept at the University until the final disposition of the remains and other artifacts is decided."

Cordelia sniffed. "I have no idea what you mean."

Nate sighed. "I'm really hoping that I don't have to get a warrant, Cordelia. I'd like to handle this in a civilized manner."

Cordelia's breathing became shallower. Her face was pinched and white lines appeared around her nose. "You are wrong, Nate Edgerton. Those remains do belong to me. They are the remains of my ancestor and I can prove it. I have all the research and paperwork that I've submitted to the Daughters of the American Revolution, and you and this town have no right to interfere with the proper burial of *my* ancestor and his personal possessions. I'll have you know I have sought legal counsel and my attorney will be bringing an action against the University to release those remains."

Lucky heard a step in the hallway and looked up to see Norman Rank standing in the archway to the parlor.

"Well, Cordelia, I can't argue legal technicalities with you. I guess that will be for a judge to decide. But in the meantime, I can and will apply for a warrant, and if that lead ball is on the premises, I would be forced to bring charges against you. Fortunately for your sake, Professor Winthorpe has no desire to cause you trouble, but the University entrusted those artifacts to him and he's compelled to return them. Completely apart from the injury he suffered that night and the emotional upset, he's personally embarrassed by the loss."

Norman glared across the room at his wife. He turned and disappeared from the threshold, while Cordelia and Nate faced each other in silence, neither one willing to relinquish a position of power. Norman returned and walked toward Nate. He handed him a small box.

Surprised, Nate looked up and took the box. He opened it carefully while Lucky peeked over his shoulder. On a pad of cotton lay the small lead ball once fashioned from family pewter that had killed a man more than two centuries ago. Horace breathed an audible sigh of relief.

"I apologize and I am very sorry for all the trouble we've caused you." Norman addressed his comment to Horace. "We never meant you any harm."

Horace stood and shook Norman's hand vigorously. "It's all forgotten. Thank you."

Cordelia's complexion had turned bright red. She opened her mouth to object, but Norman silenced her with a look. "My wife has a very good point. If the remains are those of her ancestor, she is entitled to claim those remains and artifacts. I was . . . it was very foolish to do what we did. I hope you'll forgive us. We'll handle this through legal means and let the court decide what to do."

Cordelia mustered her dignity. "The fact remains that I am still a Daughter of the American Revolution. And I'll have you know that my ancestor *was* a patriot. He was not a traitor, no matter whose bullet killed him. Anyone who says otherwise is guilty of slander. We possess a very fine record proving that Nathanael Cooper was a militiaman in the Continental Army and that's all that really counts."

Cordelia choked on her words and rushed from the room. She looked as if she were about to burst into tears.

Lucky had a moment of pity for Cordelia. That is, until she remembered the night she discovered Horace injured in the woods. Maybe Cordelia Cooper Rank deserved a little humiliation.

Chapter 38

CHARLIE LEAPED FROM the grass and landed on Lucky's lap, purring and nuzzling her face.

"You've got a fan," Elizabeth remarked. She moved around the large picnic table, lighting candles.

The sun was just starting to set. The evening promised to stay warm, the last of the days of summer before the first chill of autumn arrived. Elizabeth had decided to organize an "End of Summer" party as she called it, to celebrate her rescue and release. She had invited Lucky and Elias, Jack, Sophie and Sage, Horace, and Nate and Susanna Edgerton.

Susanna poured a glass of wine and carried it over to Lucky. "I know you don't want to disturb Charlie. He looks so happy on your lap."

"We bonded while Elizabeth was away."

Elizabeth chuckled. "You mean he's attached to you because you fed him."

"That about sums it up," Lucky agreed.

Jack and Nate sat together at the picnic table with beers in their hands, while Sage grilled steaks and hamburgers on Elizabeth's backyard barbeque. Corn on the cob lay on the rack, cooked and charred. Sophie was next to Sage at a utility table slicing vegetables and brushing them with olive oil.

"That smells so good. I'm starving," Susanna called out.

"Be ready in just a minute." Sage brushed the steaks with a ladle of marinade and let them sizzle a few more seconds. Sophie scooped the vegetables into a large platter with the corn and delivered it to the table. No one needed an invitation. They all headed to the picnic table immediately and grabbed seats. Lucky rose from her chair and Charlie leaped off her lap, protesting. Sage moved around the table, depositing a steak on every plate. He returned to the grill and brought a platter of burgers to the table. When everyone was settled, Elizabeth raised her wineglass.

"To good friends. Without all of you . . ." Her eyes filled with tears. "Well, I don't know where I'd be."

Candles flickered around the picnic table, lighting the faces of Elizabeth's friends and loved ones. Lucky spoke first. "To Elizabeth." She raised her glass and everyone followed suit.

"To Elizabeth," echoed in the night.

Later, as the evening became cooler, and the cleanup was finished, the guests moved into the living room for more drinks and dessert. Lucky had carried the lighted candles into the house, placing them on the coffee table and around the room. Charlie had now taken his rightful place on Elizabeth's lap.

"You see, Edward and I, years ago, maybe twenty-five years ago now, I guess, we became close. It might have become . . . an important relationship. I don't know for certain, but at the time, I felt it could have. Edward had been truly devastated and grief stricken years before. To lose his son like that and then his wife. If she had been stronger, better able to cope with the loss of Johnny, then perhaps they could have had another child. Things might have turned out very differently."

"You never said how she died," Sophie said.

Elizabeth glanced at Nate. He met her gaze as though encouraging her to tell the story. "She hanged herself. She committed suicide after . . . after Johnny's death. We all did our best to support Edward through several difficult years. That's when he and I started seeing each other. He seemed to be doing well, but then, in an unguarded moment, I saw what was still inside him. Understandable, surely, but I knew then he might never move on. His need to take revenge consumed him. He could not forgive what had been done to his family."

She looked around the room at the faces of her guests. "I cannot judge him, in spite of what he did—not just to Danny Harkins and Rowland. And to me and Maggie. I cannot even begin to conceive of the crushing weight of his life. I only wish . . . he could have found a way to forgive and recover."

"None of us saw it," Nate spoke. "He was quiet and kept to himself. Perhaps if Richard Rowland had never returned, he wouldn't have acted on those impulses."

"Rowland's return was a catalyst," Elizabeth said. "But don't forget what he did to Danny Harkins years before when he had the chance. That day in the woods when he held a gun pointed at me and Lucky, he didn't appear to have any remorse. He had given up the struggle, I think. When Rowland—that slick, amoral man—returned, it overwhelmed him."

"I had heard of the old history, but I never put it together," Nate said. "Rowland had an alibi for the night Harry was killed. He claimed to be in Lincoln Falls at a business meeting. But it was shaky at best. He could have come back to town at any time and knocked on Harry's door. And if I were just looking for a motive, I'd have to have a good look at Guy Bessette."

"Guy?" Sage furrowed his brow. "Why Guy?"

"Oh." Nate cleared his throat. "I guess everyone will know soon enough. Harry knew he was dying. He drew up a will with a lawyer in Lincoln Falls and left everything he had to Guy Bessette, including the business."

"Why that's wonderful!" Sophie exclaimed. "Not to mention that we'll still have an auto shop in town." Lucky didn't tell them that Guy had already confided in her. She was glad she had given Guy the advice she had that day at the Spoonful—to keep his mouth shut until Harry's murder was cleared up.

"Now we just have to keep Rowena away from him," Sophie said.

Jack laughed. "Maybe I'll have a word with Guy next time I see him—man-to-man."

Elizabeth stroked Charlie's fur, lost in thought. "I do think if Maggie hadn't been so terrorized, she would have let me go. I never felt she intended to harm me. At least I couldn't think of any earthly reason why she would. Edward must have played on her fear and her guilt. She must have felt like a social pariah. The loneliness and isolation . . ." Elizabeth shook her head. "All those emotions must have festered inside her for years. She wanted to believe that Edward wouldn't kill her. And she must have believed there was no one who would come to her aid."

"Perhaps Edward would have killed her sooner, but you turned up," Lucky said. "He needed her alive to hold you hostage."

Elizabeth nodded. "I'd like to think he didn't intend for me to die in that fire, but in his mind, he must have seen no other alternative."

"Are we sure it was Rowland who killed Harry?" Susanna asked, looking around the room at their faces.

Nate cleared his throat. "We can't be absolutely sure. There's no hard proof that we could go into court with— that is, if the man were still alive—but I'd bet my last dollar on it."

"I think Nate's right," Lucky said. "After overhearing that conversation outside Pastor Wilson's office, I did feel Harry had held a terrible secret for a long time. I'm convinced it was Rowland he needed to give fair warning to. Rowland must have panicked. If he were charged with . . . what would it be? Manslaughter? Second-degree murder? He saw his reputation and his life going down the tubes. He struck out at Harry before Harry could talk about what happened when they were young boys. He wasn't going to let that happen. Not after all this time."

"That makes sense," Nate volunteered. "A couple of people saw Harry talking to Rowland on the Green the day before Harry was murdered. They noticed it because they thought Harry might be in cahoots with Rowland about the car wash."

Sophie spoke up. "We kept trying to imagine what Harry Hodges and Richard Rowland could have had in common. You couldn't find such different men, and yet their murders, coming so close together, just couldn't be a coincidence." Sophie looked across the room. "Elizabeth, what do you think? Do you think they deliberately locked Embry's son in that house? Did they mean to kill him?"

"Maybe it was just a prank that got out of hand," Sage said. "Maybe they were just trying to scare Johnny for following them around."

"I remember them so well," Elizabeth said. "As if it were yesterday. Teachers and parents aren't supposed to have favorites, but there are just some kids you like and some you don't, as if you can see the kind of person they'll grow into. Richard Rowland was like that. I never could take to that boy. You could tell he had a mean streak a mile wide. And for whatever reason, he was able to compel other kids to follow in his wake. He was a nasty little boy, and definitely the ringleader of their small group. Harry and Danny were his followers. They'd do whatever Rowland told them to do. I do not believe that Harry Hodges or Danny Harkins could have deliberately hurt anyone else, especially a younger boy, without Richard Rowland egging them on. But I also don't think any of them were innocent, even though they claimed to be nowhere near that house that day. It's possible it was a game that got out of hand. And maybe they tried to put out the fire, but couldn't. It was too late. Too late to save Johnny Embry."

Elizabeth was quiet for a moment, her eyes taking on a far-off look. "Whatever really happened, all their lives were irrevocably damaged. Harry was a lonely man who never got close to anyone. Even if Danny had lived longer, he might have drunk himself to death. And Richard Rowland—what a hardened, unhappy man he turned out to be. Or perhaps he was simply born that way. I can't even begin to comprehend the emotions that ate at Edward all these years, losing his son and then his wife. All those lives ruined by one reckless event—if recklessness it was, and not premeditation. Did they lock Johnny in that house and play at setting it on fire? Or did Johnny just become trapped and they were unable to do anything about it and, terrified, decided to live a lie for the rest of their lives?"

The candles sputtered as everyone fell silent. The night had grown cool, but inside Elizabeth's home, it was warm and comforting, a universe away from the horror they contemplated. Lucky leaned against Elias's shoulder. Life could be snuffed out at any moment, any age, she thought. It was a shame to waste time in fear. What difference did it make if their relationship caused gossip? What was important was that she and Elias move forward with their lives, that every day be lived to the fullest.

Jack broke the silence. "Guess we'll never know for sure

what happened that day in the woods. And maybe it doesn't matter anymore."

"Amen," Elizabeth said. "There's no one who cares anymore except the people in this room." Charlie purred contentedly as Elizabeth stroked his fur.

Recipes

SAGE'S PEANUT BUTTER SOUP

(Serves 4)

1 small onion, finely chopped
2 tablespoons butter or margarine
3 cups chicken broth
1 cup cubed chicken (cooked or uncooked)
¼ teaspoon red pepper
½ cup chopped celery
¼ teaspoon salt
½ cup peanut butter

Melt butter or margarine in soup pot, add chopped onion and sauté on low heat for two minutes, until onion is softened, but not browned.

Add chicken stock, chicken pieces, celery, salt, red pepper and peanut butter.

Cover and cook on medium heat for 15 minutes until celery is softened and chicken pieces are completely cooked.

In a separate small pan, on low heat, whisk the flour and water together until the flour is dissolved, adding milk to the mixture.

Add the flour, water and milk mixture to the soup pot, and cook on high for 10 minutes until the broth has slightly thickened.

Sprinkle chopped peanuts over each serving.

CHERRY SOUP (CHILLED)

(Serves 6)

2 lbs. fresh, frozen or canned sour cherries (pitted)
1 cup water
1 cup sugar
1 tablespoon ground cinnamon
¼ teaspoon nutmeg
3 cups dry red wine
1 teaspoon almond extract
1 cup light cream
1 cup sour cream or crème fraiche

Add cherries, water, sugar, cinnamon and red wine to pot. Bring to a boil, reduce heat and simmer for 20-30 minutes until cherries are tender. Remove from heat and stir in almond extract.

In a mixing bowl, slowly stir light cream into the sour cream or crème fraiche until the mixture is smooth. Add the cream mixture to the pot. Stir gently until evenly mixed. Chill until ready to serve.

CUCUMBER YOGURT AND WALNUT SOUP (CHILLED)

(Serves 4)

1 cucumber
½ garlic clove
½ teaspoon salt
1 ½ cups coarsely chopped walnuts
1 cup cooked white rice
1 teaspoon walnut or sunflower oil
2 cups plain yogurt
1 cup cold water
2 teaspoons lemon juice
Fresh dill sprigs

Cut cucumber in half lengthwise, and remove peel from one half.

Dice both the peeled cucumber flesh and the unpeeled cucumber and set aside.

Blend garlic and salt together in a food processor.

Add cooked rice, peeled diced cucumber and 1 cup of chopped walnuts to food processor and blend again.

Transfer the mixture to a large bowl. Slowly add the walnut or sunflower oil, stir, then mix in yogurt and diced (unpeeled) one-half of cucumber. Add cold water and lemon juice to the mixture.

Pour the soup into chilled soup bowls to serve.

Garnish with remainder of chopped walnuts and sprigs of dill. Serve immediately.

CHICKEN APRICOT ALMOND SALAD

(Serves 2)

1 ½ cups cooked, chopped, skinless chicken breast
½ cup chopped dried apricots
2 stalks of celery, chopped
3 tablespoons chopped fresh cilantro
1 cup plain yogurt
2 tablespoons spicy mustard
2 teaspoons honey
2 teaspoons orange zest
10 large leaves romaine lettuce (washed and chopped)
½ cup sliced almonds

In a large bowl, mix chicken pieces, dried apricots, celery and cilantro together.

In a separate small bowl, mix yogurt, mustard, honey and orange zest, adding it to the chicken mixture. Then add chopped romaine leaves. Mix all ingredients thoroughly and garnish with sliced almonds.

WATERMELON BASIL FETA SALAD

(Serves 2)

2 cups chopped watermelon cubes
½ cup chopped red onions
½ cup crumbled feta cheese
½ cup chopped fresh basil leaves
8 leaves romaine lettuce (washed and chopped)
Mix all ingredients in a large bowl.
Serve with a sprinkle of balsamic vinegar.

Turn the page for a preview of Connie
Archer's next Soup Lover's Mystery . . .

A Roux of Revenge

Coming soon from Berkley Prime Crime!

Chapter 1

NATE EDGERTON, SNOWFLAKE'S Chief of Police, reached over and flipped off the siren and flashing light. He pulled his cruiser to the side of the road, slowing and coming to a stop behind a bright blue sports car. Two people, a young couple, sat on the rear bumper of the car. Nate could tell from their expressions there was no need to hurry.

He turned to his deputy. "Cancel the ambulance."

Nate heaved a sigh and climbed out. He already knew what he'd find in the ditch—a mangled body or bodies trapped in an equally crushed vehicle. Not how he wanted his day to go. His spirits had been high when he left home this morning. He had impulsively hugged his wife and kissed her quickly on the cheek. It was a golden October day. Summer had lingered over the countryside and a brilliant glow of crimson and orange covered the trees, leaves unwilling to submit to the coming winter.

He turned back to the cruiser and leaned into the

driver's window. "And get ahold of somebody in Lincoln Falls for a coroner's van."

Bradley nodded, and following Nate's orders, began to make the calls. He really hoped he wouldn't have to see any blood today.

"And after you've done that, talk to those two." Nate indicated the young couple by the sports car. "Get their information and don't let 'em leave just yet." Nate straightened up slowly, holding a hand against his stiff back and approached the pair. "You the folks who called this in?"

The man nodded. His arm hung around the shoulder of the woman who sat next to him. Her face was pale and pinched.

"My deputy will get your information and I'll be with you in a few minutes."

On the off chance the couple was mistaken and the victim still alive, Nate walked to the edge of the road. He gauged the distance to a white van that was tilted forward into the soft earth at a twenty-five degree angle. He grasped onto a sapling that clung to the side of the ditch, and doing his best not to slip or tumble, stepped sideways down the slope. As careful as he was, he barely stopped himself from sliding the rest of the way down into the gully.

The windshield of the van had shattered from the impact. Probably from the driver's head, he guessed. Nate peered through the open window. The body of a man dressed in casual work clothes was splayed over the steering wheel. His face, pressed into the shattered windshield, was striped with rivulets of blood. Sightless eyes were open, fixed at a place well beyond the ditch in which he lay.

Nate sighed and shook his head. *Why won't they ever wear their seat belts?*

He wrenched the door open and stood back to let gravity do the hard work. The man's sleeve and shirtfront were soaked in blood. Nate scanned the interior of the van searching for broken glass or a sharp object to explain the blood loss on the man's body but found nothing. He pulled a pen from his pocket and very carefully lifted the sleeve of the man's shirt. Humming tunelessly to himself, he replaced his pen and climbed around the van, carefully checking all sides. Then he returned to the back of the vehicle and leaned closer to the bumper for a better look.

"Bradley," he bellowed.

Nate looked to the top of the rise. Bradley's face peeked over the edge.

"Bring the camera down here." Nate knew the crime scene techs would take plenty of pictures but whenever possible he preferred to document the scene himself—too easy for a key piece of evidence to disappear or be overlooked.

Bradley appeared a few moments later, a camera bag slung over his shoulder. He slid down a lot more gracefully than the older man had done. When he reached bottom, he passed the camera to Nate, carefully keeping his gaze averted from the front seat of the van.

"Come on over here." Nate scrambled around to the driver's door. "What do you see?"

Bradley followed his boss dutifully. He looked as if he was about to retch. "A lot of blood."

"What else do you see?"

"Well, he didn't have a seat belt on. Went straight into the windshield."

"Anything else?"

Bradley shrugged his shoulders. "He bled all over himself."

"What do you think caused all this?" Nate asked.

Bradley, his face white, shrugged his shoulders.

"Look again." Nate pointed to the dead man's arm and shirtfront and waited patiently for light to dawn in Bradley's eyes. "This wasn't caused by the accident." He slid the pen from his shirt pocket again and very carefully lifted the material of the shirt away from the dead man's arm. "Now what do you see?"

Bradley squinted. "A hole." He turned to Nate, surprise on his face. "He was shot?"

"There's more. Listen and learn." Nate pointed to the rear of the van and led the way. "See here?" He indicated a dent on the rear bumper. "And here?" He pointed to a second spot of damage. "There's a lot of dings and rust spots, but there's no rust on these. A little paint in there. Maybe they can match it."

"You're saying somebody made sure he went off the road?"

"Yup. Twice, it looks like. Here, I want you to get some good shots of our man inside, his shirt and these dings on the bumper. But don't touch anything, all right?"

Jerking his thumb to the top of the rise, he said, "I want to talk to those two up there before they decide to take off."

Nate straightened his back. *Getting stiffer every day*, he thought. Getting too damn old for this job. He heaved another sigh and made an effort to climb back up to the road. Taking two steps up and sliding back one, he clung to the thin plantings and branches to give himself purchase.

The man at the car stood as Nate approached. The woman's hands were held against her face as she leaned over her knees. "Can we go now?"

"About what time did you first pull over?"

"Maybe forty-five minutes ago, I think. We saw the top of the van down below. We stopped, thinking somebody might need help, but . . ." he trailed off.

"It was too late." Nate finished his sentence.

The man gulped and nodded.

"Where are you headed, by the way?"

"Over to Bournmouth to visit my wife's parents. We live in Lincoln Falls."

"Did you happen to see any other vehicles when you first noticed the van? Anybody pass by?"

"No. Not a soul. There wasn't any traffic. We came this

way 'cause we wanted to take the scenic route." The man shook his head ruefully. "We sure as hell didn't bargain for this."

Nate nodded. "Sorry you had to be the ones. If you've given your names and home address to my deputy, you can be on your way."

Without a word the young woman stood. The couple turned away, a look of relief on their faces. They climbed into the sports car without a backward glance. The engine revved and the car pulled on to the road heading east.

Nate turned as he heard the crunch of gravel behind him. He watched as another car pulled up behind the cruiser. Elias Scott, Snowflake's town doctor and the local coroner, climbed out, a heavy black bag in his hand. Nate shook his head negatively to let Elias know there was no hurry.

"You're sure?" Elias asked as he approached.

"Sorry to drag you out here. Not much you can do now."

"Well, since I'm here, why don't I have a closer look."

"Be my guest."

Elias stepped carefully down the side of the ditch and slipped on a pair of latex gloves. Nate followed him. He looked into the open driver's door and whistled softly.

"What do you think?" Nate asked, following Elias.

"Well, the accident caused this." Elias pointed to a gash on the man's head and facial cuts. "Might have caused a concussion too. But it doesn't account for all this blood. Looks like it flowed from his left arm. See here." He pointed a gloved finger and then carefully examined the material of the shirt.

"Yeah, I caught that. A gunshot wound."

"He was alive when he went off the road. He could have been in shock from the wound, maybe that's what caused the crash. Could have died from the trauma of the wound, the blood loss or even the head injury. Can't be certain yet."

"Have a look back here." Elias followed the path that Nate had taken, careful not to slip on the damp vegetation. Bradley was returning the camera to its bag.

"There are two areas of damage. Here and here." Nate indicated the spots on the crushed bumper. "And these are new—no rust. The accident didn't cause this. Somebody rear-ended this guy—a couple of times, I'd guess."

"So you think he was shot first? Maybe whoever shot him managed to hit a vital artery."

"And maybe he was able to get away—tried to get help. But somebody didn't want him to." Nate shook his head. "Nothing's simple, is it? I'm gonna have to get the body moved and this thing towed to Lincoln Falls where the techs can have a better look. Let's go back up to the road. I want to get some shots of the tire tracks before everybody messes them up."

The three men climbed back to the road, doing their best not to slip on the soft earth or wet autumn leaves. Nate reached out and took the camera from Bradley. Elias stepped away and watched as Nate shot several photos.

"What can you tell from those?"

"See these right here," Nate said, pointing to wide tire tracks. Elias nodded. "These are the marks from the van. They start right here, off the road. No sign of an attempt to brake. This guy just flew off the road. Maybe he was already unconscious. But I still think somebody helped him along."

Elias followed in Nate's wake. "And back here . . ." Nate pointed to another set of marks. "Somebody hit the brakes real hard. See these tracks? And then it looks like he drove right onto the soft shoulder."

He turned to his deputy. "Bradley, you stay here until everything's handled and then bring the cruiser back to the station. And make sure you don't touch anything and don't let anybody stop to gawk. And especially right here," Nate said, pointing to a set of tire tracks. "Get some markers out of the trunk and make sure they get an impression of that tire."

Bradley wasn't happy to be relegated to a mop-up operation but there wasn't much he could do about it.

"I'll hitch a ride back to town with you, Elias. Bradley can handle the rest." He stood for a moment, silently surveying the scene. "Yup. I'd bet my last dollar. Somebody was after this guy. We've got a murder on our hands."

Chapter 2

JANIE SHIFTED THE branches of brightly colored autumn leaves, rearranging them in a wooden cask, one of several placed around the restaurant. "What do you think, Lucky?"

"I think it's fabulous. Maybe you should consider a career in interior decoration, even though I'd hate to lose you." Lucky's compliments were sincere. The restaurant was filled with morning light filtering through the yellow gingham curtains and reflecting off the wide pine floors of the By the Spoonful Soup Shop.

Janie laughed. "Don't think that'll be happening anytime soon. I'll be stuck in Snowflake for the rest of my life, more likely." She pushed an unruly branch back into place. "But at least we're all dressed up for Hallowe'en."

"I mean it, Janie. Look at this." Lucky waved her arm to indicate the work that Janie had accomplished—wooden casks of autumn leaves, brilliant reds and oranges from the autumn chill, cornstalks and baskets of multicolored gourds in the front window. "It really looks terrific."

Lucky's grandfather Jack had decided to hold a promotion for the Spoonful—free soup from three o'clock to five o'clock on the afternoon of Hallowe'en. Lucky agreed that would be a great idea. It would cover the time period when children were released from school and the sun went down at the witching hour. Jack had also decided to sponsor a jack-o'-lantern contest. Anyone could donate, each entry anonymous, and every customer would have one vote for their favorite by secret ballot. The prize would be three free all-you-can-eat meals for two at the Spoonful any day of the week.

Janie and Meg, the Spoonful's other waitresses, and Sage, their chef, had each contributed carved pumpkins to get the contest rolling. Janie's jack-o'-lantern sported a smile, red lips, teeth of seeds and twig eyelashes. Meg had carved one that looked like a tiny demon. Sage's was a leering witch, with a parsnip nose. The jack-o'-lanterns were lined up on a long table against the wall. Tiny battery lights twinkled inside each of them.

Lucky could hardly believe that ten months had elapsed since she had returned home to Snowflake to take over her parents' business. Their sudden death on an icy road had changed her life forever. Two more months would mark a full year. Somehow she had managed to keep the restaurant afloat. At first she had been terrified of taking over the Spoonful, and doubtful about her decision to stay. But now, this path felt the most natural one in the world.

"You can't really see the lights inside the pumpkins during the day," Janie said. "Maybe we should turn them off for now, and save the batteries 'til it's dark."

"Good idea." Lucky looked up from laying out place mats on the tables.

Janie held a wooden bowl full of gourds in her arms and was staring intently out the front window. Something about her expression caught Lucky's attention.

"Janie? What is it?"

"Nothing." Janie continued to stare across the street to the opposite sidewalk on Broadway. "It's just . . ."

Lucky walked over to Janie and followed her gaze. "What do you see?"

"That man. I've seen him before." Janie nodded her head, indicating a tall muscular man with a full head of thick auburn hair, streaked with gray. He stood on the other side of the street, in the shade of an awning as though waiting for someone.

"Maybe he's someone in town working for the Harvest Festival," Lucky said. Snowflake, Vermont, had been chosen as this year's location for a fall event, hosting a local farmers' market, pony rides and a corn maze for children. Ernie White, a very successful businessman from Lincoln Falls, a much larger town, was the moving force behind the Festival.

"You're probably right." Janie shrugged and flipped over the sign on the front door to read OPEN. "I just feel like I've seen him around a lot." She shrugged her shoulders. Janie turned and headed for the kitchen to help Sage prepare for the morning rush.

The bell over the door jingled just as Lucky finished laying out the last of the napkins and silverware. Hank Northcross and Barry Sanders, two of the Spoonful's most loyal regulars came in every morning. Retired gentlemen, they were often together and were usually the first customers of the day. Hank was tall and thin. His hair, completely gray, was cropped close to his head and he wore pince-nez glasses that constantly slid down his long nose. Barry, much shorter and very plump, was fond of brightly colored shirts that barely buttoned over his midsection. Today he was dressed in an orange and black plaid in deference to the season.

"'Morning, Lucky . . . Janie. You too Meg," Barry called out. "Jack around?"

"He'll be here shortly. He's picking up some supplies in Lincoln Falls."

"You still let the old man drive?" Hank asked in jest, but there was an undercurrent of worry to his question.

Lucky's grandfather had suffered from wartime flashbacks most of his life. When she returned home months before, she realized that Jack had other, more serious health problems. Fortunately these had since been alleviated by medical treatment, but she still worried about him.

"Couldn't stop him if I tried," she answered. Jack was the only family she had now. He needed to feel useful and she needed his support. There was no doubt in her mind that he was essential to the smooth running of the Spoonful. Lucky approached the corner table where Hank and Barry always sat. "Coffee?"

"Yes. Perfect," Barry answered.

Lucky retrieved cups and saucers from behind the counter and poured two cups for the men. She placed them on a tray with a pitcher of cream and a sugar bowl and carried them to the corner table where Hank and Barry were already setting up a game of chess. "Don't forget Jack's pumpkin carving contest. He'll be disappointed if you don't both contribute."

"We haven't forgotten," Hank spoke. "Wait'll you see mine. I'm quite sure I'll win."

"Not so fast, you old coot. I'm gonna beat the pants off you." Barry looked up. "What do you have for specials today, Lucky?"

"We have three new soups—Sage has a pumpkin rice with Persian spices, he tells me. I haven't tried it yet myself, but it smells delicious. And a zucchini leek with potatoes and a beet mushroom and barley soup. I've tried that one, I really love it."

"Hmm. I'll have to sample every one of those this week," Barry said. "We're gonna walk down to the Harvest

Festival later. I want to pick up some vegetables from the
farmers' market but I'll be sure to come back for lunch.
Make sure you save me some of that pumpkin soup."

"I will, and Jack should be back by then." Lucky turned
back to the counter and saw Janie standing at the window
again. She walked over and stood behind her. The same
man was across the street. He had disappeared for a short
while and was now back.

"You're right. He does seem to be around a lot," Lucky
whispered.

Janie had lost her father quite suddenly more than a year
before, just as she was about to graduate from high school.
Lucky tried to keep a good eye on her. Doug Leonard had
been a kindly man who adored his only child. When he
died of a massive coronary, Janie was inconsolable. Lucky
felt a deep empathy now that her own parents had been
taken from her in an equally sudden fashion. How much
more difficult for Janie, given her youth, the loss must have
been.

"I wonder who he is," Lucky said.

Janie, a troubled look on her face, didn't answer. She
turned away from the window and hurried into the kitchen.

Becca Robbins is happy to help research a farmers' market and tourist trading post—until she has to switch her focus to finding a killer...

AN ALL-NEW ESPECIAL
FROM NATIONAL BESTSELLING AUTHOR

PAIGE SHELTON

Red Hot Deadly Peppers

A Farmers' Market Mini Mystery

Becca is in Arizona, spending some time at Chief Buffalo's trading post and its neighboring farmers' market to check out how the two operate together. She's paired with Nera, a Native American woman who sells the most delicious pecans—right next to a booth with the hottest peppers money can buy.

When Nera asks her to deliver some beads to Graham, a talented jewelry maker inside Chief Buffalo's, Becca is grateful to get a break from the heat. Little does she realize that the heat's about to get cranked up even more—because Graham has been murdered, and she's the one who finds his body. She soon discovers that Graham was Nera's cousin, and that her uncle was recently killed, too, after receiving a threatening note. Becca begins to think the murders may have something to do with the family's hot pepper business. Now she must find the killer, before she's the one in the hot seat...

Includes a bonus recipe!

paigeshelton.com
facebook.com/TheCrimeSceneBooks
penguin.com

M1144T0712

*In the quaint seaside village of Cape Willington, Maine,
Candy Holliday has a mostly idyllic life, tending to the
Blueberry Acres farm she runs with her father—
and occasionally stepping in to solve a murder or two . . .*

FROM NATIONAL BESTSELLING AUTHOR
B. B. HAYWOOD

TOWN IN A
Wild Moose Chase

A Candy Holliday Murder Mystery

It's winter in Cape Willington—and trouble is about to
walk right into Candy's life. First, town hermit Solomon
Hatch stirs things up by claiming to have seen a dead
body in the woods with a hatchet in its back. Then a
mysterious white moose starts appearing around town in
the strangest of places.

Meanwhile, the town's annual Winter Moose Fest has
drawn plenty of out-of-towners who've come to enjoy the
Sleigh and Sled Parade, the ice-sculpting exhibition, and
the Moose Fest Ball. As Candy runs around town covering events for the local newspaper, she begins to suspect
a link between the body in the woods, the white moose,
and several of the town's weekend visitors. But as she
hunts for the killer, she's the one who's prey . . .

INCLUDES DELICIOUS RECIPES!

facebook.com/HollidaysBlueberryAcres
facebook.com/TheCrimeSceneBooks
penguin.com

M1181T0912